The Complicated Life of Maggie MacGregor

By Tempie W. Wade

The Complicated Life of Maggie MacGregor
By Tempie W. Wade

This is a work of historical fiction. While some of the
names in this book are the same as real-life historical
figures, the actions and words of the characters are
strictly figments of the author's imagination and any
resemblance to actual events, places, and persons, living
or dead are entirely coincidental.

Printed in the United States of America.

First Edition Print - ISBN: 978-0-9600257-5-6
Digital Edition – ISBN 978-0-9600257-4-9

For more information, please visit...
www.TempieWade.com

The Complicated Life of Maggie MacGregor

By Tempie W. Wade

Book Three in the Timely Revolution Book Series

ISBN: 978-0-9600257-5-6

ACKNOWLEDGMENTS

To all of those who have supported and encouraged me on this journey, my family, my friends, and especially to Jen….

THANK YOU!

1 CHAPTER ONE

December 1778
Beechcroft Estate
Williamsburg, Virginia

Black plumes of smoke rolled from the back of the house. The closer Maggie got to the scene, the heavier and thicker the air became, making it almost impossible to see and to breathe. Her men were already outside, running a bucket water line from the river trying to douse the flames coming from the kitchen, with Abel and Joshua at the front of the line.

Maggie pulled Onyx to a hard stop and dismounted where the men stood.

"Is everyone out of the house?" she shouted over the noise and chaos.

Joshua turned. "Yes, Ms. Maggie, the house is clear."

The kitchen was engulfed by flames and the firestorm was mere feet from making the short leap to the main part of the house. Maggie took the lead at the very front of the line, tossing buckets of water, desperate to save her home.

Duncan, Gabe, and Quinn caught up and rushed to her side.

"We need to keep the fire from spreading!" yelled Gabe, as he directed the men where to pitch the water, grabbing a bucket himself.

"Where is the closest entrance to the house?" asked Duncan. "Quinn and I can form a barrier from the inside."

Onyx whinnied for them to follow him, rearing up and disappearing around the corner.

"NO!" croaked Maggie, her throat burning from the smoke. "Do NOT endanger yourselves!"

Duncan and Quinn were already out of sight before she finished her words.

Damn it!

Maggie and Gabe handed off their spots to Abel and Joshua so they could follow their spouses. By the time they reached the front of the house, Onyx had already splintered the massive door, and the two brothers were inside. Maggie and Gabe, covered their mouths with their palms, rushing into the inferno to search for them.

Duncan and Quinn were just inside the foyer holding their hands out before them, chanting some ancient, forgotten words. A foggy mist formed in the air around them, one that they were able to control and direct into the kitchen, dousing most of the blaze. The flames that were left reversed course straight into the water line, permitting the fire to be extinguished completely.

Finished, the brothers dropped their arms to their sides.

Maggie rushed into Duncan's embrace. "Do not ever scare me like that again!" she barked, still gasping for air.

He pulled her tightly to him. "I am fine, Maggie."

Gabe embraced Quinn, "That goes double for you," he choked, trying to clear his throat.

They all moved outside into the fresh air.

"How did you do that?" Gabe heaved as he leaned over, his hands on his knees, face turned up to Quinn.

"It is one of the spells we were given to protect the house in Scotland. Not only can the fog conceal, but the mist is fine enough to put out flames," answered Quinn, rubbing Gabe on the back, concerned.

"Are ye alright, Maggie?" asked Duncan. He held her while she gulped in the fresh air.

"I will be."

They made their way around to the back of the house, Joshua and Abel meeting them half-way.

"I'm sorry you had to come back to this," said Joshua. He produced a rag from his pocket and wiped the grime and sweat from his face.

Maggie shook her head. "It doesn't matter, as long as no one is hurt. The house can be replaced, people cannot. Where is Hettie?"

A voice called from behind the group, "Maggie? Is that you? Oh, thank the good Lord you are home." Hettie and

Cecile rushed over, and the three women embraced in a hug.

"It is good to be home. What on Earth happened?"

"Looks like it started in the chimney in the kitchen, Ms. Maggie," said Abel, looking around, using a stick to rake through some of the charred remains.

Maggie looked at all of the people from the estate who had come to her aid, gratitude filling her heart, "I don't know what to say. Thank you all so much for saving my home."

"You don't have to thank us, Ms. Maggie...look at all you have done for every person standing here. You take care of us, so we take care of you," said Joshua, putting his arm around Cecile.

Everyone that had helped stepped forward, and nodded their heads in agreement, expressing the same sentiments as Joshua, before they started back to their own homes. Duncan slipped his arms around Maggie's waist from behind, resting his chin on her shoulder.

Hettie put her hands on her hips, shooting Duncan a menacing look, then took a step towards him in a defensive posture, much like a mother hen. "Who do you think you are putting your hands on OUR Maggie like that? Do I need to get my broom, boy?"

Duncan was taken aback. *Maggie? Who is this woman?*

Maggie laughed. "I want all of you to meet Duncan MacGregor... my new HUSBAND."

"Your husband?" a shocked Hettie asked. "Why would you want to get one of those, and where in the world did you find him?"

Maggie bit her bottom lip as she looked down, trying hard to conceal her amusement. "Scotland."

Hettie folded her arms, narrowed her eyes, and glared at Duncan. She looked him up and down.

Duncan mirrored her stance, clearly amused, but trying hard to conceal it.

Maggie covered her mouth with her hand to hide her grin.

"Duncan, this is Hettie. She takes care of the house, and she is very protective of me."

Hettie continued her stone-faced stare as Maggie turned to introduced Quinn. "Hmph!" scoffed Hettie, pointing her finger at Duncan, "I will be keeping my eye on you."

Duncan looked down at the ground to mask the smirk on his face while he rocked back and forth on his heels. He raised his chin to look Hettie in the eye. "Why don't ye do that?" he replied with a wink.

Maggie shook her head at the exchange.

Harm came around the corner. "The horses are settling down, Joshua. The fire had them upset, but thankfully, they didn't break the stable door." He looked up to see the new arrivals.

"Ms. Maggie! Colonel! It's good to have you back home."

"It is good to be home, Harm," said Gabe, touching the man on the shoulder.

Onyx, who had been at the corner of the house, took the opportunity to sneak up on Harm. When he was just behind him, Onyx neighed, frightening the poor man so badly that he jumped straight up. Onyx bobbed his head up and down as he appeared to snicker.

Harm hung his head before he turned around to lay eyes on his practical joker. "It's been so quiet around here. I haven't had to fix the first broken door or gate since you've been gone."

Maggie winced and pressed her index finger to her lips. "Umm.... Onyx just busted down the front door...to get in to stop the fire."

"Of course, he did." Harm shook his head. "What else would he have done?"

"If it makes you feel any better, he broke a few gates in Scotland as well," added Maggie.

Onyx slipped his head over and rested it on Harm's shoulder, appearing to grin. He stuck out his tongue and used it to lick the side of Harm's face.

Harm wiped the slobber off his cheek with his hand, giving Onyx a disgusted look before he reached up and rubbed his nose. "I reckon I missed you, too."

Maggie turned to look at the house, sighing.

Gabe came to stand beside her. "It looks like the worst of it was contained to the kitchen. The rest of the house will have some smoke damage, but it appears to be intact. I'm so sorry, Maggie."

"It's getting dark. We can get a better look in the morning," Duncan said, hugging her and kissing the side of her head.

"Joshua? How close is Gabe's house to being complete?"

"It's all done, Ms. Maggie. We finished up last week, all except the stable... and, well it isn't furnished yet."

Maggie nodded. "Good. We can drop anchor and stay on the ship another night while we figure out a plan tomorrow."

That night, Maggie sat silently in one of the chairs in their stateroom, her feet propped up on the table, polishing off a glass of whisky, when Duncan returned from securing the ship. He moved behind her, massaging her shoulders with his hands.

"This is not the welcome I wanted for you," she said softly and laid a hand up on his.

"I know, my love, but the house is not a complete loss, and everyone is safe. That is all that matters. We will rebuild."

"At least Gabe's home is finished. He, Kat, and Quinn can get settled," she said, as she frowned at her empty glass.

"Aye, and they are insisting that we stay with them while the repairs are being done."

"They will already have a full house. Gabe left as a single man and is returning with a baby, a husband, and a nanny. It will be extremely close quarters. He is also going to need a complete staff."

Duncan moved her feet to the floor, took the glass from her hand, and set it on the table. "That is tomorrow's problem." He pulled her up, into his arms and kissed her. "Let me help ye forget about all off this until then."

Duncan's kiss moved from slow to urgent.

"It may be a long while before we are alone again," he grinned.

Maggie groaned, "Oh! You are right."

She giggled, as he wasted no time removing her clothes. He laid her down, covered her with kisses and his body, and made her forget all her troubles, if only for the night.

The next morning, they had breakfast at the community kitchen. Everyone, including all of the children, came over to greet Maggie, with hugs and 'welcome homes'. The little ones eyed Duncan suspiciously, giving the rather large Scot a wide berth, which he found quite amusing.

He waved to one little girl, who ran to duck behind her mother to hide her face. Slowly, she skirted around to the far side of the table, inching her way along, until she was close enough to leap into Maggie's lap.

Duncan shook his head as Maggie rubbed his arm.

"They will get used to you, my love. You are a little big and intimidating to tiny ones."

He took a good look around at all the people so well cared for and happy in this place they called home. Their love and respect for their Mistress was apparent.

"Maggie, ye have built something very special here. I can see why ye are so protective of it."

"This is the only place they are treated like this. Slavery everywhere else in the colonies is cruel and inhuman. People are beaten for minor offenses, taken from their families, and forced to work intolerable hours for no pay. I would not be able to sleep at night if I used other human beings that way."

He kissed her hand. "Ye are a good soul, Maggie. Just one of the many reasons I love ye."

Maggie saw Gabe, Quinn, Kat, and Cora approaching through one of the windows. She and Duncan rose and greeted them at the door.

"Good morning," said Gabe, coming over to kiss Maggie's cheek.

"Morning," Maggie said as she kissed Kat.

"Been up to the house yet?" asked Quinn.

"Not yet," said Duncan.

"I have been stalling," added Maggie, "Besides, I know one little girl who needs to meet Hettie," she said, pinching Kat's cheek.

Gabe smiled as they went inside.

"Oh, Hettie?" He called out.

The beloved housekeeper stuck her head out of the other room. "Yes, Colonel?"

"Come out here. I have someone for you to meet."

Hettie came out, wiping the flour from her arms. She tossed the towel she was using over her shoulder and placed her hands on her hips when she saw him with a child.

"Whose baby you got, Colonel?"

"She is my baby!" he said. "Meet my daughter, Kat, and her nanny, Cora. This is Hettie."

Hettie raised an eyebrow. "Colonel, the last time I checked it took nine months to have a little one. You ain't been gone that long."

Gabe explained to her how Kat had come to be his daughter.

Hettie looked over at Kat, who was blowing bubbles and cooing. She reached out to take her. "Well, bless her little heart. This poor thing has had a rough start in this world." She spoke to Kat, "But, you found a fine father and he is gonna take good care of you. We all gonna make sure he does."

They had breakfast and headed up to the main house. Some of the men were already there, cleaning up.

David Percy was also there by the time they arrived.

"Maggie! Gabe! The men said you were home."

"Yes, we arrived just in time for the glorious bonfire," said Maggie, dryly.

"I am sorry that you had to come home to this. I was in town and had no idea it had happened until this morning."

"Thank you, David." She waved her hand indicating for him to follow. "Come over and meet my husband, Duncan MacGregor and his brother, Quinn." Maggie turned to Duncan and Quinn, "This is David Percy, my personal attorney."

"Your husband? You married while you were away?"

"I did indeed."

David offered a shallow bow, then held out his hand to Duncan. "It is a pleasure to make your acquaintance...and congratulations to you both."

Duncan shook the offered hand. "Thank ye."

"You are Scottish? Do you have family here?"

"Nay! We are from a small clan. There would be none of our kind in the colonies."

"Oh! Well, welcome to you, just the same." David turned to Maggie. "I will handle any legal issues that need to be taken care of for you."

"Thank you, David."

Cora came around the corner with Kat.

"Oh, David, let me introduce you to my daughter," said Gabe, taking Kat into his arms.

"Your daughter?" he asked, surprised.

"Yes. Her name is Katherine, and this is her nanny, Cora Roberts."

"Oh, a pleasure to meet you, ma'am," said David as he removed his hat, bowing, a slight tinge of blush appearing on his cheeks.

"It is very nice to meet you too, sir," said Cora, looking down, a coy smile crossing her lips.

David turned his attention back to Gabe, who explained the entirety of the situation. He listened intently, absorbing every detail.

"Legal paperwork was filed in England by my family's firm, but I may need your help with some things here."

"Of course, Gabe. I am at your disposal, as always."

Gabe bounced Kat on his shoulder, trying to comfort the little one; she was starting to fuss.

"Colonel Asheton, I will need to get some things for the baby," Cora said to Gabe as she reached to take her from him.

"Certainly!" Gabe looked to Maggie. "Can you spare someone with the carriage?"

"Harm should be able to help you." She looked in the direction of the stables.

David waved his hand. "Maggie, I would very much like to be of assistance, but I am afraid I will not be much help here with the cleanup. I would, however, be more than happy to escort Ms. Roberts and the baby into town, if you wish."

Maggie nodded. "That would be wonderful, David, and actually, if you don't mind, there are a few other things you can do for me while you are there."

"Anything to help!" he replied, enthusiastic as always. "Just tell me what I can do."

"We will need some supplies and furniture for Gabe's new house that must be ordered. I can make a list." She turned to Cora. "I have accounts set up at all of the stores in town. Put whatever you like on them."

Duncan located Maggie standing in the foyer of the house, her hand over her mouth, surveying the destruction. There, thankfully, was very little damage to the main part of the house, other than from the smoke. The worst of it was the big gaping hole that went into the kitchen and the busted front door. Thanks to Duncan and Quinn, most of the house had been saved.

"Want to show me around?" asked Duncan.

"Why not?" She pointed to the charred wall. "That is what is left of the kitchen."

"I gathered that much," he chuckled.

Maggie took him by the hand and led him around, giving him the full tour.

"Maggie, this house is absolutely amazing."

"It was...and it will be again," she said and turned to face him, laying her hands flat on his chest. "I was actually thinking that the fire may have been fortuitous."

"What do ye mean?" he asked, wrapping his arms around her.

"Well, the hidden room that I have will hold the books, but there will be no room left for anything else. If we must rebuild, we can make additional space, and a better place for the part of the collection we have."

Duncan nodded. "Aye, that sounds like a wonderful idea."

"There was a hidden cellar under the kitchen. Hettie is the only one who knows about it. You can take a look at what's left, but I think it can be modified for our benefit.

Now is as good a time as any. I actually have an idea that may work very nicely."

"Quinn and I will have a peek when no one else is around. In the meantime, I am going out to join your...rather...OUR people with the cleanup."

"And I will begin in here," she said, as she placed one hand on each side of his face and kissed him.

"Good! We are just in time."

Maggie and Duncan turned to see from whom the voice had come, still embraced.

Cecile came through the hole where the front door had once been, along with ten more women behind her, all carrying buckets and rags.

"What's all this?" asked Maggie.

"Well, we figured if we all jumped in, we could get the main part of the house cleaned and aired out. It's still warm for December, so it's best to do it now."

Duncan kissed Maggie on the top of the head. "I will be outside, my love." He nodded as he passed by the women. "Ladies," he said and left to find the others.

"Thank you all, again," said Maggie, pushing her hair back out of her face.

Cecile came over and hugged her. "It's alright, Maggie. We're gonna get this house back in shape in no time. We should get started upstairs."

Maggie, Cecile, and Sadie began in her bedroom, while the other ladies started work on the other bedrooms. They freely chatted away while they worked.

"How are you liking married life, Maggie?" asked Cecile, wiping down the chairs.

"I am still getting used to it, but so far so good," Maggie said with a smile as she stripped off the bedclothes. "Duncan is a very special man."

"He is a handsome one too, Ms. Maggie. Do all the men in Scotland look like those two brothers?" grinned Sadie, as she started on the wall.

"No!" laughed Maggie. "Those two, and their three brothers, are cut from a very different cloth."

"There's five of them? And they all look like that?"

"Yes, they do."

"Y'all gonna have some mighty fine-looking children, Maggie," said Cecile.

"I always wish we could have had some," Sadie said with a sad smile. "The doctor said he didn't think we could ever have any and, well, if we ain't had none in ten years, I don't reckon we ever will."

Maggie stopped what she was doing and moved to put her arms around Sadie. "I'm so sorry," she said with a tight squeeze of the shoulders, wishing there was something she could do to ease the other woman's pain. Maggie felt a strange tingling sensation in her hand, that turned into a white, hot scaring pain that shot throughout her entire body, from her head to her toes, lasting for a few long seconds.

Stepping back, Maggie looked down at her hands, opening and closing her fingers, that felt rather numb and prickly. *That's weird.*

Moving to the open window to take in a deep breath of fresh air, Maggie could see the men working below from the windowsill. Duncan stood above them all, stripped to the waist, his hair loose with beads of sweat glistening off his chest.

Cecile walked over next to her. "You good, Maggie?" she asked.

Maggie smiled wide. "Yes, I am! I'm just taking a minute to appreciate the view."

Cecile followed her gaze. "Uh-huh! I see what view you are appreciating," she laughed.

"I don't think I shall ever tire of looking at that man."

Duncan's head lifted; his eyes fixated on her. *What's weird?*

I am just feeling tingly all over for some odd reason.

Duncan smirked and raised an eyebrow. *Missing your husband, are ye?*

Maggie shook her head as she rolled her eyes and grinned. *Always!*

They soon all reunited at the community kitchen for dinner. Hettie and some of the other ladies had cooked all morning and managed to lay out a grand feast for everyone that had been working hard.

"How is the outside coming?" asked Maggie, stuffing a piece of bread in her mouth.

"Very well," replied Gabe.

"With everyone pitching in, we have almost cleared it all out," said Joshua.

"We will finish, then temporarily seal the wall in case the weather turns," Duncan added.

"How is the inside coming?" asked Quinn.

Maggie shrugged. "The house itself is fine beyond the kitchen, but the smoke damage is much more extensive than I first thought. I think all the furnishings and fabrics will have to be replaced."

Gabe set down his fork. "That will be a great many things, Maggie."

"I know, but we don't have much choice."

"So, we start our married life with a whole new house," said Duncan, squeezing her thigh reassuringly under the table.

"Well, the furnishings in the house were the ones that came with it when I bought it. I picked out nothing myself, so this will give us a chance to really make it our own. Speaking of which…" she turned to Joshua, "I want to make some changes to the layout when we rebuild, if you think you can handle them."

Joshua broke into a huge grin. "You want me to do them?"

"I would not trust anyone else."

"Yes, Ms. Maggie. I would be proud to do them for you," he beamed.

"In the meantime," said Gabe, "you will stay with us, even though we have no furniture yet. Our floor is your floor."

"I have David checking with the cabinetmakers in town today to see what is readily available. Maybe, we can pull together enough things to get your house set up and somewhat in order."

"Maggie," admonished Gabe, "do not concern yourself with my home, you have your own household to replace."

"Gabe, you have a baby now. Taking care of her comes before anything else."

"Aye," added Duncan, "the bairn and her nanny need to be provided for. Besides, all Maggie and I need is a bed." He grinned as he leaned over and kissed her.

David, Cora, and Kat returned later that day. The cabinetmaker had promised to bring four beds, a crib, and a table with chairs in the next few days, while the rest of the furniture for Gabe's house would be ready in two weeks. Maggie made the decision that they would continue to bunk on the ship for the next couple of days, at least until the beds had been delivered.

Maggie was not comfortable storing the Fae collection on the ship, so that night, when no one else was around, Duncan, Gabe, and Quinn loaded everything onto a wagon and moved it into the secret space in the drawing room. Once all the books were placed in there, the door barely closed, but it did with a little effort, and all the items were securely inside the house. Quinn went out one final time to make sure that they had gotten everything but returned carrying something that was wrapped.

"What is this?" he asked, curiously. "It was with the collection, but I do not remember packing any portraits."

"Nay," said Duncan, coming over to get a closer look, "all the paintings were left in Scotland."

Duncan unwrapped the packaging, then stepped back.

Maggie moved to his side, astonished by what she saw.

"Duncan! It's beautiful! But, where did it come from? We didn't sit for this."

It was a stunning likeness of Maggie and Duncan on their wedding day. The image was as perfect as a modern-day portrait, the color and brushstrokes so amazing, the images looked lifelike.

Duncan looked closer. "There is a note here."

Maggie tugged it loose, opened it, and read it aloud.

A small wedding gift for the happy couple.
One of three...
One for your home.
One for the collection in Scotland.
One for your parents...personally delivered.
I have done as ye asked.
Your parents are well.

"Oh, Finn!" Maggie whispered, her voice cracking, her eyes watery, "Wherever you are...thank you."

Duncan took the note to see it for himself.

"It is a remarkable image of the two of you," said Gabe, examining it further, smiling. "I think you have your first new piece for the house."

Looking at Maggie, a bit perplexed, Duncan held up the parchment. "How were ye able to read this?"

Maggie looked at Duncan puzzled. "I just READ it. Why?"

Duncan handed the page to Quinn, who, in turn, showed it to Gabe.

"Maggie, it is in the ancient language."

"It is NOT!" Maggie exclaimed and snatched it back. "Let me see that!"

Maggie looked again. "It is in English."

"No, Maggie, it is not," said Gabe.

"But...it looks like English to ye?" asked Quinn.

"Yes!" Maggie took another look, only this time, the letters started to morph into something resembling symbols. "Whoa! The words just changed around on the paper. How did that happen?"

Duncan took the note, looking bewildered. "I guess you can read the ancient language now?"

"I am jealous, Maggie," said Quinn, "Mother made us study for years before we were able to understand it."

"But how?"

Duncan shrugged. "If I were to venture a guess, I would say that Finn had something to do with it."

"You know what?" Maggie threw up her hands. "I am too tired to even care tonight. Let's just chalk it up to being one more strange occurrence for the day."

"Another? What else happened?" asked Duncan, his brow furrowed.

"I am sure it was nothing."

He took her hand in his. "Tell me!"

Maggie frowned. "I was talking to Cecile and Sadie earlier upstairs when a strange, tingly jolt shot throughout my body. My fingers were numb for a good while afterward."

"Is that what ye meant before...at the window?"

Maggie nodded.

"That is very odd," mumbled Quinn.

Duncan pulled her close to him, giving Quinn and Gabe a concerned look over her shoulder. He pushed her back slightly and cupped her face, stroking it with his thumb as he forced a smile on his own face. "It has been a long day. I think we all could use some rest."

2 CHAPTER TWO

The next few weeks were a flurry of rebuilding and refurbishing their residence. Maggie had Joshua draw up the new plans for the house. The current dining room would be extended over the part of the kitchen with the cellar and would be converted into the library. The current library would be extended and made into the new dining room, where it was connected by a short hall to the new kitchen. Maggie told Joshua about the cellar and how it needed to be kept a secret with a concealed entrance. He readily agreed to keep that information between them. Duncan and Quinn sealed the cellar door that went to the river so no one could ever slip in unannounced. Once the extension was added, they would remodel the cellar to make it a better place to store the collection.

Captain Russell took the ship in for much-needed maintenance, so Maggie and Duncan moved in with Gabe, Quinn, Kat, and Cora. Gabe only had three bedrooms, it being more than he needed at the time, but now, the house was bursting at the seams. Hettie even had some of the men bring her bed over from her house, and had it set up in the kitchen, so she would not have to trudge between her house and Gabe's while the repairs were being done, to make sure they were taken care of for breakfast and supper. Between the tight quarters and the work at the house, Maggie and Duncan had not been alone together in weeks. They were both extremely frustrated, and in desperate need of some private time to be physically together with each other.

They were having dinner at the community kitchen when Maggie slipped her hand on Duncan's thigh underneath the table.

Duncan closed his eyes, sighed, and did the same, sending her a silent message. *If we are not alone soon, I am not sure I will survive.*

Maggie tilted her head at him with a sympathetic look on her face. *I know exactly how you feel.*

They were smiling at each other when someone caught Maggie's attention.

Askuwheteau, from the Native American village on the edge of the property, appeared in the doorway, looking around, his gaze locking in on Maggie.

"Hello, Maggie!" he waved.

"Askuwheteau! Come in and have something to eat with us."

He crossed the room and took a seat across from Maggie while Hettie brought him a plate and Maggie made formal introductions.

"Is everything well with the tribe?"

"Yes!" he said, taking a bite of food. "Better than it is here. I have been away on a hunting trip. I just found out you were back and about the fire. I am very sorry about your house," he said.

"No one was hurt, and we are slowly getting back to normal." Maggie smiled.

"Some of the children from the school said that you had taken a husband. Mingan sent me since he cannot travel as well as he used to. He would like you to come to visit at sunset for the wolf moon tonight. He wishes to have Powaw perform a marriage blessing ritual over you and your new husband, as a gift."

Maggie slipped her arm around Duncan and smiled. "That is very kind of him. We would be honored to accept. Thank you."

"I will tell him to expect you." He nodded, popped another morsel of cheese in his mouth, and stood to go. "Thank you for the food. We will prepare for you tonight... and bring your horse. Powaw wishes to commune with him."

Askuwheteau left as quietly as he appeared.

Duncan, Gabe, and Quinn all gave Maggie a strange look.

"What does he mean by 'commune' with Onyx?" asked Gabe, leaning in toward Maggie.

Maggie shook her head. "Who knows? Powaw and Onyx have... conversations...of some strange sort. I do not ask about what. I don't think I really want to know."

That night, Maggie and Duncan rode slowly, side by side, holding hands as she told him all about the Native Americans that were her neighbors.

"They sound much like the clans of old in Scotland."

Maggie looked at him thoughtfully. "You know, I suppose they do." She lowered her head, sadness in her eyes. "The future is not kind to the Native American people, and it breaks my heart to know what is to come for them, but, here and now, I will do everything in my power to protect them." She squeezed his hand and smiled. "You will love them as I do. They are a very special group of souls."

They were met by Askuwheteau, his wife Wawetseka, and Mingan as they dismounted. Maggie introduced Duncan and they cheerfully welcomed him with open arms.

"Come! Join us," said Mingan, speaking in English that he had learned in his visits to the school over the years. He led them to the large bonfire that had been built in the middle of the village and invited them to sit next to him and his wife.

People were laughing and talking, while healthy, happy children played all around them.

"Maggie," said Mingan, "our village thrives because of you. Your kindness has sustained us and allowed our numbers to grow. We thank you and wish to honor you and your new husband with one of our ceremonies."

Maggie took Duncan's arm.

Powaw came to them, taking each of them by the hand, to stand in front of him; the crowd grew quiet.

He performed the ceremony in the Algonquian language. Though neither of them understood what was said, the words sounded much like a sweet, loving melody. When he was done, he dipped his finger in a bowl and made symbols on their foreheads with a sweet oil. Afterward, Powaw seated them in a place of honor, and a group of dancers performed a sensual, hypnotic dance complete with chanting and drums. A woodwind flute played softly somewhere in the background.

Maggie and Duncan were lulled into a state of dreaminess.

When the performance was finished, a group of giggling women came and pulled Maggie away. A group of men did the same to Duncan. They watched each other go in the opposite direction, both laughing, and wondering what they had gotten themselves into.

The women took Maggie into one of the longhouses, Wawetseka leading the pack. She had learned English, and quite well, from Askuwheteau.

"Wawetseka, what is happening?" asked Maggie, as she felt hands all over her.

"We are preparing you for your night with your husband." she smiled. "Askuwheteau and I had a marriage bed prepared for you."

It dawned on Maggie that she and Duncan would FINALLY be completely alone for the first time in weeks.

"Oh, Wawetseka...I think I love you." Maggie laughed and embraced her. "I wish there was something I could do to show you JUST how much I appreciate all of this."

The strange, powerful sensation that Maggie felt before in the house happened again. She shook her head and looked down at her hands, her fingers now numb from whatever it was. *Seriously? Are there any neurologists in the 18th-century?*

The women shepherded Maggie over to a raised platform in the middle of the longhouse, removing her clothes as they moved. Maggie was more than a little surprised when they stripped her completely nude, gently urged her to lay face down on the bed and, rubbed every inch of her skin with sweet oils and herbs, giving her a type of massage. They brushed out her hair, then gave her something sweet to drink that tasted much like wine. Maggie had never felt so pampered in her life.

When the eldest woman was satisfied, she wrapped Maggie in a soft deerskin blanket, like a robe, and led her outside to another nearby longhouse. She smiled, said a few words, and pushed Maggie in, closing the makeshift door behind her.

Maggie laughed to herself, giddy from the wine, as her eyes adjusted to the dim interior to see that a fire was burning in the middle for warmth and that there was something very special waiting for her against the far wall.

Duncan was there, propped up on one elbow, his hair hanging loose, and lying on a bed made of soft blankets and deerskins. He was strategically covered from the waist down, smiling a seductive smile, as he patted the bed.

Oh, dear God, I am such a lucky woman! Maggie grinned and sashayed over to the bed, dropping the robe she wore along the way.

He raised the covers as she slipped in beside him.

"Oh, Maggie," he growled, slipping his arms around her, "You were right. I LOVE these people."

Maggie purred as Duncan kissed her neck.

"Ye smell and taste like Heaven, my love. What is this stuff?" he asked as he rubbed her oil-covered breast with his hand, before catching her nipple with his mouth.

Maggie groaned. "I don't know, but I think we need a big supply of it in our bedroom," she said, sucking in a breath, arching her back, and pulling him tighter to her.

Duncan moved up, biting her lip, teasing it with his tongue. "And your lips are so sweet." He thrust his tongue into her mouth, in one swift movement, taking her breath away completely.

Wrapping her arms around his neck, Maggie met his vigor with her own.

He ran his hand down the length of her body, down to her sweet spot, and worked it until he brought her right to the edge just before he slipped inside her, and they found their release together. Duncan remained inside her, throbbing, taking his time loving her until he was once again ready to begin his welcome assault upon her, the pattern repeating several times that night before they drifted off to sleep in each other's arms, still physically entwined with every part of their bodies.

Maggie awoke when she shifted and they separated, feeling the loss within her instantly. She kissed his chest before she slipped down below the covers and woke him with her mouth upon him.

He groaned, placed his hand on her head, and guided her. She worked him up to the point of release, before climbing atop him, a deerskin blanket pooling around her waist. He held her hips and pumped into her; they worked in perfect tempo, until they both lay sated, Maggie out of breath, upon his chest.

"I love ye with every part of my soul, Maggie," Duncan whispered, stroking her back.

"I love you more, Duncan," said Maggie, snuggling in closer to him... warm, loved, and more blissful than she ever thought possible.

The next morning, he woke her with his body, and took his time making love to her one more time before they had to leave.

"I think we should build one of these close to the house," Maggie splayed her fingers over his chest, not wanting to move.

Duncan lay with one arm around her, the other folded behind his head. "Aye, I am all for that. The past few weeks have been...trying...to say the least."

"Don't I know it? But our bedroom furniture should be ready this week and I do not see any reason why we cannot live out of the one room while the rest of the house is being finished. The fireplace in there will keep us plenty warm. I am sure Gabe and Quinn would appreciate some alone time, as well," she said as she circled one of his nipples with her finger.

"I'm sure ye are right. We should finish closing in the house in the next day or so and the rest will be inside work that can be done as we go. I suppose we should head back to hurry that along." He kissed her. "I look forward to christening our new bed."

Maggie kissed him back. "Me too." She paused. "Duncan?"

"Yes, Maggie?"

"How are we going to get out of here? They took my clothes."

He chuckled. "They took mine, too." He grabbed her and rolled her onto her back, grinning. "I guess we will just have to stay a bit longer."

They reluctantly dressed when they found their clothes had been slipped inside the longhouse, emerging in each other's arms. They thanked their host and went to find the horses.

Maggie rubbed Gavina's head as Duncan saddled her. "Gavina, you are so sweet. I wish we had a dozen more just like you."

The pain shot throughout Maggie again, this time, strong enough to cause her to take a few steps back.

"What is it?" Duncan demanded.

Maggie shook her head. "I don't know. It is that weird thing again...where I feel something like a shock throughout my body and my fingers go numb. I think it might be some issue with the nerves in my hand. That's twice in two days, and it seems to be getting worse."

"Let's get ye home." he frowned; the concern apparent on his face as he cupped her cheek.

They rode up to the house. Duncan helped Maggie dismount and Harm took the horses. They went around the outside of the house, where Gabe and Quinn were admiring their progress.

"Where have you two been all night?" asked Gabe with his arms folded, his eyebrows raised like an overprotective father.

"The village. The ceremony lasted longer than we thought," said Maggie, winking at Duncan.

"That must have been some ceremony by the looks of the two of ye this morning," teased Quinn.

Gabe stepped closer to Maggie, narrowing his eyes. He ran his finger along the side of her neck, examining the oil on his finger, and showed it to Quinn.

"What's this?" he asked, his tone amused.

"I don't know, Gabe, but Duncan seems to have a little here, as well," answered Quinn, touching Duncan's ear in jest.

"It's nothing!" grumbled Duncan, slapping his hand away.

Quinn and Gabe laughed.

Duncan shook his head at their antics. "If ye two are done, we have work to do. I want to get this house sealed up so I can be alone with my wife at night without having to worry about the rest of ye hearing it."

Cora came around the corner with Kat. "We are heading into town, Colonel Asheton," she announced.

"Hold on a minute, Cora," said Gabe. "Maggie, you have been cooped up here for weeks dealing with all of this. Cora and Kat are going into town for some supplies today. Why don't you take a break and go with them?"

Duncan squeezed Maggie's hand. "Gabe is right. The house will be finished soon, and we need new things for it. We will have it closed in by the end of the day and it would be good for ye to take some time to get away from here. The distress from the house fire may be what's causing ye to feel so strange."

Maggie sighed. "Why not? I need to restock the rum anyway." She kissed Duncan slowly, then started towards the stables with Cora and Kat.

Gabe looked over at Duncan, picking up on his uneasiness. "What's going on?" he asked in a hushed tone.

"I'm not entirely sure, but it concerns me greatly," whispered Duncan.

Maggie had a lovely day with Cora and Kat; they cleared out the stores and dined at the Raleigh Tavern. The townspeople stopped to congratulate Maggie on her marriage and to inquire about the repairs at the house;

word traveled fast in a small town. Maggie stopped by the cabinetmaker to inquire about his progress. He assured her that the new bedroom furniture would be delivered in the next two days, and the other furniture shortly thereafter. She had ordered a specially built bed to accommodate Duncan's height and was having it carved with the same symbols on their wedding rings as a surprise.

When they arrived home, the house had indeed been sealed closed, now ready for the inside work to begin. They were just about to go over to Gabe's house for the evening when Harm rushed in, out of breath.

"I'm sorry, Ms. Maggie, we tried to stop him, but once he broke through, there won't nothing we could do to stop him."

Maggie sighed. "What did he do this time, Harm?"

Harm took off his hat, hung his head, and shifted on his feet, as if he were embarrassed to say.

"Harm, nothing surprises me anymore when it comes to Onyx. Just tell me. I have restocked the rum cabinet; I think I can handle it."

"Ms. Maggie...he broke through the stable that... Gavina was in."

Harm's eyes widened, looking at Duncan, as if he were afraid for his life.

"Did that beast hurt my horse?" Duncan asked, anger forming on his face.

"Well...I wouldn't say he...hurt her exactly. She ...didn't seem to mind too much."

Duncan narrowed his eyes. "WHAT did he do?"

Harm closed his eyes, bracing for the worst. "He...um... mounted her."

His face red with rage, Duncan spoke slowly and deliberately. "Are ye saying...that bloody creature...defiled...MY horse?"

Harm shrank back and nodded.

Maggie's hand flew to her mouth. "ONYX!"

"I will KILL that fecking beast!" Duncan stormed out of the front door before Maggie could stop him.

"I'm so sorry, Ms. Maggie," said Harm, looking miserable.

Maggie placed her hand on his shoulder. "Harm, Onyx does what he wants. We all know that. It is not your fault, and no one blames you for his behavior."

"Thank you, Ms. Maggie," he said, somewhat relieved, before leaving.

Turning to Gabe and Quinn, who burst into the laughter they had been trying to hold back, Maggie warned, "Don't laugh you two...this is very bad." She snickered, unable to help herself, "Duncan's head may very well explode."

Quinn finally got his laugh down to a chuckle and was able to speak. "I will go and check on my brother," he said, squeezing Gabe's shoulder.

After he left, Maggie shook her head and turned to Gabe. "Just when I thought things couldn't get any stranger around here."

Gabe pulled her into a hug, kissing the top of her head. "Never a dull moment."

Duncan was still furious with Onyx when he and Quinn returned.

Onyx had the good sense to disappear before he could be found, and Maggie hoped to quell her husband's hot temper before he returned. After supper, they lay in bed, whispering.

"I am sorry about Gavina, Duncan. I don't know what got into Onyx."

Duncan simply growled in response, still upset.

"Maybe I can take your mind off of things."

"What do ye mean?" he mumbled.

Duncan softened slightly as Maggie pulled him into a deep kiss.

"Maggie, we can't," he said tenderly, disappointment in his voice. "Everyone will hear."

"Not if we are careful," she whispered, obvious need in her voice.

Maggie turned her back to him and lifted her gown, rubbing her bottom against him, moaning simply from the heat and nearness of his body.

"Oh Maggie," he groaned. Running his hand up her thigh and right to that very special spot, he felt how completely ready she was for him and instantly became aroused.

He buried his head in her hair and slipped into her from behind. They moved slowly, deliberately—and silently—until they both sighed, Duncan's frustration tamed, his anger with Onyx forgotten. They fell asleep just like that, tangled in each other's arms, locked in a tight embrace.

Two days later, the furniture for their room arrived. Maggie had everything set up and the following evening, after supper, she surprised Duncan.

"Close your eyes." She checked to make sure he wasn't peeking. Maggie opened the door and led him inside, looking around. Everything was perfect, including the roaring fire and the many candles lit all around the room. "Okay Duncan, open your eyes."

She watched his face light up with amazement, delighted by his reaction.

"Maggie! It looks just like my bedchamber in Scotland."

Maggie had recreated it as closely as she possibly could. "Do you like it? I know you miss Scotland and gave up a great deal to be here with me. I just wanted to make you feel like THIS was home."

He pulled her tight and kissed her thoroughly. "Maggie, don't you know that home is wherever ye are?" He looked around, "But this is a nice reminder."

Pulling her over to the bed, he got a better look, rubbing his hands over the intricate woodwork. "It is beautiful...and the carvings match the design on our wedding rings perfectly. Maggie, this is wonderful. Thank you!"

He pulled her into a deep kiss.

"I think it is time we give this bed a try," he grinned.

"Oh!" giggled Maggie as he wrapped his arms around her thighs, picking her straight up and playfully laying her down, their gazes never breaking. They undressed quickly, but made love slowly the rest of the night, the first of many times in their new bed.

3 CHAPTER THREE

Towards the middle of March, the restoration was complete. The entire house had been refurbished in a style more befitting Maggie and Duncan's tastes. It had been transformed into a warm, comfortable home, greatly resembling the house in Scotland. Large area rugs with vibrant colors covered the floors, intricate Scottish tapestries, sent by Lady Aurnia, lined the walls and their wedding portrait was proudly displayed over the grand fireplace; it was the first thing anyone entering the residence saw. The new library was over the old cellar, that had been turned into the perfect chamber for the collection, a secret door added to it for security. Duncan, Gabe, and Quinn had worked tirelessly to get everything in order.

Hettie moved back into her own home and was ecstatic to resume her duties in the main house in a much larger kitchen that she'd helped Joshua design, making life easier for her.

Gabe and Quinn had a little more privacy but were still careful of themselves around Cora. A small house was planned in the spring so that she would have her own place close enough by to come nurse Kat, and Gabe and

Quinn could be together freely in their home without worrying about being seen.

Kat continued to grow and thrive into a healthy child. They all still gathered for dinner each day, becoming as close as four people could be.

They were enjoying after dinner drinks in the drawing room when Hettie appeared at the door. "Maggie, there is a messenger here for you. He says he needs to see you, personally."

Maggie set her drink down and went into the foyer. "You have a message for me?" she called to the man.

"Are you Mistress Maggie Bishop?" he asked.

"I am."

"Ma'am, I have confidential correspondence for you," he said, digging through his bag, producing a sealed envelope.

Maggie frowned and took the letter. "Thank you. Do you need to wait for a response?"

"No, ma'am." He tipped his hat and departed.

Maggie came back into the drawing room while looking down at it in her hands.

"What's that?" asked Duncan.

"No idea," Maggie said, breaking the seal, as she came to sit by the fireplace. "Oh, it's from John."

"How is he?" asked Gabe.

Maggie skimmed the letter. "He has been promoted to Major...."

"That is wonderful news." Gabe smiled, nodding. "No one is more deserving."

Maggie read on further, as her face started to grow with concern.

"FUCK!" she exclaimed. "Fuckity fuck!"

They all spun in their seats to stare at her.

Maggie looked up. "This is bad! This is VERY bad! Duncan, close the doors."

He rose and did as she instructed.

"What is it, Maggie? What does John say?" questioned Gabe.

Maggie closed her eyes and blew out a long breath. "He says that General Clinton plans on recalling you back to active duty."

"What?" a stunned Gabe asked, coming over to take the letter from her.

"Can he do that?" Quinn moved to rest his hand on Gabe's back, looking over his shoulder.

"Yes! He can!" said Gabe. "And, if he has already decided upon it, there is nothing I can do."

Gabe's face paled and he slowly sank down in one of the chairs.

Maggie took the letter back and continued to read. "Wait! We have some time. John says here that Clinton knows you are out of the country but is awaiting news of your return."

Gabe looked at Quinn. "What about Kat? I can't leave her."

"Not only that," added Maggie, standing and pacing in front of the fireplace, "Gabe, you cannot be part of the British army when this goes belly up for them. You will be lucky if the worst that happens to you is that you have to go back to London."

Maggie sat back down in the chair, in deep thought, chewing on her fingernail.

"What's on your mind, Maggie?" Duncan walked to stand next to her, knowing that she was mulling something over.

She looked down at the letter. "General Clinton is very fond of John and, not only that, he listens to him. If we can talk to John and explain that Gabe is a single father now, how Kat has no one else after losing both of her birth parents, maybe, just maybe, he can dissuade Clinton from his decision."

"And this John…he would do that for Gabe?" asked Duncan.

"He, Maggie, and I have become close friends," answered Gabe. "Yes, I think he would. I can send a messenger out right away."

"No..." Maggie stood to stand at Gabe's side, "you cannot. John sent this by private courier so the wrong person would not lay hands on it. If General Clinton finds out that he warned us, he may be in a great deal of trouble and we cannot bring that down upon him for helping us. It will require a personal visit."

"I will leave tomorrow."

Maggie took Gabe's hand. "YOU cannot go."

"Of course, I can," he argued. "I have to."

"Gabe, if General Clinton sees you, he very well may pull you back to duty on the spot, and right now, he still thinks you are out of the country. It's best if John takes his time working on him. You know how persuasive John can be. He will have Clinton convinced that is in the best interest of the British army to NOT bring you back. It's better if I go."

"Maggie," Gabe shook his head, "this is not a good idea."

Maggie looked down at the letter again. "This correspondence is dated just a few days ago and it appears that John is currently in Oyster Bay, New York. I can slip the ship straight into port, meet with him, and return the next day. It will be a quick and easy trip."

"Where have I heard that before?" asked Gabe, dryly.

"WE can slip in, ye mean," said Duncan, folding his arms.

Maggie moved next him and touched Duncan's face. "I should probably go alone for this."

He grasped her hand and kissed it. "Nay! I go where ye go. This is not up for discussion, so don't even attempt to argue with me."

"Easy trip? That's what you said about Scotland." Gabe became visibly upset. "This is too dangerous, Maggie!"

"Gabe!" Maggie attempted to calm him. "This isn't about me. This is about that little girl upstairs. She has already lost two parents and I will not allow her to lose you too. Besides..." she winked, trying to lighten the mood, "you and I made out pretty well in Scotland."

Gabe dropped his head in his hands as Quinn sat on the arm of the chair, rubbing his back.

Maggie kissed the top of his head. "Don't worry, Gabe. I will take care of all of this, I promise."

It was decided that Maggie and Duncan would leave the following day. While everyone was busy preparing for the trip, Maggie slipped into the small bedroom that had been converted into a nursery in the main house for Kat for when she visited. Kat was lost in a faraway world, smiling in her sleep.

Maggie rested one arm on the crib, reaching down to touch her little hand. "You have my word that I will not let anyone separate you and your father," she whispered, her tone soft. "You both need each other too much for me to ever let that happen."

Kat smiled as soon as the words left Maggie's mouth, acknowledging the promise that her godmother had just made.

Two arms slipped around Maggie's waist; she knew who they belonged to without even turning.

"We need to talk," he whispered in her ear.

"In a bit, Gabe. Let me watch her sleep another moment."

Gabe rested his chin on her shoulder. "I slip in every night just to make sure she is breathing and to gaze upon her as she dreams. I never thought a child could change my life as much as she has."

Maggie took in a deep breath. "That is what they do."

She leaned back against him and he tightened the embrace.

"Have you told Duncan about you and John?"

Maggie shook her head.

"Do you plan on telling him?"

"Should I?" she asked.

Gabe blew out a deep breath. "He will be furious if he finds out in a way that does not come from you."

Maggie sighed. "I suspect he will be furious either way. Those few days with John are in my past and I think it may be best to let sleeping dogs lie on that one. John is too much of a gentleman to say anything in front of Duncan anyway."

"And, what about Ben?"

Maggie turned around to face him. "Duncan knows everything about Ben."

"That's not what I mean, Maggie. What if you run into him? The New York area is where he is based, is it not?"

"I expect he will be staying more on the Connecticut side around this time, and I do not plan on being in New York long enough to see anyone except John. But, on the off chance that does happen, I will tell him that I have married, and hope it is enough to help him move on." Maggie proceeded to look out the window.

"There was a stack of letters when we returned from London from him, all saying the same thing. He is still holding out hope that I will see him when things settle down and this war is over. At some point, he will need closure to move forward with the life he is destined to have, and I will have to be the one to shatter any expectations that he has about us." She closed her eyes. "I never wanted things to end up like this. Hurting Ben is the last thing on Earth that I ever wanted to do. A part of me still cares a great deal for him."

Gabe came over and took her into another hug. "I know, sweetheart." He pulled her tighter. He knew that she blamed herself when she was as much a victim of circumstance as Ben.

"Maggie, stay here. I will take my chances going to see John. You do not need to be anywhere near New York…or Ben, for that matter."

Kat started to stir in her crib, her eyes opening, and she reached up for Gabe as soon as she saw him.

He picked her up, his face beaming with joy, as was hers, Kat cooing and smiling. The two of them had formed an extraordinarily special bond in the short span of time they had known each other.

Maggie moved next to them, taking Kat's big toe between her fingers. "I think you have your answer, Gabe. The two most important women in your life have spoken and we both say that you belong here."

Gabe and Quinn remained at the main house that night as they made final preparations for the trip. The next morning, Gabe and Quinn rode out to the ship with them.

Gabe hugged Maggie tightly. "Please be careful and stay out of trouble."

"Gabe, don't worry. We will be in and out, and back before you know it."

"Those sound like famous last words," he said dryly.

4 CHAPTER FOUR

Maggie and Duncan were on deck when they pulled up to the dock at Oyster Bay. The closer they had gotten to the shore, the more anxious Maggie had become.

"This place is crawling with soldiers," Maggie said, scanning the area. "I had no idea there were so many here."

"Are ye sure your friend John will welcome us?"

"Yes, but Duncan," she turned to him, "you must let me take the lead here, control your temper, and watch everything you say. Any word out of turn could put us on the wrong end of a rope before we know it. This is not Scotland and things are very different here at this time."

He kissed her. "I will be on my best behavior, my love."

The ship was met by a group of British soldiers that boarded and started searching it, as the captain of the soldiers detained Maggie, Duncan, Captain Russell, and the rest of the crew.

"I am Captain Wilson, in charge of search and seizure of all ships coming into Oyster Bay. State your name and business for the record."

Maggie stepped forward. "I am Mistress Maggie Bishop MacGregor of Virginia and I am here on a personal matter."

"What matter?" he spat, obviously annoyed by having a woman address him.

"I am here to see Major John André on private business. I must insist that you contact him and make him aware of my presence without delay."

"We are not yet finished searching this ship and I do not answer to WOMEN!" Captain Wilson took a step closer to Maggie, looking her up and down. "Least of all, one of Major André's cock-sucking whores. You all regularly come through here demanding special attention and I have had quite enough of it."

Maggie closed her eyes. She knew what was coming and that there was no way to stop it, so she merely took a step to the side to get out of the way.

Duncan was on the man before he knew it, pounding him to a bloody pulp. It took five soldiers to pull Duncan away, and two more to get the ill-mannered captain back on his feet.

Wilson bent over and spit out a mouthful of blood along with a few broken teeth.

"Take him and the crew to the gaol. Escort this woman to my office; I will deal with her personally. This ship and all contents onboard are hereby seized by order of the Crown."

Maggie turned to Duncan; her arms folded, like a mother scolding her child, as she sent him a silent message. *Didn't we just talk about this? Seriously? Less than half an hour ago.*

No man speaks to my wife that way. He smiled. *It was worth it.*

Maggie shook her head. *I will get you out as soon as I can. Try not to make things any worse.*

He winked. *I love ye, Maggie!*

I love you too.

After Duncan had been taken away, two soldiers took her by the arms and led her to a small office in a building by the dock, placing themselves on either side of her.

Glad they didn't search me.

Maggie leaned with her back against the desk, eyeing her guards. "How would you gentlemen like to make a week's wages for a few moments work?"

The two soldiers looked at each other, unsure of what their answer should be.

Captain Wilson appeared shortly thereafter and dismissed the men, leaving the two of them alone. His right eye was swollen completely shut, and his nose was obviously broken; he still pressing a handkerchief to it to staunch the blood that continued to gush from his nostrils. "Your man will hang for this! I will supervise it myself."

Maggie shrugged. "I doubt that."

He leaned over the desk towards her. "I wouldn't be so smug if I were you. He assaulted an officer of the Crown, and that is a very serious charge."

Taking a seat, Maggie acted disinterested as he came around the edge of the desk and eyed her lustfully up and down.

"I may, however, be persuaded to drop the charges—if you perform for me as well as you do for Major André."

Maggie inwardly gagged. "I don't think so. I am not that kind of girl. Besides, you are not my type."

He leaned down, sneering. "I do not need your permission. You are colonist filth. I can do what I wish with you and no one will stop me; they will not even come when they hear you scream."

Maggie shifted in her chair. "You could try, but I will not be held responsible for what fate befalls you if you do."

"Are you threatening me?" He threw the bloody rag down on the desk.

Maggie leaned forward, narrowing her eyes, turning to face him. "No! I am promising you that you will never lay your disgusting hands on me."

He roughly grabbed her by the arm. Maggie reached for the dagger in her boot, ready to slit his throat.

A noise outside distracted them as the door flew wide open.

"Get your filthy hands off of her!" Standing in the doorway, seething, Major John André set his hand on the hilt of his sword. He must have been nearby when the men she paid went to locate him.

Captain Wilson released her and moved to take his seat. "I am merely interrogating a traitor, MAJOR André. She sailed in on a ship that has been confiscated."

John stalked across the room and leaned across the desk. "This woman is no traitor and she carries my FULL protection. Her ship and all her property are to be released immediately. Is that clear?"

"You cannot do that Major André," he angrily protested.

"I... JUST...DID!" he spat, "And, I will deal with YOU later, CAPTAIN Wilson."

John turned, offering Maggie his hand to help her stand, then escorted her out of the building and onto the street. As soon as they were clear, John turned to her, smiled, and took her into a long embrace.

"Maggie! It is so good to see you," he said, kissing her cheek.

"Your timing is impeccable, as always, John!" she leaned against him, still a little shaken from the day's events.

He placed his hand on the small of her back. "Come! I have a carriage waiting."

He helped her inside and once they were alone, he asked, "Maggie, what are you doing here? Where is Gabe? Is he with you?"

"No," she sighed, leaning back. "He is actually the reason I came to see you. I am in need of a personal favor...actually, I now need two of them."

"Of course! Whatever I can do." He took her hand and noticed the wedding ring as he looked down. He lifted his gaze and gave her a puzzled look as his smile slowly faded. "You have married?" he whispered, taken aback.

"I have," said Maggie gently, offering him a sympathetic look.

"Gabe?" he asked in disbelief.

"No," she squeezed his hand. "My husband's name is Duncan MacGregor. I met him in Scotland while we were away."

"I see," he said, dismay in his voice. He forced a slight smile. "Congratulations. Although I must say, I am... disappointed, to say the least." He frowned. "Please, tell me you married for love, Maggie!"

She smiled. "I did indeed! I love him very much and we are extremely happy."

John nodded. "Well for that, I am... grateful." He cleared his throat as he regained his composure. "I wish to hear all about it, but I must ask, why is he not with you? Oyster Bay is not a safe place for a woman alone."

Maggie sighed. "Your Captain Wilson has him locked up."

"That man," John spoke with contempt in his voice, "is a vile, disgusting human being. He is a cancer on the British army that needs to be surgically removed. Why

General Clinton keeps him around is beyond me. What are the charges?"

Maggie winced. "You saw his face? It was courtesy of Duncan."

John chuckled. "I see! I have to say that I think I like your husband already. But what brought it about?"

"I am pretty sure it was because when I requested to see you...Captain Wilson called me one of...what was it... 'Major André's cock-sucking whores who demand special attention'. Duncan fell upon him before I could stop him."

John's eyes widened, and his mouth dropped to reveal looks of shock and embarrassment on his face.

"My...God...Maggie," he stuttered. "I am so sorry that he spoke to you that way. It is unconscionable that man would dare say such a thing to you...of ALL people. I do not know what to say to such abominable behavior."

"John, can you get him released?" She asked.

He nodded his head. "I can, but it may take some time and it may require filing formal charges on your part. There will be a process that will need to be worked through. Where did they take him?"

"To the gaol."

"That's good! I can ensure his safety while seeing that he is, at the very least, comfortable there. Thankfully, he was not sent to one of the prisoner ships that are out of my control."

"Thank you, John."

He nodded just before he broke into a horrible coughing fit.

"John, are you alright? You sound awful, and you look a little pale." Maggie leaned forward, very concerned.

He removed a handkerchief from his coat pocket. "I contracted a fever a few weeks ago on my travels. I found myself in Oyster Bay when the worst of it hit, so I have been recovering at a friend's residence ever since."

Maggie touched his arm. "I am so sorry to bring all of this to you, but I am glad to see you, John. I have missed you very much."

"I have missed you as well, Maggie. I think of our time together often...and fondly." He kissed her hand. "And, what of this other favor that you need?"

"Oh yes! My reason for coming to begin with. First of all, thank you for the warning about Gabe's recall. He wanted to write, but I did not want to take the chance on getting you in trouble with General Clinton for letting us know."

"I greatly appreciate that."

"I am here on Gabe's behalf hoping that you might be able to sway General Clinton from his decision. You see, Gabe is a new father."

John looked surprised. "What? Gabe? He never mentioned being involved with anyone."

Maggie explained how Gabe's new title came about.

"That is quite a story. And, he just took the child in...like that?"

"He did, and he is such an amazing father. Gabe's loss of his wife and baby took a great toll on him, but this has given him a second chance. Katherine does not have another soul in this world. Surely, General Clinton will understand if you explain things to him, or I will gladly go beg him myself. Whatever it takes. I made young Kat a promise that I intend to keep."

"I will do my best Maggie, but I will have to handle something as delicate as this in person. I will be rejoining General Clinton soon."

"I understand. I am grateful for anything you can do."

"Of course!" John smiled. "It sounds as if you two had quite the trip. Did Gabe make it to his mother before she passed?"

"Oh yes, that! She actually made a full recovery and remarried while we were there...to her physician who is half her age."

John laughed. "Oh my! London must be abuzz with gossip."

The carriage came to a stop and Maggie looked outside. "Where are we?"

John opened the door and stepped out, holding out his hand to assist her. "This is where I am currently residing; the headquarters of Lt. Colonel John Simcoe of the Queen's Rangers."

Maggie gazed upon the lovely two-story home as John escorted her inside to a parlour, taking her cloak.

"John?" Maggie asked, taking a seat, "Is there any way I can see Duncan?"

John poured two drinks, handing her one as he answered. "I can arrange for a brief visit to see to his welfare." He sat down opposite her, "In the meantime, I will write the orders to have your ship and crew released."

Maggie nodded. "Thank you. And might you know where they would have taken Onyx?"

John looked surprised. "You brought your horse with you?"

"You know me and Onyx, we are joined at the hip, so to speak."

John laughed softly. "He would have been seized. I can inquire as to where he is." He caught sight of something in his peripheral vision, outside of the window as he looked past Maggie. He turned his head slightly, as if the view before him were a figment of his imagination. Setting down his drink, he moved to the window, drawing the curtains further back for a better look. "Or, you could just go outside."

Maggie stood, set down her glass, and moved next to him to see that Onyx was standing in front of the house. She shook her head and grinned. "Onyx! He can always find me no matter what."

Maggie patted John on the back and was about to go outside when a voice stopped her.

"John? Any idea who this fine horse outside belongs to? I may need to commandeer him." A man appeared in the doorway, looking apologetic as soon as he saw Maggie.

"Forgive me. I did not realize that you were...entertaining."

He stepped back.

"John, come in. I wish to introduce you to my dear friend, Mistress Maggie Bishop... MacGregor. Maggie, I would like you to meet Lt. Colonel John Graves Simcoe, Commander of Her Majesty's Queen's Rangers."

Simcoe removed his hat and bowed, before he came over to greet her.

"Mistress, it is my pleasure to make your acquaintance."

Maggie offered her hand. "Thank you, and yours as well."

"That is Maggie's horse outside," said John, "and I am afraid you would have a devil of a time taking that one. He is fiercely loyal to Maggie....and he bites."

"I see. Wherever did you find him?"

"He followed me home one day and just never left," teased Maggie.

John poured Simcoe a drink and they moved to sit. "Maggie needs our assistance. That damnable Captain Wilson had her husband arrested earlier and then tried to accost poor Maggie in his office. Thankfully, she had the forethought to send for me."

Simcoe shook his head. "That man is a despicable disgrace to the uniform. What is he charged with?"

"Assault, I am assuming," said John. "Mr. MacGregor did not react kindly to his wife being insulted by that piece of trash."

"Did he at the very least get a few good licks in, my dear?" Simcoe asked Maggie.

"I would say so. I am fairly certain the captain's nose is broken and that he is shy a few teeth this afternoon."

"Very good," chuckled Simcoe. "I only wish I had been present for the show."

John smirked. "You should see him, John. I think Mr. MacGregor deserves a commendation personally. I, for one, am anxious to shake the man's hand and buy him a drink." He broke into another coughing fit.

Maggie moved to his side, feeling his forehead then taking his face in her hands. "John, you should be in bed, not running all over the place for me. Your color is horrid."

He placed his hands over hers. "Thank you for your concern, but I am fine."

Simcoe set down his drink. "Mistress MacGregor is right, John. Go get some rest before dinner."

"Nonsense," said John. "Maggie needs to see her husband and I have to ensure that her property and crew are released. I will write the necessary papers and escort her there."

Simcoe stood. "You write the paperwork and I will see her into town. It will give me the perfect opportunity to get a gander at Captain Wilson while I am there." He winked.

John shook his head and laid back in the chair, exhausted.

Maggie placed her hands on her hips. "No arguing, John. You are going to bed if I have to drag you there myself."

"Don't tempt me," he teased. "You are a married woman now."

An hour later, Maggie waited for a soldier to open the gaol door. Once open, she rushed into the cell. "Duncan!"

He was alone, sitting against the wall, his knees propped up. He stood as he heard the door open. "Maggie!"

He pulled her tight to him and kissed her.

She placed her hands on his face, gently stroking over his numerous cuts and bruises. "Are you alright? How badly did they hurt you?"

"I am perfectly fine, my love."

He winced when she leaned into him.

"You are lying." Maggie lifted his shirt to see the area around his ribs, only to reveal that he was black and blue.

"Duncan! What did they do to you?"

He pulled her hands down. "This is nothing. I am more concerned about ye. Did that bastard hurt ye?"

Maggie shook her head. "I was able to get the word out to John and he came immediately. We are working on getting you out, but it may take a few days. Captain Wilson is pressing charges, but John has asked me to file a grievance against him for HIS behavior. He is going to make sure they keep you here safe and not allow you to be taken to one of the prisoner ships, which would be very bad. I just do not want to be away from you for another minute."

"Dinna fash about me. What of the ship and crew?"

"The paperwork has been signed to release all of them. It is being handled as we speak."

"Good."

Maggie slipped her arms around his waist carefully. "As soon as we get you out, we can be on our way home to our nice warm, comfortable bed."

He hugged her. "I look forward to that."

The guard banged on the door to indicate their time was up.

"Duncan, I am not sure how often they will let me see you, but I will be back as soon as I possibly can. I love you."

"I love ye too, Maggie. Stay safe and out of trouble."

Maggie scoffed. "Says the man in jail."

Simcoe needed to stay in town, so he sent Maggie back in the carriage alone, which gave her a chance to get her first good look at Oyster Bay. It was in a sad state of affairs.

British soldiers were on every corner, and the townspeople looked afraid for their very lives. Uniformed men shoved residents to the ground, and dragged others out of their homes, before they ransacked the buildings, and stole their livestock. Williamsburg and Maggie's estate had remained relatively unaccosted thus far, but this small town was in the thick of it and it was not a good place to be. Even the church had been decimated, turned into barracks for the soldiers. Maggie's heart broke for these poor souls and she just wished this war was over for all concerned.

She arrived at the house just before dinner and found John dozing in a chair in the parlour. She went over to him, and felt his face for fever, as his eyes slowly opened. She kissed his forehead.

"Hello, my sleeping beauty."

"Hello, my sweet, Maggie."

"How are you feeling, John?"

"Better, now that you are here," he said and kissed her hand. "How is your husband?"

Maggie sat down across from him on the sofa, her face in her hands, closing her eyes. "They beat him, John."

John sighed and moved to sit next to her, wrapping his arm around her. "I am so sorry. I will see that he gets medical attention."

"How did all of this happen? We just came to try to keep Gabe and his daughter together and look where we are now."

"You have my word, Maggie, I WILL get this sorted out." John reached down and took her by the hand, rubbing it, when he noticed her wrist.

"How does your husband feel about you wearing the bracelet another man gave you?"

She looked down at it. "I told you before John, it is a part of me; I never take it off."

He leaned closer and whispered, "Does he know about us? About the time we shared together?"

"No, and I would prefer to keep it that way. There are some things better left unsaid."

"As you wish."

A man appeared at the door, clearing his throat.

"Major André?"

John lowered his head, annoyed by the interruption. "Yes, please come in." He stood.

"Allow me to introduce my dear friend, Mistress Maggie MacGregor. Maggie, this is our host, Mr. Samuel Townsend."

Townsend. Of course, his name would be Townsend. A name associated with Washington's spies and his network. This man's son would become Samuel Culper Jr. and provide invaluable information to the General. It was foolish to believe this would ever be a simple trip.

Maggie composed herself and stood. "Mr. Townsend. It is a pleasure to meet you."

"Mistress." He nodded. "Dinner is served."

At the table, Maggie was introduced to his wife, Sarah and two teenage daughters, Phebe and Sally.

"You have a lovely home. Thank you for your hospitality," said Maggie, taking a good look at Samuel Townsend. The man was not well, very underweight, fatigued by stress, and aged well beyond his years.

"Mr. Townsend runs a store out of the back of the house," said John. "I am surprised the two of you have not crossed paths."

"Oh?" asked Mr. Townsend.

"Maggie owns a shipping company out of Virginia."

"Is that right Mistress MacGregor? What do you import?"

Maggie laid down her fork. "A little bit of everything from all over the world. I recently brought back a great many books from London. My partner's nephew owns a bookstore there. Which reminds me, John, I have several on the ship for you, if Captain Wilson didn't throw them overboard in his anger."

John acknowledged Samuel's unspoken question. "Captain Wilson had Maggie's husband arrested. We are trying to sort through it now."

Their host frowned.

"Who is your partner, Maggie?" asked John.

"I gave half of the business to Gabe. He resigned his commission to take care of me; it was the least I could do for him. Besides, he has a child to support now."

"That was very kind of you. I must say, I do wish Gabe had been able to come along with you. I miss our friendship, and I would love to meet his new daughter. Maybe I can visit when this war business is done...if my invitation still stands."

"Always," said Maggie sadly, knowing he would never get the chance.

After dinner, Maggie and John spent time in the parlour catching up.

"John, as much as I hate to leave, I really need to go find a room for the night."

"Nonsense! You will stay here."

Maggie looked around. "I do not want to be more of an imposition than I have already been. Besides, I think you have a full house here already."

The front door opened, interrupting their conversation; Simcoe entered the house with Captain Russell.

"Mistress MacGregor," said Captain Russell, taking off his hat.

Maggie stood and went to greet him. "Are you and the crew alright, Captain?"

He frowned. "We are, but Lt. Colonel Simcoe just told me that they are still holding your husband in the gaol."

"Yes, we are working to get him freed, and as soon as we do, we will be sailing for home, without delay."

He shook his head. "I am afraid that will be impossible, Mistress."

"What? Why not?" asked a very agitated Maggie.

"I just left the ship. It seems that Captain Wilson was more than a little infuriated by his more than well-deserved beating. He had his men destroy the inside of it and burn all the sails."

Maggie blinked in disbelief, unable to form words for a moment. "He...destroyed... MY ship? My PERSONAL ship?"

Captain Russell nodded.

Maggie closed her eyes, trying to contain her ire, pinching the area between her brows. "Of course, he did."

"It will take weeks, if not months to make all of the repairs, and that is only if I can locate what we need. I am sorry, ma'am. The crew and I will get to work as soon as possible," replied Captain Russell, before he excused himself to go back to town.

Maggie moved to the window to watch him depart as John and Simcoe discussed the matter.

After Simcoe left, John moved to her side. "I cannot tell you how dreadful I feel about this, Maggie. Something has to be done about that man, the sooner the better."

He touched her face, tucking a stray piece of hair behind her ear before leading her to a chair. He handed her a glass of sherry. "You will stay under my care, for your own protection. I would never forgive myself if any harm were to come to you."

Maggie watched the flames in the fireplace, realizing that she was trapped...and at the worst possible time. The Culper Ring would just be getting started, not having yet recruited one of its most crucial members, the son of her host, no less, Robert Townsend. The least little thing could upset the entire process, derailing the outcome of the war. Once again, her good intentions had landed her right smack dab in the middle of it all, and it was the last place that she needed to be.

That night, unable to sleep, worrying about Duncan, Maggie slipped downstairs to take a seat on the sofa in front of the fireplace. She was so lost in thought, she didn't hear John come in. He touched her shoulder, breaking her concentration.

"I had a feeling you would be awake."

Maggie covered his hand with hers. "No need for both of us to be. You should be resting, John."

He brought over two glasses, taking a seat on the sofa next to her. "I can't. My curiosity has the better of me. Tell me about him...the man who has stolen you away from me."

"Oh, John! I know you have not been pining away for me here all by your lonesome," she teased, accepting the glass.

He grinned sheepishly. "I admit, I have not been alone, but you are still the one I think of the most. I had hoped this war would have been over with by now so we would have had our chance to explore where things might have gone."

Maggie touched his arm. "I owe you a debt of gratitude."

"For what?" he asked.

"In Philadelphia, when we were together. I was in a very bad place, as you well know. When I lost so much at one time...a piece inside of me was...broken. That time with you helped me to heal. I would have never been able to fall in love with Duncan if you had not been there for me in THAT way when I needed you the most."

He looked down, took her hand and kissed it, feeling truly touched by her confession.

He cleared his throat to hide the fact that he was choking up. "Tell me about him," he whispered. "How did you end up in Scotland to begin with?"

"I was actually assisting Gabe's nephew. The boy had gotten himself into some trouble at the local brothel. Gabe had just gotten Kat, so I insisted he stay in London and I went in his place. It was to be a quick and easy trip, much like this one was supposed to be."

John raised an eyebrow, "A whorehouse?"

Maggie laughed. "Yes, and I went inside his room to retrieve him." She told him all about the scene until he was roaring with laughter.

"Oh, my dear Maggie, you are an extraordinarily brave woman."

"Anyway, since I was already in Scotland, I decided to nose about a bit to look for information about the crest on my sword."

John's eyes flew open wide. "I had completely forgotten! The shield on your sword! It belonged to the 'Gregor' family. The same?"

Maggie nodded. "Indeed. The sword was a part of their collection, as was a book that I came into possession of that they had lost. I met the family when I returned it."

John was astonished. "That is...unbelievable. I have to say, Maggie, it sounds as if you and your husband were, for lack of sounding too cliché, 'meant to be'. It seems that fate played a tremendous role in your relationship."

"I would have to agree with that, John. He and I fell in love almost immediately and, now I cannot imagine my life without him." She looked into her glass, swallowing the lump in her throat. "This is the first night we have been apart since we wed, and it physically hurts."

John put his arm around her shoulder. "I will reunite the two of you, I give you my word."

She leaned into him. "Thank you. Between this and the fire..."

"What fire?"

"Oh! My home was ablaze when we stepped off the ship after returning from London. A chimney fire destroyed the kitchen part of the house. We had just finished settling in from rebuilding when your letter came."

"Your marriage is off to an interesting start."

"I suppose it is."

A noise in the hall caused Maggie to sit up, giving John a curious look.

He inclined his head that way. "Lt. Colonel Simcoe and the young Miss Townsend have been keeping company."

"Does her father know?"

"He does, although I expect he is not thrilled about it."

"Is it serious?"

John leaned closer as he took a sip of his drink.

"I am not really sure, if I am being completely honest. He gifted her a valentine with a bit of poetry that set her heart all aflutter," he smirked behind his glass, "It was some of my best work, if I do say so myself."

"You wrote it?"

John laughed softly. "I had a hand in it, but he was the one who actually wrote down the words on paper. He winked. "Let's keep that between us."

"Ever the romantic, aren't you John?"

"I do my part," he chuckled, but then started to cough.

"Alright mister...up to bed you go."

"It is nothing, Maggie."

She stood, holding out her hand. "Come on, I will tuck you in and tell you a bedtime story if you are a good boy."

After breakfast, John had some correspondence to answer so Maggie went outside for some fresh air to clear her head. She noticed a decimated area off the side of the house and moved closer for a better look. Whatever had grown here, was completely destroyed except for one little pitiful sapling, a mere few inches tall, trying to hold on for dear life.

"That apple orchard was my pride and joy," a voice said from behind her.

Maggie turned to see Samuel Townsend walking towards her, his hands clasped behind his back.

"What happened to it?" asked Maggie, turning to look back across the field.

"The Queen's Rangers tore it down for firewood. God's beautiful creation destroyed for something so mundane. I suppose that is what happens when the serpent is set loose in the Garden of Eden."

"I am so sorry, Mr. Townsend. This war has taken far more than it has given back, affecting so many."

"Indeed, it has, Mistress MacGregor. Sometimes, I wonder if this country will ever recover from all of the loss it has experienced."

Maggie offered a reassuring look. "We must remind ourselves that God has a plan, sometimes so monumental, that it is too much for us to see in the moment."

He looked at her thoughtfully. "You sound very sure of that, Mistress MacGregor."

Bending down, Maggie gingerly touched the tiny sprig trying to spring to life in the middle of so much emptiness. She felt horrible for Townsend, knowing how badly he must feel, especially after knowing how much her mother's own gardens meant to her. Maggie knew what was to come. The war would bring devastation to this countryside, a cleansing if you will, before it's grand rebirth into what it would become, but she wished the destruction was not as hard on these poor people in its path as it was. The thought brought a well-known phrase into Maggie's mind.

"From the ashes of the fire, the phoenix shall rise," she whispered, almost as if in a trance.

As soon as the words left her mouth, Maggie felt a heat spread throughout her entire body, a white flame far more powerful than anything she had ever experienced before, setting alight every nerve inside of her. The impact was so strong, that it knocked her backward on the ground, depleting her of all energy, leaving her almost too exhausted to breathe. Her eyes closed, and she slipped into oblivion.

She was being carried inside by one of the soldiers when she came to.

"Lay her on the sofa," she heard John say, "and send for the surgeon."

"No," Maggie managed. "I do not need a doctor."

John pulled up a chair beside her, looking very concerned. "Maggie, you collapsed."

"I am fine now, John. I just need a drink, please."

Mr. Townsend poured her one and handed it to her; she slowly sat up to take the proffered libation.

John helped her with the glass. "Maggie, I must insist you receive medical attention."

She looked down at her hand, her fingers completely numb. "It will pass. It always does."

"This has happened before?" he asked incredulously.

Maggie nodded. "It usually involves a numbness in my hand and a shooting pain, but I have never lost consciousness."

John's eyes went wild.

Maggie attempted to assure him. "I am certain it is from the distress of the past few days, that's all. It seems to happen when things are in an uproar."

"Just the same, Mistress MacGregor, perhaps you should get some rest," said Mr. Townsend.

"Yes," agreed John. "I have some things to handle in town. Will you, at the very least, lie down while I am gone?"

Maggie was still feeling devoid of energy. "I think I will."

He helped her upstairs, into bed, and kissed her forehead before departing. "I will return shortly."

As soon as Maggie cleared her mind, a message from Duncan came across.

What happened? I felt something!

She sent a response before she drifted off to sleep. *Nothing that you need to concern yourself with, my love. I just need to rest for a bit.*

Maggie? Maggie!

5 CHAPTER FIVE

Maggie was dreaming of Duncan, his hand gently touching her face, softly calling her name. Coming to, she desperately tried to hold on to it, only it wasn't a dream. As her eyes fluttered open, she saw his face and smiled.

"Duncan!"

"I am here, my love."

Maggie sat up, pulling him close and burying her face in his chest. "How ARE you here? Have the charges been dropped?"

"No!" John answered from the doorway. "I was, however, able to convince the powers-that-be to release him into my custody for the time being because of the distress all of this is causing you. He is confined to the inside of the house when he is not accompanied by me, but he will be safe and the two of you can be together."

Maggie looked over at John. "Thank you, John."

He nodded. "I will leave you two alone," he said, and closed the door behind him.

Duncan took her face in his hands. "What happened to ye?"

"It was that strange nerve thing that has been happening, only it was much worse this time. It caused me to black out and when I came to, I was too exhausted to move. How did you know?"

"I felt something odd...a shift of some sort, as I did when Finn was onboard the ship. I cannot describe it."

"You don't think he has anything to do with this, do you?" she asked.

"I do not know, Maggie, but it would be best if ye were seen by the doctor to be sure."

Maggie leaned against his chest, and he wrapped his arms around her. "No, I feel fine now, besides I have a strange feeling that none of this has anything to do with my health."

"I cannot wait to get out of New York," he muttered.

Maggie cringed. "They destroyed the ship."

He pushed her back to look her in the eyes. "What? Who?"

"Captain Wilson was more than a little enraged about what you did to him. He burned the sails and broke the sailing instruments. Captain Russell and the crew are trying to piece it back together, but it could take weeks...or even months."

Duncan dropped his head. "Och! This is all my fault. I should have controlled myself as ye warned me to."

Maggie pushed the hair out of his face. "It is what it is. All we can do is deal with it. But right now, I am just happy you are back by my side where you belong."

By suppertime, Duncan had bathed, and Maggie was feeling much better. After a quiet meal, Maggie, Duncan, and John retired to the parlour, and the Townsend family to their own part of the house. Simcoe was not expected until later.

"I must thank ye Major André for your help," said Duncan.

"Please, call me John. I feel as if I already know you, and you are welcome. I could not stand to see Maggie so upset, but then again, I have never been able to."

"Yes," said Maggie. "John is always coming to my aid, it seems."

Duncan looked confused.

"John was the one who found me the night I was shot."

"Oh," replied Duncan. "I did not realize."

"One of the most frightening nights of my life, I must say. Although, today was a close second," he said with a glance toward Maggie.

John's coughing fit began again, and when he leaned forward, it became much nastier. Maggie stood and went to him, rubbing his back.

"Forgive me."

"John, this is getting worse," said Maggie. "What does the doctor say?"

"He said it is left over from the fever and will go away, eventually."

Duncan looked at John. "Does the owner of the house have an herb garden?"

John nodded. "I believe so. The servants would know."

Duncan set down his drink. "I will be right back." And he left the room.

"I rather like him, Maggie," John said, wiping his mouth with his handkerchief.

"I am pretty fond of him myself," she replied. "I think I will keep him."

Duncan returned a short time later with a cup of tea. "Drink this. It will help."

John looked at the cup. "What is it?"

"An herbal remedy for coughing. It is an old, family recipe, passed down through the years." Duncan winked at Maggie.

How old?

Ancient.

Duncan smiled slyly.

John took a sip. "It is quite good."

Maggie eyed Duncan. "Is that one of Quinn's concoctions?"

"Aye, he has been teaching me a few things."

Maggie folded her arms and looked at John, chuckling. "You might want to find a bed soon. Some of Quinn's drinks will have you forgetting who and where you are in a matter of moments. The first one I had, snuffed me out like a candle."

"Who is Quinn?" asked John.

"My brother. He came with us to Virginia. He is back there with Gabe and Kat looking after things while we are away, and that particular mixture will not knock you out, simply soothe your chest. I will stir up a batch and leave it with the kitchen servants so ye can have it whenever ye need it."

"Thank you. That is very kind of you."

Duncan moved to Maggie, taking her into his arms, staring into her eyes. "John, if ye will excuse us, I would like to retire with my wife. I have been away from her for entirely too long."

Maggie and Duncan were already lost in each other's gaze, oblivious to anyone or anything around them.

John smiled impishly. "Of course. Good night."

An hour later, they lay in bed tangled up in each other's limbs. Maggie ran her hand over Duncan's bruises on his chest and abdomen, and frowned, still disturbed by the sight of them.

He pulled her hand away and kissed it. "Dinna fash, it is nothing, my love," he whispered, drifting off to sleep, exhausted from his stay in the gaol.

Maggie was wide awake, so she decided to go downstairs for a drink, in hopes that it would help her sleep. She wrapped herself in a robe and slipped down quietly. Maggie paused when she heard John and Simcoe talking.

"My man, Brookes, in Washington's camp is working out very well," said John.

"The information we are receiving is proving invaluable. No one suspects their secrets are coming straight from their own encampment. It's amazing how cheaply disgruntled soldiers can be bought."

"A toast," said Simcoe, "to General Washington's first trip out of winter quarters. As soon as he announces to the men where he is going, we will be waiting for him to cut off the head of this rebellion, once and for all. No Washington, no war."

Damn!

Maggie closed her eyes. She had just heard information that she could not ignore, even if she wanted to. If Washington was to be captured or killed, all would be lost, and the war would be over. Now, what was she going to do with the news that she had just learned?

She turned to go back up the stairs when the bottom step creaked.

"Who is there?" called out John.

Fuck! Busted!

"It is just me, John." She moved to the doorway, pulling her robe tightly to her. "I was coming down for a drink. You know I do not sleep well."

Simcoe and John exchanged a grave look.

"Oh, Lt Colonel Simcoe, I did not realize that you were back. We missed you at supper."

John stared at her; his face solemn. "How long have you been there, Maggie?"

Damn it!

"I just came down," she said with a smile. "Duncan fell asleep and I did not want to disturb him with my restlessness."

John stroked his chin, silent.

"If you two are engaged in something, I can just take a glass and go back up. I do not want to intrude," she said sweetly.

John took in a deep breath, as he tried to read her, pausing a long moment before speaking.

Maggie thought for sure she was done for.

"Of course, you are not intruding. Let me get you that drink." He watched her intently as he poured.

"John and I were just discussing his relationship with Miss Townsend."

He handed the glass to Maggie and led her to a chair.

Act normally, Maggie. John can spot suspicious behavior a mile away.

"Oh! She is a lovely young lady."

Simcoe looked at John, then back at Maggie, and forced a smile. "Yes, she is."

Maggie sipped the drink.

Lighten the mood.

"You should be careful," Maggie smirked. "This one over here may steal her away from you."

Simcoe shot a narrow-eyed look at John, before his face broke into a grin. "Oh, I keep my eye on him. John can't romance all the ladies at once, no matter how hard he tries."

Maggie laughed as John blushed.

"You are making me look like a cad in front of Maggie, old friend."

Simcoe pointed towards the desk. "That stack of letters from Philadelphia is making you look bad enough. I can smell the perfume from all the way over here."

Maggie winked at John. "Philadelphia? Anyone, I know?"

John looked down, as he shook his head. "I merely keep in contact for the news in town."

"Is that what they are calling it these days?" Maggie quipped.

Simcoe watched the banter between the two of them with amusement.

"So, who has been in the 'news' while I have been out of the country."

John bit his lip. "I have thought of no one save you, and you break my heart by running off to marry another."

"Forgive me!" Maggie waved her glass in a grand gesture. "I am a heartless shrew. Take comfort in the fact that another saved you the misery of my company."

"I wouldn't exactly call it misery," smiled John, a touch of melancholy in his voice.

Maggie leaned forward, reaching for the St. Michael necklace hanging from his neck.

"You still wear it?" she asked.

He leaned closer. "It is a part of me. I never take it off." He touched her face, then kissed her forehead.

After Maggie was convinced that John did not suspect she'd overheard their conversation, she returned upstairs to bed and safely back into Duncan's arms. He stirred slightly as they settled together.

Maggie was still awake when the sun rose.

They dressed and went down to join John for breakfast.

"Maggie," said John after they were seated and eating, "I have been giving Duncan's situation a great deal of consideration. You need to file a grievance against Captain Wilson. The man you need to see is currently in Setauket and will not be here for another week. I think it may be best if you get to him first to file your complaint so that by the time Wilson's reason for filing charges are heard, it will simply appear that the Captain is doing so in retaliation. If you explain the circumstances, I feel he will be sympathetic to your cause. I will also write a report in support of you and Duncan."

"Whatever you think is best, John," said Maggie.

He laid his napkin on the table and sighed. "Unfortunately, I cannot escort you there, and Duncan will have to remain here since he is in my custody."

Duncan pushed his plate away and rested his arms on the table. "Nay! Maggie is not traveling alone, my freedom or not," he said adamantly. "It is not safe, and I will not allow her to be put in danger."

"Oh!" said John, sipping from his glass. "I did not mean to imply that she would go alone. I will send armed guards to ensure her safety. The wooded areas between the towns are full of ruffians and are not safe for anyone unaccompanied. Maggie, you should be able to be there and back by nightfall. If it does take longer, however, the guards will secure your lodgings for the night. But, only IF, you are feeling up to it after yesterday." John rubbed his forehead with his index finger, a troubled expression on his face. "I am still gravely concerned about your health. I do wish you would let the surgeon look you over."

"I appreciate your concern, but I am quite well, John," she smiled, reassuringly.

Duncan looked at Maggie and shook his head, "There must be another way!"

She laid her hand on top of his, intertwining her fingers in his. "It will be fine, Duncan. We need to get this settled if we are to ever return home." *Please, trust me, my love! Let me do this for you.*

John sighed. "I would not suggest this if I thought it unsafe, Duncan. I would never do anything to put Maggie in jeopardy, and I truly believe this is your best option to have these charges completely removed."

An hour later, Maggie was in their room packing her saddlebag, when Duncan came in, looking extremely unsettled.

"Close the door," she said, then pulled him close to the window so they would not be heard and told him the details of what she overheard the night before. "I have to warn them."

"Maggie..." Duncan began to protest but she laid her finger over his lips to quiet him, and whispered, "They have contacts in Setauket. I merely need to get word to one of them and that is ALL it will involve. I will take no unnecessary chances, but if the opportunity presents itself, I will seize it."

"I do not like this at all!" His voice was strained.

"I know, Duncan, but if Washington is killed, this country is doomed before it has a chance to begin. I cannot sit by and let something like that happen if it is in my power to prevent it."

Duncan looked down at her, then closed his eyes and pulled her tight. "No unnecessary chances? Ye give me your word?"

"I promise, Duncan."

He cupped her cheek and stroked her face with his thumb. "Make sure ye come back to me. I love ye too much to lose ye."

"I love you too, Duncan."

Maggie rode Onyx out later that morning, flanked by four British soldiers, who had been ordered to remain by her side at all times. Three hours later, they arrived in Setauket, a little town that very much resembled Oyster Bay.

Soldiers were everywhere and the citizens had the same terrified looks as the people in the town she'd just left. Her escorts led her to the building where she needed to plead her case: yet another quaint church, gutted and destroyed by the British army for their own personal use.

Maggie spent two hours waiting to be seen by the Provost Marshal.

When it was finally her turn, she explained to the man how Captain Wilson had insulted her and then, in turn, destroyed her ship without any proof of treachery against the Crown.

"Mistress MacGregor!" he said in an exasperated voice without looking up. "Do you have any idea how many complaints I receive each day from the fair ladies of this area who have found themselves insulted by a mere compliment from one of our brave soldiers?"

"I am fairly certain that Captain Wilson was not offering me a compliment, sir," replied Maggie, in a rather annoyed tone.

"What exactly did he say?" He reclined back in his chair with his arms folded, finally lifting his head to acknowledge her.

Maggie leaned close. "He called me one of 'Major John André's cock-sucking whores in front of my husband, a rather large Scotsman that did not appreciate the implication."

"I suppose he did not," he mumbled, with a grimace on his face.

He stared at her thoughtfully for a moment. "I will need to speak to Major André about this situation."

Maggie pulled a large packet of papers from her bag, which she laid in front of him. "Major André had the foresight to write you of the incident. He is recovering from an illness in Oyster Bay and is unable to travel. He is the one who advised me to come here to lodge the complaint."

He glanced down at the packet on the desk, disinterested. "Come back tomorrow after I have had time to review his correspondence."

Maggie nodded. "Thank you, sir."

Leaving the church, the four soldiers who were stationed outside the door, moved immediately to her side.

Well, this is going to get old quick.

She turned to glare at one of them. "Looks like we are spending the night, gentlemen."

After inquiring in town, Maggie was directed to a tavern for the evening. It was packed full of rowdy, drunk soldiers when she slipped in, and moved discreetly to the front to locate the tavern owner.

"Pardon me, but I need a room for the night."

The man looked around at the men in the room. "We are all booked up, ma'am," he replied, pouring a tankard of ale.

Maggie pursed her lips. "Yes, but I have money, and I pay very well—in advance."

Some things never changed; cash would always be king, and it would open the doors that words could not, especially in an area whose residents were desperate for money because the British were running up tabs that they would never bother to pay.

Producing her purse, Maggie removed several coins, and slid them across the counter. "Preferably, a private room that is NOT big enough for my entourage," she whispered, tilting her head back towards the four soldiers behind her.

The man laid his hand over the money and slid it underneath the counter. "I think I may have just had a room open up."

He turned to indicate an unoccupied table hidden away in a corner. "Why don't you have a seat and let me bring you something to drink while I have your room readied? What can I get you?"

"Thank you," she smiled, "...and the strongest thing you have."

She returned to her guards and informed them that she would be in the corner, nodding to the table. Two moved outside while the other two planted themselves in open chairs nearby. The tavern owner brought over her drink.

"Thank you, Mister...I am sorry, I did not catch your name."

"Austin Roe, at your service ma'am," he said with a slight bow.

Maggie thought she heard wrong for a brief moment. She immediately recognized that name, because he was one of the original Culper spies. Although he wasn't as well known as the others, Maggie recalled the name from a museum tour somewhere in New York that her father had taken her on, and Roe had certainly been a part of it in the beginning, traveling around to gather information as he purchased supplies for his business.

"Thank you, Mr. Roe. I am Mistress MacGregor."

One of her guards eyed them cautiously.

"You seem to have some admirers, Mistress MacGregor," he glanced over at the soldiers.

"Not by my choice," she muttered.

A thought occurred to her. Maggie reached in her purse and removed a few more coins. "As a matter of fact," she laid them on the table, "why don't you see to it that my shadows get PLENTY of ale tonight, on me?"

He smirked and eased them into his apron pocket. "Whatever the lady desires." He left to attend to his customers.

Maggie blew out a long breath. She had information that needed to be passed along and no idea how to do it. One of Washington's spies was a mere six feet away from her and her guards were standing between them. So close, yet so far. Damn it! Why did John have to be so overprotective of her? Or, maybe he was suspicious. She thought she had diffused the situation the night before, but John was a keen man. What if he were having her watched? She knew the information was credible because they had no idea she was on the staircase when they had spoken freely, but he may indeed be having her kept under surveillance to see what, if anything, came from it.

Maggie closed her eyes, and massaged her temples, trying to figure out what to do next.

"I know that look," she heard a voice say. "That's the look of a woman with 'man' trouble."

Chuckling to herself, Maggie looked up to see a pleasant face smiling back at her. It was a lady she had noticed earlier, delivering eggs to the tavern.

"More like 'men' trouble," answered Maggie dryly, glancing towards her guards. "One is bad enough; multiple ones are a hellish nightmare."

"I can only imagine," the woman laughed softly, her smile fading as she noticed the soldiers were paying attention.

Maggie perceived her concern. She propped her elbow up on the table with her cheek in her left hand and drummed on the top with the fingers of her right. "Would you like to join me? I seem to find myself in dire need of some interesting conversation with another woman. All of these men are irritating, to say the least."

The woman looked as if she might consider it.

"All you can eat and drink, on my bill," offered Maggie.

The woman shrugged. "Why not?" She pulled out a chair to sit as one of the guards stood and moved towards Maggie.

She held up her hand. "It's quite alright. We are just chatting and getting a bite to eat."

"The Major will not like this!" he said gruffly.

"Oh, well in that case, perhaps you would like to take this lady's place. You see, I seem to have forgotten to pack some items I am currently in need of and my monthly courses have caught me off guard. She is assisting me with my problem...however, if you would rather run around town to locate those things for me instead, I can make a list…"

His eyes widened, an abhorrent look on his face. "Enjoy your meal, Ladies."

"Uh-huh!" mumbled Maggie, rolling her eyes.

Maggie's guest burst into laughter as soon as the guard was out of earshot, and Maggie shook her head.

"These men will not hesitate to gut another on the battlefield but mention anything about a woman's natural monthly issues and they disappear so fast, that you cannot even tell the color of their coat."

"If I had known that conversation would have worked so well in getting rid of soldiers, I, and the rest of the ladies in town, would have done it a long time ago," whispered the woman, still giggling.

Maggie motioned to Mr. Roe to bring more drinks.

"My name is Maggie MacGregor, and I am very pleased to make your acquaintance."

"It is very nice to meet you. My name is Anna Strong."

Maggie froze. Another member of the Culper Ring and an important one at that. This was the woman who could signal someone on Washington's side. Maybe, for once, her luck had changed for the better.

Mr. Roe came over with another drink for Maggie. "Please, bring Mrs. Strong whatever she would like, and we will have two of your finest meals."

"Mistress MacGregor…"

Maggie cut her off by holding up her hand. "Please, call me Maggie."

She nodded. "Maggie, and please, do call me Anna. Why do you have so many escorts with you, if you don't mind me asking?"

Maggie shook her head. "Not at all. I needed to file a grievance against a captain in Oyster Bay, and my friend, who is extremely overprotective of me, insisted that I travel with them because of the trouble in the surrounding areas."

Mr. Roe brought their meals and they chatted as they ate. Maggie kept a wary eye on the inside soldiers that Mr. Roe was plying with alcohol. When he returned to refill their glasses, she leaned over.

"Mr. Roe, there are two other men outside who may be thirsty as well. Please, treat them as well as you have the two inside."

"Yes, ma'am," he said as he discreetly cut his eyes over at the two in the chairs, who were well on their way to becoming sloppily drunk.

After they had finished their meal, and were enjoying more drinks, Maggie leaned close, as she kept watch on the guards.

"Anna, I know we have just met, but I need to ask a favor."

Anna nonchalantly slid her chair closer to Maggie's.

"I must get a private message to an old friend of mine. It is extremely important, and I find myself unable to get away from my 'unwanted companions'."

"Go on," said Anna.

Maggie pretended to sip her drink, holding up the glass to conceal the movement of her lips. "I believe you know my friend...Benjamin Tallmadge."

Anna hesitated, looking down, before she answered. "I do know him, but I have not seen him in a very long time."

Maggie looked out the window. "But I am fairly certain that you can pass along a message to him."

"What makes you think that?" she asked.

Maggie had to take a chance; she had no other choice. She pretended to wipe her mouth with her napkin, concealing her speech. "I do not have a great deal of time. Just send word to him that there is an extremely dangerous traitor in his camp by the name of Brookes. Washington is in extreme danger and this man must be removed, immediately."

Anna looked down, remaining silent.

Maggie had to figure out a way to let Ben know the information was true. She dropped the napkin to the floor and, as she bent to pick it up, she slipped her mother's necklace over her head and off. She wrapped it in the napkin, brought it back up to the table, and slid it to Anna. "Give this to Ben. He will know who it is from, and that the information is true."

One of her guards had gotten up from his chair and was stumbling in her direction.

"Please, just get the message to him, however you can, I beg you. This is the only chance I have to warn him."

Maggie smiled and announced loudly, "Thank you for a lovely evening, Mrs. Strong. It has been a pleasure meeting you."

Anna stood to go as she spoke. "Thank you, Mistress MacGregor, for the meal and the company."

Watching her go, Maggie hoped to God that what she had done had been enough. There was nothing else she could do at this point.

6 CHAPTER SIX

The next morning, Maggie returned to see the Provost Marshal.

He was busy penning a letter when she came in and he did not bother to look up as he spoke. "Mistress MacGregor, I am not convinced that mere words warrant such a harsh response against one of the men. You ladies of the colonies get yourselves all worked up over nothing, and I fear Major André's personal feelings may be clouding his judgment. I will, however, speak with him further on the matter when I am there next week. You may see yourself out." He dismissed her with a wave of his hand.

You skeevy fucking bastard!

"Thank you for your time, sir," she forced out, attempting to hide the contempt in her voice. She stepped outside, and took in a deep breath to calm herself, as her entourage gathered around her.

Now, how was she going to get Duncan freed?

Maggie and the four guards were traveling just outside of Setauket, headed towards Oyster Bay, when they came upon a fallen log that blocked the main road. The men dismounted to clear the way, while Maggie slid off Onyx to get a flask from her saddlebag. Sipping from it, she watched them work.

Suddenly, two of the guards pulled their swords and dashed in her direction. One of them shouted, "The tree trunk has been cut. It is a trap."

Her mind was still trying to register what the man had said, when several other men with their faces covered, poured out of the woods, and easily overtook the soldiers.

Seriously? Now what?

Maggie reached over her shoulder for her sword before she remembered that she had left it with Duncan, afraid that her escorts might see it. Reaching down for a dagger from her boot, she felt the muzzle of a gun against the side of her head. She raised her hands slowly, completely disgusted with herself.

The man reached down and removed both daggers from their hiding places, and slipped them into his belt, while never moving the gun.

He grabbed her from behind and pressed the barrel closer to her temple. "You must be pretty important to the British to travel with four of the Queen's Rangers. Let's find out how much you are worth to them."

Damn it!

Maggie was never caught off guard by anyone, yet here she was, in the woods, without her sword, completely disarmed, and at the mercy of common highway bandits. She should have never let herself depend on four British soldiers to do what she should have done for herself. Onyx pawed at the ground, anxious to protect his mistress, but Maggie shot him a look to stand down, afraid that the man that held the gun might become trigger happy if startled, and accidentally blow her brains out.

The man dragged her into the woods, where two other men joined them. They tied her hands and gagged her, before sitting her down on a log while they spoke in hushed tones. The man who had kidnapped her watched her intently.

Maggie casually turned her head, pretending to wipe her nose on her shoulder as she looked at her surroundings. She caught a glimpse of Onyx in the woods. He was trailing them but remained well out of sight.

Good!

The man came over to her and crouched down. "Let's go find somewhere a little more private, shall we?"

He jerked her up roughly, and loaded her onto a saddled horse, before he mounted, sitting directly behind her, in order to trap her and keep her from getting away. They set off in a gallop through the woods. They rode for what seemed like hours, Maggie's arms and legs cramped from the uncomfortable position. She had no idea where they were, New York being unfamiliar territory to her. All she saw were trees, and no other souls in sight for miles. The man did not speak to her the entire time, only sang an annoying, off-key tune that was starting to give Maggie a massive headache.

They finally arrived at an old cabin in the middle of nowhere, that appeared to have been deserted long ago. He dismounted and pulled Maggie down, the leg cramps causing her to stumble. She looked back; Onyx was still close by. As soon as she got the chance to free her hands, she would get to him, and have him whisk her back to Oyster Bay.

The bandit grabbed her by the arm, steadied her on her feet, and led her inside to where there was a table and chairs. He sat her down, removed her gag, and set a canteen of water in front of her.

Maggie licked her lips, her mouth dry from the gag. "Hey!" she croaked, shrugging her shoulders. "It is kind of hard to drink with my hands tied," she pointed out.

He regarded her for a moment before he moved over to her, and held the canteen up pouring the water into her mouth. She tilted her head to catch as much of it as she could. When he decided she'd had enough, he set it on the table. He then pulled a chair directly in front of her, to face her, and took out one of her knives from his belt to examine it closer.

"I will be needing those back very shortly," she said. "I am personally attached to them."

He leaned back in his chair and stared at her before he finally spoke. "Why would a lady like you need two fine blades such as these—and in her boots, no less?"

"Oh, I don't know," said Maggie sarcastically, "to protect against thieves and rapists in the woods? It seems my guards weren't doing a very good job."

He smirked. "You think I am a rapist, do you?"

Maggie shrugged. "You have me tied up in an abandoned house, all alone. What AM I to think?"

"Why were you traveling with four guards of the Queen's Rangers? I know of no one who gets that kind of treatment, not even wives of high-ranking officers...or...are you one of their… 'other' ladies?"

Maggie let out a large sigh, annoyed. "Why does everyone automatically assume that I am a whore? Is it my hairstyle? The way I dress? The way I speak? I don't powder my face, I do not wear rouge, and my breasts are not exposed on a daily basis. Can you please explain this to me, so that I may promptly correct it, because it is starting to irritate me just a little?"

The man looked down, doing his best to suppress a wry smile. He turned his head to the side and cleared his throat to compose himself. When he turned back, his face was once more serious. "Who are you?" he demanded.

"You first," she countered.

He was still watching her intently when the door behind her opened. "Caleb, I am here. What is so damned important that you needed to pull me away from what I was doing?"

Maggie closed her eyes and lowered her head. *Oh, God! She knew that voice... a little too well.*

Her kidnapper nodded his head in Maggie's direction, and the man who'd just came in, stepped in front of the chair she was sitting in, still looking at his friend before turning to get a good look at her.

The blood drained from his face and his legs appeared to slightly buckle. "Maggie?"

Maggie took in a deep breath. "Hello, Ben."

7 CHAPTER SEVEN

Ben leaned against the table for a moment, needing to gather himself, before he kneeled in front of her. He took her face in both his hands to make sure it was really her. "What are you doing here?" he whispered.

Maggie pulled her arms against the chair. "Your rapist friend brought me here."

Ben turned to face Caleb, a look of absolute horror on his face. "My... what?... Did you..."

"No!" an affronted Caleb exclaimed. "You have known me all my life, Ben Tallmadge, I am NO rapist. I would pay for it before I did that."

Ben turned back to Maggie, questioningly.

"I am tied up in an abandoned cabin, I'm just saying..."

He saw the ropes, pulled out a knife, and cut her loose while shooting a disgusted look in Caleb's direction.

"I take it you know this woman, Ben?"

"Yes, very well," he replied, freeing her, then pulled a flask from his coat, and offered her something stronger to drink.

Once her hands were no longer bound, Maggie rubbed her wrists where the ropes had been, to stimulate the blood flow. She took the flask and had a nice, long swig. After she handed it back, he set it down on the table, and pulled her into an embrace.

"Are you alright?" he asked, greatly concerned, pushing her tangled hair back from her face.

"I am."

Ben looked over his shoulder at Caleb. "What the hell is going on here? Why is Maggie tied up in this old cabin?"

Caleb looked back at him and pointed to Maggie. "Ask her. She is the one who asked Anna Strong to pass along a message to you." The man dug around in his pocket and produced Maggie's necklace, then handed it to Ben. "I figured it was important when she sent this."

Ben took it from his hand, a confused look on his face when he turned to Maggie. "Your mother's necklace? You never take this off. Why did you send it?"

Maggie placed her hand on his chest. "There is information that you need to know, and I didn't know how else to get it to you. There is a man in your camp by the name of Brookes. He is a spy for the British, and he is giving them a great deal of information. He is also going to pass along the itinerary of General Washington's first trip out of winter quarters, so the British can ambush and assassinate him."

Ben shook his head, as the dire implication of the information hit him at full force. "It would be over. We would not stand a chance without Washington," he paced with his hand over his mouth.

Maggie nodded. "I know, and that is why I needed Anna Strong to get the message to you."

He turned back to focus on her. "Maggie, why are you even in New York? Why aren't you at home in Virginia?"

She pinched the bridge of her nose. "It is a very long story, Ben."

He looked to Caleb. "I need you to ride to camp and warn the General."

"What are you going to do?" he asked.

Ben tilted his head towards Maggie. "Maggie and I have some things we need to discuss...alone."

Caleb looked back and forth between them curiously, and finally nodded before heading to the door.

"Wait!" Maggie called. "It needs to look like an accident, otherwise it will be traced back to me, and I suspect I am already under heavy suspicion."

Ben walked over to Caleb. "Inform Washington, and just have our loyal men keep a close watch on him until we can figure out the best way to deal with the spy."

"I will be back as soon as I can," Caleb said and departed.

Maggie stood to stretch her legs as Ben moved in front of her to take her in his arms again. He hugged her tightly to him and whispered, "I have missed you so much."

Maggie held on for a long moment before she pushed him back a little to look into his eyes. "There is something that I need to tell you," she swallowed, a hard lump forming in her throat.

The hope in his eyes was almost too much for Maggie to bear, but she had to do it, no matter how much it hurt them both.

"Ben, I have married."

Ben's arms dropped to his sides and he turned pale, taking a step back, the pain apparent on his face. "I see. I..." he stuttered, searching for the words.

She took him by the arms. "I am sorry, Ben," she whispered, "I still care for you so much, and a part of me always will for as long as I have breath in my body, but after what happened...after the baby...I just...I couldn't...it was all too much." Her voice cracked and she wiped the tears that leaked from her eyes. She had tried to hold herself together but had failed miserably. "I need you to understand."

Ben took a seat in one of the chairs.

Maggie sat down across from him and took his hand. "I never wanted to hurt you. I would have been very happy if we could have been together and made things work, but..."

Maggie's mind went numb. She had this conversation many times in her head, but the reality was so much worse, and a thousand times harder.

"Please don't hate me," she whispered, slumping and hanging her head.

Ben lifted her chin with his finger; he looked at her with tears in his own eyes.

"I could never hate you, Maggie!" He choked out. "Please don't ever think that. I understand, I honestly do."

He pulled her to him, and she broke into a sob against his chest.

"I hope you can forgive ME for not being there for you when you needed me. If I had known about our child, I would have never let you go. I should have never let you go, to begin with, child or no child, but you had to shoulder that pain alone and, for that, I will never forgive myself."

"I wasn't alone," she whispered, wiping her nose with the back of her hand. "Gabe was there for me. He took care of me, and when I did not have the will to live, he pulled me back from the edge. I was so lost after what happened that I truly did not care if I lived or died."

Ben wiped his face with his palm, trying to gather himself. "Is Gabe the one you... married?" he asked.

"No," Maggie shook her head. "I married a man from Scotland, just a few months ago."

"Are you happy with this man...do you love him?"

Maggie nodded her head. "I do! I love Duncan very much, more than I thought possible, and we are very happy together."

Ben's gaze fixated on the floor. "That is all that matters, Maggie. Your happiness is all that I have ever wanted."

"Promise me something, Ben. Promise me that you will marry someone that makes you happy when this war is over, have loads of children, and live a long and joyous life."

"Is that what you want, Maggie?" he asked softly, defeated.

"It is."

He intertwined his fingers in hers and kissed her hand. "Then, I shall do it for you."

They embraced again, holding each other tight, allowing themselves to mourn the loss of their child, and of their life together that was never meant to be.

As the sun started to go down, the temperature turned cold.

"I need to start a fire. I cannot have you freezing to death," he finally said.

Ben went outside to gather firewood, using the time to take in some air and compose himself, even though he was still very much reeling from the news. He built the fire, and they spoke more, sitting in front of it on the floor.

"Why are you in New York, Maggie?" he asked, focusing on something besides his pain.

"I came on Gabe's behalf. The army may be recalling him to active duty, but he now has a daughter that he adopted, and she needs him at home. I was pleading his case to a friend that is in a position to help us."

"Is that how you learned the information?"

"I overheard it while staying at the headquarters of the Queen's Rangers."

"The Queen's Rangers?" he asked, angst in his voice. "Maggie! You placed yourself in a pit of vipers, then beat them with a stick. Do you know the risk you took even coming to Setauket?"

"I had no other choice," she sighed. "Duncan has gotten himself into some trouble and is under arrest in Oyster Bay. I had to come here to file a complaint against a British captain to try to get him free, but I am afraid things are much worse than that now."

"What do you mean?"

"Four Queen's Rangers were escorting me when your friend took me. I am sure they are tearing up the countryside as we speak. There is a very good chance I was already under suspicion, but this just made things ten times worse." Maggie massaged her temples.

"Ben, the information I overheard...the officers involved know I was there when it was spoken of, and if Brookes goes missing right after I do, it is not hard to ascertain where that tip came from. I had hoped Anna Strong would pass along the message with the necklace, and that would have been the end of it, but now I am not sure how much damage control I can do."

"What kind of trouble is your husband in?"

"Captain Wilson, the one in charge of ships coming in, insulted my reputation and later threatened to rape me, so Duncan expressed his displeasure by beating him to a bloody pulp. Then, the bastard turned around and destroyed my ship, so we are stranded here until the repairs are made...not that the ship would be any good right now, because it seems my attempt to discredit Captain Wilson with the Provost Marshal did not go as well as we had hoped, so now I am at a complete loss on many levels." Maggie blew out a breath in frustration.

Ben shook his head in utter astonishment. "Can you do nothing simply?" he teased.

"Obviously not," chuckled Maggie, amused by the absurdity of it all.

He put his arm around her. "It is good to hear your laugh again, Maggie. I have missed you."

"Oh, I have missed you too, Ben," she leaned against him.

"I have my bedroll. Why don't you get some rest, and let's see what we can do about getting this suspicion off you while getting you back…to your husband."

"Thanks, Ben."

"It is I who owes you the gratitude. Once again, both General Washington and I are in your debt for saving his life."

Ben made a pallet for her before going outside to secure his horse.

Maggie was exhausted. She lay on her side gazing into the fire. As soon as her mind quieted, Duncan's message came through loud and clear.

Maggie! Are you hurt?

No, my love. I am well.

Where are you? The soldiers said you were taken.

I was, but I am in safe hands. I will explain when we are together. I love you.

Maggie was fast asleep when Ben came back inside the house. He moved silently to her side and watched her as she slept. She was the one he had missed so much, for so long, the one that haunted his dreams each time he closed his eyes, and now she was the one lost to him. He took off his coat and gingerly spread it over her, careful not to wake her. Taking his flask from the table, he emptied it and sat down in one of the chairs, wondering how he would ever carry on without the hope that he had been desperately clinging to of someday getting her back.

Maggie was still sleeping the next morning when Caleb returned. Ben motioned him outside, so they wouldn't disturb her.

"I thought you two might be hungry, so I brought food and ale," said Caleb, holding up a bag.

Ben winced. "Damn it! Maggie must be starving. I completely forgot last night."

"Worked up an appetite, did you?" joked Caleb.

"No! We did not! Maggie is a married woman now," a despondent tone in his voice accompanied the wretched look on his face.

Caleb took a good hard look at his oldest friend. "Ben, how long have we known each other?"

"All of our lives. Why?"

"How is it that, your best friend, has never heard you once mention that woman that is asleep in that cabin? You obviously know her VERY well."

Ben lowered his gaze, hesitated, then whispered. "Maybe one day I will tell you about her...when it doesn't...hurt as much...although that day may NEVER come." He took the bag Caleb brought and went inside the house.

Caleb watched him go, wondering about the one woman who had gotten under the tough, thick skin of Major Benjamin Tallmadge himself.

Maggie heard the door close when they went out. She took her time opening her eyes. Sitting up, she realized that Ben's coat was laid over her. She was snuggling into it when the door opened.

"Oh Maggie, you are awake."

"How late is it?" she asked.

"It is the middle of the morning."

"You should have woken me sooner," she said, stretching, and clambering to her feet.

"You looked so peaceful; I did not want to bother you. Besides, you had a rough day yesterday. Caleb brought food. Are you hungry?"

"Starving!" she replied, walking to his side.

They sat down to eat.

Caleb took a chair and straddled it backwards.

Maggie grinned. "So, how are we going to do this? How do I get back to Oyster Bay and back to the same level of trust that I had before I overheard what I did?" she asked. "If the British think that Washington's army took me, and they already suspect that I may be passing information, it will only confirm their suspicions when

Brookes is removed. They have to be convinced that I was, indeed, taken against my will."

"I have been giving that some thought," said Ben. "I think it is best if we continue to let them believe you WERE taken by bandits. The Continental Army would never hold an innocent woman, but common thieves would. We just need to emphasize it."

"Ben's right. The men and I had our faces covered. They have no reason to think we weren't anything but ruffians looking for money."

Ben snapped his fingers. "A ransom note would do it and get us something in return."

Maggie took a sip of the ale. "I do not think the British army will give up money for me."

"We don't need currency," replied Caleb. "It is too easy to track. What we do need are supplies for the men."

Ben grinned. "A load of supplies would come in very handy right about now."

"So, we write a note, make some demands, and figure out a way to deliver it. Getting it to the headquarters of the Queen's Rangers will be the hardest part," said Caleb.

"Maybe not!" Maggie looked out the window. "Onyx was trailing us yesterday. He is close by, and he can ride straight to the headquarters without being bothered."

"Who is Onyx?" asked Caleb.

Ben chuckled. "Maggie's horse."

"There is no way he followed us. I would have known."

Maggie rose, looked at Caleb, and smirked. "Oh really?" She backed up to the window to watch Caleb's expression and tapped on the pane. Onyx's head instantly appeared.

"Bloody Hell!" Caleb darted to the window, stunned.

Ben folded his arms and grinned. "Caleb, meet the strangest, and most remarkable, horse you will ever meet." Pulling paper and ink out of his saddlebag, Ben handed them to Caleb so he could start composing the note.

Maggie paced the floor, watching Caleb and Ben decide on what to ask for.

"A horse and a wagon with a list of supplies," Caleb suggested.

"One horse? Is that all I am worth?" asked an insulted Maggie. "You DO know that I am a wealthy woman, right?"

Ben shrugged. "Maggie IS one of the wealthiest women in the colonies."

Caleb grinned. "Oh really? Are you sure you aren't looking for a second husband? I would be happy to be a kept man on the side...for the right price, of course," he joked.

Ben smacked him on the back of the head to express his irritation with the statement. "NO! She is NOT!"

Caleb grimaced, then winked at Maggie with an amused look on his face that Ben could not see.

Maggie shook her head but smiled to herself.

An hour later, the list of demands, including a meeting time and place, was ready to be delivered.

"We need some way to prove that we have you and are serious."

Maggie thought a moment and looked down at her hand. She pulled off her wedding ring and gave it to Caleb. "This ring is one of a kind. Duncan forged it himself, and he will recognize that it came from me."

"That should do it."

Maggie spoke to Onyx as Caleb affixed the note and ring to his saddle where it could be seen. 'Onyx! Ride straight to Duncan where we were staying and make sure he sees this. Do not lead them back to me."

Onyx acknowledged the orders with a dip of his head and was off.

"Are you sure your horse will get that note where it needs to go?" asked Caleb.

"I am betting my life on it," said Maggie, watching Onyx gallop off.

Ben and Caleb stepped inside to discuss some other matters.

Maggie closed her eyes and focused in hard on Duncan. The further apart they were, the more effort it took to get through. *Onyx is delivering a ransom note to ensure my safe return. Make sure John believes it. It carries my wedding ring, so do not lose it.*

Are you still safe?

I am, and I will be back in your arms soon, my love.

Not soon enough. I love ye, Maggie.

Duncan was in the parlour of the Townsend house arguing with John. "I need to find my wife!" he shouted, planting his palms flat on the desk.

John shook his head. "If you leave this house, I will be in jail in your stead and your charges will never be dropped. Maggie would never forgive me for that."

"John! Maggie is out there somewhere. She could be hurt, men could be..." Duncan closed his eyes, trailing off, his face strained. "I NEED to find her, NOW!" he demanded, slamming his fist down.

"I understand how worried and upset you are, Duncan." John spoke calmly, but he understood the man's frustration. "I feel the same way about Maggie. We have men combing the entire area between here and Setauket. We WILL get her back."

"But what kind of shape will she be in when ye do?" spat Duncan, enraged, his eyes ablaze. "We cannot continue to sit around and hope for the best."

"John is right, MacGregor," interjected Simcoe, sipping from a glass. "Let my men do their job."

Duncan narrowed his eyes at Simcoe. "If your men had done their job, my wife would be here with me, and not being held by a bunch of men who are doing only God knows what to her."

Duncan slammed his hand flat down on the table in frustration.

John seriously considered releasing him to go look for her because he wasn't the only one out of his mind with concern for what might be happening to Maggie. John's guilt for being the one who sent her to Setauket to begin with, was eating away at his very soul.

A commotion outside drew their attention.

Duncan ran to the window. "It's Onyx...and he would not have left Maggie without good reason."

Striding to the door, Duncan opened it as Onyx reached the front of the house, John and Simcoe close on his heels.

Onyx whinnied and pawed until Duncan searched him and located the note. Skimming it, he handed it to John, who snatched it from his hand and read it carefully. "The men who have her want a ransom."

Duncan noticed Maggie's ring tied to the saddle, which he quickly retrieved.

"Are we sure whoever sent this note even HAS her?" asked Simcoe, skeptically. "Everyone knows we are searching for her."

"Yes," answered Duncan, holding up the ring. "She would not have taken this off willingly."

John took the ring from him, inspecting it.

"I will pay whatever price it takes to get my wife back."

"No!" said John. "The army will pay it. Maggie was under our protection and we failed her. It is the very least we can do."

John marched inside, pulled out paper and ink and made a list. As soon as he was done, he sent three men into town to secure a wagon and horses along with the requested items. The meeting time was scheduled for the next day.

"They will not kill her, Duncan, they want their demands met," he said in a vain attempt to console him.

Duncan sat down on the couch with his hands covering his face. "John, there are worse things for a woman to experience than death," he said in a low, matter-of-fact tone.

John's blood ran cold, realizing that Duncan was right.

"I will be at the meeting point with ye tomorrow," Duncan said to John. "Ye will have to kill me to stop me."

Ben came in with a load of firewood to find Maggie staring out of one of the windows, lost in her thoughts.

"I know that look," he said.

"What?" she asked, turning toward him.

"THAT look...the one that says that you carry everyone else's troubles upon your own shoulders."

"Oh, that one. I am afraid that never goes away." Maggie moved closer to the fire, as he added the wood to it.

"I am sorry about the conditions here. If I had known Caleb was going to KIDNAP you, I would have made better arrangements."

Maggie chuckled. "I will be sure to send word next time so you can prepare for my arrival."

"I did send Caleb into town for a few things that should make tonight a tiny bit more comfortable for you."

She sat down on the bedroll, still out from the night before. "It's not so bad. The company is pretty good."

Caleb returned with food, candles, another bedroll, and rum.

Ben held up the bottle. "Still your favorite?" he asked.

"A girl's best friend," she grinned, taking the bottle from him.

Maggie pulled out the cork and poured the liquor into the three tin cups that Caleb had brought with him. The trio ate and drank, enjoying each other's company away from the war, even if it was for a short time.

The next day, they prepared for the exchange.

"The other men will meet us just up the road from where we are taking Maggie."

"Good!" said Ben. "I will change before then."

"I think that is a bad idea, Ben," said Maggie. "If someone on the other side happens to recognize your voice, I am done for."

Caleb agreed and it was decided that Ben would watch from afar.

It was almost time to go.

"You are going to have to sell this Maggie," said Caleb. "It has to look like you have been through a really bad time."

Maggie took her dagger off the table and used it to cut up her clothing. Next, she took some of the ash from the fireplace, applying it to her face and clothes and then, she had Caleb bring in a tree branch that she used to brush up and down her arms, scratching them, giving the appearance of being dragged through the woods. She pulled her hair free, letting it hang loose and shaking it out to give herself a more disheveled look. Slicing her blade across her hand and drawing blood, she rubbed it all over her face and clothes for a final touch.

"How do I look?" she asked.

"Like you haven't been robbed," said Caleb, sarcastically.

"What do you mean?"

"Your jewelry."

"Oh!" said Maggie. "You are right." She hesitated before she took off her necklace and bracelet, then she handed it all to Ben.

"I will keep them safe and find a way to return them to you, Maggie, I promise," said Ben. "I know how much your mother's necklace means to you."

Maggie nodded. "Keep my bracelet and daggers safe, too. They have sentimental value, as well."

"Of course."

Caleb walked around her, giving her a good once over. With a nod of approval, he said, "Let's go trade you in."

They met the other men near the drop-off area.

Ben pulled Maggie off to the side, took her hand and kissed it. "Please take care of yourself, Maggie."

"You too...and Ben," she paused, "I do not want you to blame yourself for not being there when we lost our child. I think it is time we both released this guilt that we have been carrying around for so long. It was no one's fault; it just was not meant to be."

He kissed her forehead and whispered, "I will always love you, Maggie."

"And I you, Ben. Be well and if you ever need anything, I am still always here for you." A few tears slipped down Maggie's cheek.

He wiped away one of his own, before he tied her hands, and helped her up on Caleb's horse. His hand lingered on her leg for a moment before he nodded, mounted his own horse, and rode off into the woods to observe.

Caleb watched the whole scene before he came over and climbed atop the horse behind Maggie.

"You alright?" asked Caleb.

"Yes. Nothing like a few tears to sell the story, right?" she whispered.

"What's Ben's excuse?" He looked in the direction of his oldest friend.

"He is back to being stuck with you. That's enough to make anyone cry."

Caleb laughed a hearty belly laugh. "I hope he tells me about the two of you one of these days. I bet it's one hell of a story."

Maggie laughed. She really liked Caleb and she knew what great lifetime friends he and Ben would continue to be. She decided to throw him a bone. She leaned back and whispered, "Ben was a virgin...until he met me, that is."

"What?" Caleb asked in astonishment, his mouth wide open before he started to chuckle.

"Oh, my dear Maggie, you have just given me the greatest gift ever."

"Take care of him for me, Caleb," she whispered.

"Always!"

Caleb covered his face with a handkerchief before they rode forward to the appointed meeting place where Duncan, John, Simcoe, and several other soldiers were waiting. He dismounted, then pulled Maggie down. He grabbed her by the arm and walked a few steps ahead of his horse.

Maggie could see Duncan's eyes wide with rage at her appearance.

I am unhurt, Duncan. We had to make this look real. Ye succeeded.

Maggie caught a glimpse of John's face. He was trying to remain stoic, but his eyes betrayed him. She felt horrible doing this to him, but then again, she would have felt much worse swinging from the end of a rope.

Caleb leaned closer to her. "Come on, Maggie. Make them feel good about handing over all those much-needed supplies to our boys. Play the part."

She lowered her head so they would not see her lips moving as she spoke. "Oh, for goodness sake, Caleb."

"Make us proud, Maggie."

She groaned. "Oh, all right."

Maggie pretended to stumble and fell on her knees, crying out in pain as Caleb jerked her to her feet.

John's face flushed red and his hands curled into tight fists at his side.

"Nice going, Maggie. You missed your calling; you should have been an actress." Caleb whispered.

"I really SHOULD get paid for all these performances."

He pulled her to the middle of the road, and Duncan led the horses and wagon to meet them halfway.

Making the exchange, Caleb moved close to Duncan with his eyes narrowed and whispered. "Nice to meet you, Mr. MacGregor. Your wife is a remarkable woman."

Duncan sneered at him. "She is pretty amazing. I trust she is unharmed?"

Caleb spat on the ground. "Of course, and she has been most helpful. Thank you."

"Thank ye, sir."

They shoved each other for a bit for the benefit of the British before Duncan led Maggie back to their side.

Caleb and his men immediately rode off with their new-found bounty.

Duncan pulled Maggie close to him, breathing a sigh of relief that she was back in one piece.

Maggie planted her forehead against his chest.

John and Simcoe dismounted, and rushed to her side.

"My God, Maggie!" exclaimed John. "What have those bastards done to you?" He turned to Simcoe. "I want those men hunted down and these woods cleaned out."

She closed her eyes. "Can we please just go home?"

"Yes!" said John, and shouted orders to the men.

Duncan pulled out his knife and cut her hands free. He helped her onto Onyx and climbed on behind her, holding her tight as they rode for the house.

"Safely back in my arms, where you belong," he whispered, kissing her shoulder.

"Thank goodness," replied Maggie, snuggling back against his chest.

In the parlour, Maggie reclined against Duncan as he held her tight and John handed her a drink.

"Thank you, John."

John swallowed hard, forcing the words out as he looked upon Maggie, pity and regret written all over his face. "I will send for the doctor to tend your...wounds unless you would prefer Mrs. Townsend," he said gravely, turning his head to hide his own distress.

Maggie knew how upset John was over her perceived condition, and she could not, in good conscience, bear to let him continue to believe as he did. "That is not necessary, John. Other than a few cuts and bruises, I am unharmed."

John stared at her, trying to decide if she were indeed telling the truth, or simply trying to spare the feelings of the ones she loved.

Maggie seemed to read his thoughts. "Truly, John. My only troubles are that I am filthy and tired. They wanted to make sure that the condition of their hostage didn't affect the price they received. Not much profit in damaged goods."

John wiped his mouth with the back of his hand, letting out the breath he had been holding, relief flooding throughout his body. "Oh, thank God."

He knelt in front of her and took her hand. "Those two things causing you discomfort, I can easily remedy." Rising, he stepped out of the room to order a bath and to have food sent upstairs for Maggie.

Simcoe appeared inside the doorway. "Mistress MacGregor, we are all relieved by your seemingly safe return, but we need to know where they held you. Where was their camp? Were any of them in uniform?"

Before Maggie could answer, John stormed back into the room. "All of these questions can wait. Maggie has been through an ordeal, and she has needs that must be attended. You can get your answers tomorrow."

"They may be gone by tomorrow, John," protested Simcoe.

John's face became red with anger and disgust.

Maggie straightened up.

"It's alright, John," she said, to calm him. "I really have no answers. I was blindfolded, and I had no sense of where I was. I know there were other men, but I only saw the ones with their faces covered. I do not think there were any soldiers. I believe they were just thieves looking for their next victim, and we happened along at the wrong time. They took everything on me including all my jewelry, even my wedding ring."

Duncan shot her a look and a thought. *Ye are too good at lying, ye know that? Should I be concerned?*

Maggie cut her eyes sideways.

"That reminds me, my love," said Duncan. "Those filthy scoundrels sent your wedding ring as proof that they were holding ye, so at the very least, ye have that back."

He pulled it off his pinky finger, where he had placed it, and slipped it back in its proper place on her hand, before kissing it. "Now, gentlemen, if ye will excuse us, I wish to take my wife upstairs so she can rest."

He stood and helped Maggie to stand.

"Mistress McGreg-" began Simcoe before John cut him off by grabbing his shoulder.

"Leave them. Can't you see they need to be alone?"

As soon as they were safely in the room with the door closed, Duncan pulled Maggie tight, and kissed her.

"Do you think they believed me?" she whispered.

"Oh aye, they did. Now, will you please tell me what is going on? I have been out of my mind with concern."

"I am so sorry. I didn't mean to worry you, and I did not intend for any of this to happen."

"Do ye ever?" he snarked. "What happened to 'no unnecessary chances'?"

Maggie pulled him away from the door and whispered. "I sent a message to Washington's camp, and thought that was the end of it, but some of his men wanted to verify the information first. They staged the robbery to take me to a safe place to question me."

She looked down. "Ben was the one that eventually came. He did not know it was me."

Duncan's eyes and nose flared. "Ben? The one whose bairn ye carried? That Ben?"

Maggie nodded. "We just talked. I gave him the information, and when I told him I would be suspected, he came up with this plan as a cover to ensure me safely back to you."

"I see," Duncan turned away. "And what did ye talk about for two days?"

Maggie caught his arm. "Duncan, this is the first time I have spoken with Ben since we lost our child. He needed forgiveness and closure to move forward with his life, and I was able to give it. Please don't be upset with me. I did not seek him out, but I will not apologize for granting a suffering man some peace in his life...and finding a little for myself, if the truth be known. You are my husband. I love you, and I would NEVER be unfaithful to you. You are the only man I will ever want for as long as I live."

Duncan folded his arms and stared out the window, his face solemn.

"Duncan, you and I both had pasts before we met. It is what has made us who we are today. If the situation were reversed, and you had lost a child with another woman, I would have been grateful if she had released you from your guilt and pain so you would have been free to become mine."

He reached down and took her hands, shifting to face her. "Is your life always this complicated?"

Maggie bobbed her head up and down. "Pretty much. If you wish me to grant you a divorce so you can go back to the quiet life in Scotland..." sighed Maggie.

Before she could utter another word, Duncan pulled her into a forceful kiss, before pressing his forehead to hers. "There is not one chance in Hell of me EVER wanting that, Maggie MacGregor, understand that!" he growled. "We belong to each other, and nothing will ever change that. Besides…" he smirked, "Mother would kill me."

"You are afraid of your mother?" she teased.

"Absolutely!"

They both laughed softly and there was a knock at the door.

Three of the servants had come to prepare her bath and to bring a tray of food. As soon as they left, Duncan helped her undress and into the tub, noticing her flinch as her hand touched the side of it. A look of concern crossed his face, as he gently examined the gash across her palm.

"Explain this!" he demanded.

"I did it myself, knowing that the blood would make it more convincing," she shrugged.

He pulled her palm to his lips and planted a tender kiss upon it. "Maggie, you cannot continue to put yourself in these dangerous situations, the fate of the future or not. Your luck WILL eventually run out."

She touched his face lovingly. "I know," she said softly.

"I cannot lose ye, Maggie. I would not be able to live."

He helped her to wash, then out of the tub, and into one of his shirts. After they ate, Maggie immediately fell soundly asleep in his arms.

The next morning, Maggie found John in the parlour, sitting in a chair in front of the fireplace, a letter in his hand.

"Good morning, John."

He stood when he saw her. "Good morning, Maggie. How are you feeling?"

"Much better, thank you. It is amazing what a hot bath and a good night's sleep can do for a girl."

"I am very pleased to hear that." He reclaimed his seat and became unusually quiet, seemingly distracted.

"Is something troubling you, John?" she asked.

"You mean other than your kidnapping?"

"I am fine," she said, leaning down and kissing him on the cheek.

John waved the letter. "I have just received word from General Clinton. I am being sent to New York City in two weeks."

"Oh... I see." Maggie nodded. "Well, I am sure New York will be more to your liking than this sleepy little town of Oyster Bay. It will have a great deal more in the way of entertainment and the arts."

"Yes, well, there are things that I need to handle here first, most pressing, Duncan's charges. I also have to ride to East Hampton next week to meet with General Clinton beforehand...he needs to see me for some unknown reason." John appeared concerned by the orders, staring down at the paper.

"What did you find out in Setauket?" he asked, folding the letter and stuffing it in his coat pocket.

"Oh! In all the excitement, I completely forgot to tell you." Maggie shook her head and sat down. "I do not think he is going to help us, John. He does wish to speak with you, but I am not in the least bit hopeful, judging by his words to me."

John rose from his chair, then came to sit down next to her and took her hand. "In that case, we will figure out another way. Please don't trouble yourself, you have had entirely enough upset this week."

She squeezed his hand. "Thank you for all that you have done, John. I am in your debt...once again."

He shook his head in disbelief. "Maggie, your manners are impeccable. You are thanking me for getting you kidnapped in a plan that I suggested in the first place; one that didn't even succeed. When I saw you, in that condition, my heart stopped and...." His voice was full of raw emotion.

He trailed off and forward, his elbow on one knee, hand on his forehead, clearly dismayed.

Maggie rubbed his back, to comfort him. "Please, do not blame yourself for mere coincidence. If they had not taken me, they would have taken someone else, and that person may not have had the great friend that I have in you to help get them back."

John closed his eyes, attempting to regain his composure. "What ever will I do in New York without you, Maggie?" he whispered.

Maggie patted his back and grinned. "Lots of women, I imagine."

Eyes twinkling, he laughed at her impropriety, his face turning red. "Yes, well, but none of them will be you, will they?"

He broke his gaze away. "Well, I have a great deal to do. Please, rest today, for me, and try not to get yourself kidnapped again."

"I will do my best."

Maggie and Duncan were in the parlour discussing John's transfer and the bad news from Setauket, when Mr. Townsend appeared. "Mistress MacGregor, I cannot tell you how good it is to see you safely back."

"Thank you, sir."

He tapped his fingers on the desk as if trying to decide upon something, then spoke. "I was wondering if the two of you would mind taking a walk with me, if you are up to it. There is something I should very much like to show you outside."

Maggie and Duncan followed behind him, stopping to let the guard know where Duncan would be.

Mr. Townsend led them out to the remains of his apple orchard. straight to where a small tree stood, about three-feet high. "Mistress MacGregor, you said something very prophetic the other day that struck me as rather odd. Before you collapsed, you leaned over a tiny little sprig and said something to the effect of a phoenix rising from the ashes."

Maggie nodded, "Yes, I remember. Why?"

"Well, that pitiful little piece of nothingness must have heeded your words and taken them to heart." He motioned to the tree. "Because, in just a few short days, look what it has become."

Maggie looked at him and then at the tree. "This cannot possibly be where we were that day. The thing I touched was barely six inches tall."

Mr. Townsend smiled. "Oh, it is indeed." He pointed to the ground. "See the boot prints of the soldiers who came to your aid?"

Maggie and Duncan looked down and around; there was no mistaking that it WAS the same place.

Maggie reached over and touched the tree. "That is not possible. Apple trees do not grow that fast."

"How big was it?" questioned Duncan.

"No higher than my hand," she responded.

"Not only that," said Mr. Townsend, "look around you."

"Oh my God!" exclaimed Maggie, scanning the area.

The entire orchard, that a few days before was nothing but blackened soil, had now started to spring to life with the growth of nearly two dozen little saplings.

"Did you replant, Mr. Townsend?"

"No, I did not. This is strictly a blessing sent by the grace of God Himself. I thought you might appreciate seeing your words come to fruition, so to speak."

Maggie stood in stunned silence.

A customer on horseback arrived at the house, so Mr. Townsend excused himself, leaving Maggie and Duncan alone.

Before he left, he turned to Maggie and said, "You, my dear Mistress MacGregor, have given me hope for our country and it's future. Perhaps, we may yet rise from the devastation of war as well as this orchard has."

They watched him go before turning back to the tree.

"Are ye sure, Maggie, that ye did not misjudge it?"

"I am positive, Duncan. How? It was the height of my hand and on the verge of death before I collapsed, and now it is three-feet tall and the picture of health."

"What words does he mean?" he asked.

"I remember speaking a phrase that I had heard somewhere before... 'from the ashes of the fire, the phoenix shall rise', while I was touching it, and as the words left my mouth, I felt that weird hot pain throughout my body, only a great deal worse than it has ever been before. It literally knocked me back on my ass."

Duncan and Maggie turned to each other in disbelief.

"What in the world is going on?" asked Maggie.

Duncan whispered, "Perhaps, it is Fae related?"

"Why would the Fae heal a small apple orchard in Oyster Bay, New York of all places in the world?"

"Because, YE are here," answered Duncan. "And, maybe THEY didn't...maybe YE did."

"What?" asked Maggie.

He took her hands. "Maggie, ye touched this tiny plant on the decimated ground, felt that surge, and now look around ye. Your mother WAS the goddess of harvest and rebirth and, if ye think about it, it only makes sense that some of that ability would already be in your veins. Even after she gave up her immortality, ye said that she always grew the most beautiful gardens around. What if you inherited some of that?"

Maggie shook her head. "My mother was mortal when I was conceived and born."

"It would not matter, Maggie; her blood is still pure Fae, even if the rest of her is not. I do not pretend to understand any of this, but it would make sense."

She stared back at him. "So, let's say that I did this just by touching that little dying tree? Then, why are things not jumping to life all around me? I touch SOMETHING every day, but things aren't growing an extra three feet high. I mean, I touch you every day, and you haven't grown taller."

Duncan smirked. "It depends on WHERE ye touch me," he teased, as he bit his lip and winked.

"Oh my God," said Maggie, dropping her head, amused. "I am trying to be serious here."

He pulled her close as they both laughed. "The tree growth would have fallen under your mother's domain. Each god and goddess is limited to the realm they hold influence over, and they do not interfere with another's, but, if truth be known, they do not even bother with their own anymore."

A sudden thought occurred to him. "What were ye doing, or feeling, when it happened?"

"I was just thinking about how bad I felt for Mr. Townsend and wishing that he had not experienced such a loss. I know what the future holds, and that America will grow into something great after all this destruction. But these people, they do not know that they will even win the war. It is what made me think of the rising of the phoenix, for some reason."

Duncan looked back across the field. "Maybe, it was the intent? When ye said those words, life sprang back from the ashes, just as the phoenix did. It is the bird of rebirth."

"Are you trying to say, that because I thought it, it happened?"

"Not thought, desired. Because ye wished his land had not been destroyed and that coupled with the words ye said; it may have just been enough to form a spell, if ye will, like the one Quinn and I use for the fog. Ye have far more Fae blood than we do, so maybe the words from your lips, along with that desire, because of your bloodline, made it far more powerful than mere words."

"So, what you are saying is that I can get things to grow?"

Duncan looked around. "At a great rate it appears."

"Well, that will come in handy on the estate...if we ever get back there. You have no idea what I would give to be home right now."

"I know," said Duncan, kissing the top of her head. "We will get there soon."

"We still have to get you free of all of your charges first."

Maggie lay in bed, watching Duncan undress.

He pulled back the covers and slipped in to face her, propping up on his elbow. He ran his hand down the length of her body.

"What's wrong, my love?" he asked.

"I am just trying to figure out how we are going to get out of this trouble."

Duncan brushed the hair back from her face. "Ye worry too much." He groaned, and gently kissed her lips, completely absorbed in his mission.

Maggie started to feel a familiar numbness in her mind, the one that came when Duncan took her to bed with the full intention of purposefully making her forget about everything else. She tried to push back. "But, Duncan…"

He kissed her again, this time deeper and more forcefully. He stopped and pulled back to see Maggie half drunk on desire, her eyes barely open and breathing heavy.

"Dunc…" she began, but his lips found her neck and he pulled her closer against him.

He knew he had her right where he wanted her; mind cleared of everything that weighed her down, focused only on him, and how he was going to make her feel.

"What were ye saying, my love?" he asked with a sly smile.

Maggie shrugged. "I do not remember," she murmured.

"Good!" he whispered in a low, sultry voice.

He managed to keep her mind 'cleared' for the entire night.

8 CHAPTER EIGHT

Maggie slept in late the following morning and, when she reached for Duncan, she realized that he was gone. After dressing, she went downstairs to look for him, but he was nowhere to be found; neither was John or Simcoe.

The entire house was unusually quiet, and most of the guards were gone.

That's strange.

Maggie sent Duncan a silent message. *Where are you?*

No response.

Concern flared; Maggie went around to the store part of the house to locate Mr. Townsend. "Have you seen my husband this morning?"

"Yes," he replied. "He rode out earlier with Major André, Lt. Colonel Simcoe, and the majority of the guards."

"Do you know for what reason?" she asked.

"I did overhear Simcoe tell one of his men that it concerned some allegations that needed to be settled."

Maggie leaned against the counter. They were going to do something with Duncan. The Provost Marshal must have come early and made his decision, probably an unfavorable one if they had left her behind. She rushed to the stable to saddle Onyx when she was stopped by two of the remaining guards.

"We have orders to keep you here, ma'am. You are not allowed to leave."

"I need to find my husband right now!"

They pulled her back.

"I am sorry, ma'am. We are under strict orders from Major André, informed that we would be court-martialed if we let you leave."

Maggie felt herself go weak, as they escorted her back into the house. She tried time after time to reach Duncan mentally, but he never responded. There would be only one reason he would not answer.

Maggie was frantic by the time John came inside the house around noon.

"Where is he? What have you done?" she asked, half out of her mind.

John gave her a confused look. "Who, Maggie?"

"Duncan!" she demanded. "What have they done with him?"

Maggie was on the verge of becoming hysterical.

John took her by the shoulders. "Maggie, you need to calm yourself this instant!"

"Calm myself? You take my husband out of here without my knowledge to answer for charges, have me held here against my will, and you expect me to sit here and do nothing while his life hangs in the balance? While he..." she trailed off as her voice cracked.

John narrowed his eyes. "Maggie, you do not understand!"

"Is he even alive?" she half-sobbed.

"Maggie!" shouted John.

"WHERE IS HE?" she cried.

Duncan appeared in the doorway, his hands and shirt completely covered in blood. "Where is who?"

Maggie raced to him, embraced him, and wept into his chest.

He wrapped his arms around her, rocking her, attempting to soothe her. "What has happened?" he demanded.

She looked up and touched his face just before he wiped her tears with his thumbs. "I thought you were dead."

John was stunned, a look of bewilderment on his face as he moved closer to them. "What on Earth made you think that, Maggie?" he asked.

She turned to look back and forth between them. "Mr. Townsend said that you had taken Duncan into town, and there were allegations that needed to be answered for...and when they told me I could not leave under your orders...I thought..."

"Christ, Maggie!" exclaimed John, affronted, covering his mouth with his hand, "I would never do something so cruel to you. How could you think that?"

Maggie gave Duncan a good once over and started checking him for wounds. "Where are you hurt?"

Duncan stopped her, catching her arms and gently pushing them down. "I am not hurt, Maggie. I am perfectly fine. This is not my blood."

"What?" asked a very confused Maggie.

He moved her to a chair and asked John to bring over a glass of whisky. Duncan forced her to drink until she had sufficiently calmed down, terrified that she might delve into one of her panic attacks at any moment.

John leaned back against the desk, with his arms folded, obviously worried about her state of mind, as well.

"Allow me to explain. I received intelligence from one of my agents behind enemy lines late last evening about a British officer in Oyster Bay that was sending information to the Continental Army. We questioned him, and of course, he denied any wrongdoing, but when we searched his residence this morning, we found proof of his treachery in the form of papers that were hidden inside his mattress. He obviously wasn't smart enough to burn them, which is of no surprise to anyone, who has the misfortune of knowing him. Not only that, we located damning evidence that he was involved, if not masterminding, your kidnapping."

Maggie looked at Duncan, baffled.

He was suppressing a grin. *Just go along with it.*

"Who?" asked Maggie, puzzled.

"That is the best part," answered Duncan. "It was...Captain Wilson."

Dumbfounded, Maggie was momentarily unable to form words.

John smirked. "I must say, taking HIM into custody has been one of the most satisfying moments of my entire military career."

Maggie shook her head. "I don't understand. Why did you take Duncan?"

John shrugged. "Simcoe and I had a discussion earlier this morning, and we both agreed, that if anyone deserved to take part in that interrogation, after all that man had done to you, it was your husband." He moved next to Maggie and laid his hand on her shoulder.

"My sincerest apologies, Maggie, I had no idea that you would think the worst when we were gone. I should have left word and been more forthcoming with you."

Duncan squeezed her hand. "I should have told ye as well, but ye were sleeping so peacefully, and I did not want to wake ye." Duncan smiled apologetically. "I DID keep ye up all night, after all."

John softly chuckled into his hand and looked down.

Maggie raised her palm to her forehead. "So, what happened to him?"

"The Queen's Rangers will take care of him," answered John, "and, since the man has been proven untrustworthy, I am very pleased to report that all charges against Duncan have been dropped."

Maggie looked back and forth between John and Duncan. "Truly?"

John nodded. "Truly!"

Maggie released a nervous laugh and pulled Duncan tightly to her, covering his face with kisses. Then, she stood to hug John.

"Thank you," she whispered.

John was caught off guard, but slowly returned her embrace, lingering for as long as he could without being inappropriate in front of her husband.

Duncan stood. "I think I am going to clean up so we can celebrate."

Maggie reached across and pulled him into a kiss. "That sounds like an excellent idea."

He went out of the room to go upstairs, leaving Maggie and John alone to talk.

She took John by the arm, a contrite look on her face. "I am so sorry, John, for jumping to the wrong conclusion. I should have known better than to think that you would have done something so awful. Please, forgive me."

John took her face in both his hands, smiling. "Do not apologize for loving someone as much as you do that man. Love like that is a glorious thing to behold."

He kissed her forehead, then reached into his coat pocket. "I have something for you." He held up her bracelet.

"Where did you find it?" she asked, excitedly.

"It was in Wilson's home, along with your mother's necklace and your daggers, which is how we knew he was involved with your kidnapping. Duncan has the rest of your things, but I wanted to return this piece personally. May I put it back on for you?"

Maggie smiled and held out her wrist so he could fasten it.

"That's better." He righted it on her arm.

"Back where it belongs," she said, hugging him. "Thank you."

She pulled back, he stopped her, held her in place, and whispered, "If Duncan is ever fool enough to let you get away…" he trailed off as he bit his lip. He kissed her on the cheek and left the room.

Maggie watched him leave, looked down at the bracelet, and smiled. She went upstairs to find Duncan.

"How does it feel to be a free man?" asked Maggie, watching him change.

"I have no idea how this all came about, but I am so grateful that it did," he replied.

Maggie leaned close and whispered, "I do!"

It was Duncan's turn to be confused.

She pulled him toward the window so they wouldn't be overheard. "Ben had my jewelry and daggers. He promised to find a way to get them back to me, and he kept his word. I told him about what Wilson did to me and about your charges. Ben has become a master at intercepting and forging letters and using that information to his advantage. I suspect they tortured the British spy, Brookes, until he told them of his way of sending information to John, and then, wrote a letter from "Brookes" implicating Wilson as an American spy, knowing it would come to exactly the right person. I am sure that he probably had one of his men slip in and plant all of that 'evidence' so well that even Wilson himself didn't know it was there. He did this to protect us both."

"That is...something else," said Duncan. "I should feel bad that Wilson was arrested for something he did not do, but I must admit, I will sleep a great deal better knowing that bastard is not on the streets anymore."

"You and me both."

Maggie pulled him into a kiss, and that night, they celebrated.

The next day, Maggie and Duncan were about to go downstairs to breakfast when they heard angry voices coming from below. Reaching the downstairs hall, they saw that John and Simcoe were engaged in an intense argument.

"You should have hanged that bastard on the spot!" shouted an enraged John, raking a pile of letters off his desk. "God only knows where he is now, and how much damage he is inflicting."

"John!" defended Simcoe, "We need whatever information we are able to get from him. I will not apologize for trying to torture what we could out of that man."

"And now?" spat John, laying both hands flat on the desk. "How much information will you torture out of him while he is safely entrenched in Washington's camp? How many people are in danger because he is free? Find him and deal with him like the traitor that he is!"

Simcoe stormed past them, out of the house.

Maggie and Duncan peeked inside the parlour to see an infuriated John glaring through the window.

"John?" asked Maggie cautiously.

John closed his eyes, as he appeared to try and find his presence of mind.

He cleared his throat. "Yes, Maggie?"

She and Duncan moved guardedly into the doorway, noticing the mess on the floor.

"Are you alright?" she asked.

John's nostrils flared, as he blew out a breath. "No, I am not!" he stated.

"What can we do?" asked Duncan.

"Nothing, I fear," John scowled. "It seems that Captain Wilson has escaped custody. Instead of hanging him, without delay, as I insisted, Simcoe unwisely made the decision to keep him around to torture him for information. He must have had guards on the inside that saw fit to come to his aid."

"Do we have any idea where he is headed?" asked Duncan.

"I am inclined to believe that he will ride straight for the enemy's camp, begging for sanctuary."

Maggie bent down and began picking up some of the papers on the floor. "What will you do?"

John straightened his shoulders. "The Queen's Rangers are searching as we speak, and other than that, there is not much we can do."

As John took notice of Maggie cleaning up, he reverted to his usual, well-mannered self. "Maggie, please... I made this mess. I will clean it up." He touched her arm.

"I don't mind, John," she smiled, standing up, and straightening a stack of papers, before placing them back on the desk.

He quickly gathered up the rest.

"John, Maggie and I were going to check on the repairs to the ship today, but, if ye will lend me a horse, I will join Simcoe's men with the search," said Duncan, staunchly.

"I can manage in town alone," said Maggie.

"No!" replied John. "Maggie, you should not be unescorted. If Wilson is still in the area, he may very well blame you for his current circumstance. It would be prudent if you were in someone's company at all times until this matter is resolved."

Maggie started to protest; John interrupted her before she had the chance, adamant in his stance.

"If you are not with myself or Duncan, you WILL be escorted by an armed guard. This is NOT up for discussion and there will be no argument. It is an ORDER."

"John is right," agreed Duncan. "The man will be desperate for retaliation against anyone whom he perceives has wronged him."

Maggie assented with a sigh; she knew it was pointless to argue with the both of them at once, and they stood united on this front. It was decided that Maggie and

Duncan would ride out to the ship, check the repairs, and return quickly.

Captain Russell greeted them when they arrived.

"How is the ship coming?" asked Maggie.

The Captain grimaced. "Not well, I am afraid. We are having a devil of a time finding replacements for the damaged parts here, so I have already sent back to Virginia for what we need, along with word to Colonel Asheton that we have been delayed."

Maggie smacked her forehead. "In all the excitement, I completely forgot to send word to Gabe. He must be worried to death."

"I thought it may have slipped your mind," the Captain said sympathetically. "You have had your hands full. I did not give him details, just said that the ship was docked and in need of repairs."

"Thank you!" she said gratefully. Maggie folded her arms and looked around at the damage.

"Where are our other ships?" asked Duncan.

"Both out to sea, and not expected to be back to home port for a few weeks. I am hoping that the crewmembers I sent to Virginia can secure safe passage with what we need, and soon. I am not very keen on remaining here much longer."

"Neither are we," replied Maggie.

"Begging your pardon, ma'am," said the Captain, "but, now that the charges have been dropped, there is no reason that the two of you cannot return home on another ship headed that way. I will see to everything here and sail her back as soon as we are ready."

Maggie sighed. "John will be meeting with General Clinton next week. I would rather wait and return with a sense of what direction he is leaning in regard to recalling Gabe. Besides, I am wary of leaving you and the crew here alone. As long as Duncan and I are here, we can head off any trouble from the British side since we are under John's protection...and on the Patriots side, with my other friends, if need be. I think it is best we remain."

Duncan and the Captain were discussing details when Maggie strolled down the gangplank onto the dock. She was looking out over the water, leaned against one of the posts, her arms folded, lost in thought. An old man, wearing ragged clothes, with a floppy hat, and walking with a seemingly painful limp, moved to rest on the pillar next to hers.

"There's that look again."

Maggie smirked without turning around, not wanting to draw attention to him. "You should be nowhere near this place."

He sat down on the dock to take off his boot, shaking out a nonexistent rock. "I wanted to make sure your mother's necklace made it back to you."

"It did...and that was an ingenious plan that you came up with, by the way. Thank you."

"Captain Wilson should trouble you no more."

Maggie cleared her throat. "Oh, if only that were true. He managed to escape."

He pulled on his boot and took off the other. "Leave it to the British to muck that up."

"He may show up in your camp looking to switch sides."

"We will be on the lookout and deal with him if he does."

"And what about our other 'friend'?"

He slipped his other boot back on. "Officially? He fell from a horse this morning, tragically dying from a broken neck."

Maggie looked down. "And, unofficially?"

"He died the way all traitors do, swinging from the end of a rope."

"Sounds like a terrible way to go."

"The worst."

Duncan appeared on the top deck of the ship and smiled as soon as he caught sight of her.

Maggie acknowledged with a smile and a small wave.

"So, that's him."

Maggie nodded. "It is."

"I should go." He pretended to struggle as he climbed to his feet. "Be well, Maggie."

"You too, Ben."

A few moments later, Duncan had his arms wrapped around Maggie in a protective embrace, rocking her to and fro, the cool sea breeze blowing the chilly air against their faces. "Who was that man, Maggie?"

"It was Ben. He was making sure that my mother's necklace made it safely back to me."

Duncan looked toward the direction Maggie's former lover had disappeared, no longer seeing him. "Did he now?" He kissed the top of her head. "Come on. Let's get ye back to the house."

9 CHAPTER NINE

The next few days, Maggie looked for ways to occupy her time while waiting for the ship parts to come in. Duncan had joined the search for Wilson, leaving Maggie in John's care since he was already chained to his desk finishing up correspondence before his departure to East Hampton to meet with General Clinton. Duncan had been gone with the Queen's Rangers for two nights and Maggie was feeling claustrophobic from being confined to the inside of the house.

"John?" she called out.

He shook his head and grinned without looking up from what he was writing, knowing the exact words about to come out of her mouth; the same ones he had heard many times over the past few days.

"Yes, Maggie?" he played along.

"May I PLEASE take Onyx out for a teeny, tiny, little ride?"

John laid down his quill, more amused by her childlike behavior than annoyed. "For the third time in three days, NO, you may not, as long as Wilson is on the loose."

"But I am SO BORED, John," she whined. "I am not used to being stuck in the house like this. I mean if Duncan were here, I would at least have SOMETHING to keep me entertained."

John raised an eyebrow. "I would be more than happy to fill in during his absence, if you like," he bantered.

Maggie rolled her eyes. "Always willing to make the ultimate sacrifice for the ladies, aren't you John?"

"I do my best," he quipped.

She plopped down in a chair, and sprawled out like a rag doll, defeated. "I am not above begging. PLEASE, I am desperate!" Maggie gave her best puppy dog eyes.

John sighed. "You cannot go out riding alone; however, I will be more than happy to escort you to one of the local taverns for dinner. Would that suffice?"

Maggie leapt from her chair, a huge smile on her face. She moved to his desk, and hugged him from behind, kissing him on the cheek. "I will go get ready. Thank you, John."

John watched her go, thrilled to see her so excited.

They took a carriage into town and found a quiet table at one of the better taverns. They ordered drinks while waiting for their dinner.

"Are you all packed for your trip?" asked Maggie.

"Almost. I am still unsure as to why the General wishes to see me before moving to New York, but I will seize upon any opportunity to visit Gardiners Island. It is a magnificent place, and the family that owns the manor house are the finest you will ever meet. The Colonel does not allow any talk of politics at his dinner table, and people from each side are always welcome. It is a much-coveted respite from the dreariness of this war."

"Sounds like a little piece of Heaven."

"It truly is! The sunsets are so magnificent, and the views are beyond anything I have ever seen."

A sudden thought occurred to John. "Why don't you and Duncan come along with me? I know you are bored here...so am I. We could all use a change of scenery, and maybe your charm can help to sway General Clinton in Gabe's favor."

"What are the chances that he will not recall him, John? Truthfully?"

John shook his head. "I am not sure. On one hand, General Clinton is a single father himself. He has four remaining children, having lost his wife and oldest child a few years ago. I think he will be sympathetic on that end; however, he is the Commander-In-Chief, and as a military man, he knows that we are in need of someone with Gabe's level of knowledge in the intelligence field, now more than ever."

"Wait! I thought Gabe only handled paperwork."

"He did in Philadelphia, but in the few years prior to that, he was one of the finest intelligence officers that we ever had. His resignation was a great loss to our side."

"That must have been during the time he was in New York, and we were out of touch. I cannot believe he never mentioned it."

John chuckled and sipped his drink. "Comes with the job. You get in the habit of not telling people things."

"I suppose you are right."

"So, are you and Duncan up for a little trip for a few days, before I have to move to New York? It will give us some more time together."

"I will discuss it with him as soon as he returns."

Duncan and the Queen's Rangers returned later that evening empty-handed; Wilson had disappeared without a trace. They left John and Simcoe to their private discussion, while Maggie went upstairs with Duncan, so he could get cleaned up.

Maggie looked out over the orchard that was growing by leaps and bounds as Duncan washed his face in the basin bowl. "I still cannot believe those trees are coming back to life the way they are."

Maggie turned to see him scratching at his face. "You are looking a little scruffy there."

"Aye, and it itches like hell." He picked up the straight razor off the dresser, after lathering up with soapy water.

Maggie slid out a chair from the small table in their room. "Here, let me do that." She took it from his hands.

He sat down, and she stood between his opened legs, placing a towel over his shoulder. She started the blade at the base of his throat and worked her way up.

Duncan put his hands on her hips, then began moving them around to her backside, playfully.

"Careful there," she scolded. "I would hate for my hand to slip and slit your throat wide open."

"As would I," he joked.

Maggie continued to focus on her work. "John has asked us to go with him to see General Clinton."

"Aye? What do ye think?"

"I don't know. On one hand, I am not sure it would serve any purpose. I am not convinced that the General will see things our way, but on the other hand, it never hurts to make a few acquaintances higher up. You never know when those things may come in handy." Maggie shrugged. "It would be nice to take a break. John said that the place is lovely, and the owner allows no talk of war at his dinner table."

"Och, that WOULD be a welcome change. Besides, we are doing nothing here but wasting our time and inconveniencing the Townsends," replied Duncan.

She sighed. "Yes, you are correct. Remind me to reimburse them for their hospitality before we leave. There is no doubt that they will never see any form of payment from the British."

Laying down the razor, she took the towel from his shoulder and used it to wipe off his face. "That's better. There's the face that I love." She kissed him on the nose.

Duncan wrapped his arms around her waist, pulling her in close, as she took his face in her hands.

"Are you hungry?" she asked.

"Starving, but I think we are going to be late for supper," he groaned.

Four days later, Maggie, Duncan, and John were on a small British boat sailing up to the dock at Gardiners Island.

"My God! Look at this place!" exclaimed Maggie, as she and Duncan looked on.

"I told you it was something else," said John, walking up to join them.

And it was.

The island itself appeared to be about six miles long and half that wide. It was a glorious area in the middle of the water just off Long Island that had been turned into a flourishing plantation. A grand manor house was just up from the dock, appearing to have been recently built. The view was especially spectacular.

"Wait until you see it at dusk," smiled John.

John escorted Maggie and Duncan to the front door, where they were met by a most pleasant older man, the owner, Colonel Abraham Gardiner.

"John! Come in, come in! How good it is to see you." He and John shook hands, warmly.

"Abraham, you are looking well!"

Abraham smiled at Maggie and Duncan.

"Colonel Abraham Gardiner, allow me to introduce my dear friends, Mistress Maggie MacGregor and her husband, Duncan."

Abraham bowed to Maggie and offered his hand to Duncan. "Any friends of John's are friends of mine. Welcome to the Manor House."

He led them into the parlour room, and had a servant bring wine for his guests.

"What brings all of you to our little neck of the woods, John?" he asked.

"I have been summoned, I'm afraid. Where is he?"

"He is set up in an office at the back of the house."

John excused himself to apprise the General of his arrival.

"Ye have a wonderful place here, Colonel," said Duncan.

"Oh, thank you. We enjoy it. Where do the two of you hail from?"

"Virginia," said Maggie. "We have a little estate there, but our views are nothing compared to yours. I hope we are not putting you out with our unexpected arrival."

"Of course not. What's a few more people? I am just happy to have guests who are not in uniform, for a change. We seem to have more than our fair share as of late."

"Abraham, you didn't tell me John was here," a lady stuck her head in the doorway. "Or that we had other guests," she added when she saw Maggie and Duncan.

"He has just arrived. Come and meet our new friends that he has brought with him."

He and Duncan stood.

"Allow me to introduce my dear wife, Mary. This is Mr. and Mrs. MacGregor."

"Maggie and Duncan, please," said Maggie. "We are not big on formalities."

"It is a pleasure to meet you both, and welcome to our home."

"Thank ye for your hospitality," said Duncan.

"Dinner will be in an hour. Why don't I show you to a room so you will have time to rest before then?" she offered.

Mary took them to a large suite overlooking a lovely part of the island.

"This room has a wonderful view of the sunset," she said. "And, it is right next to John's usual room."

"John visits often?" asked Maggie.

"Whenever he can. He has become more like family. If you need anything, please do not hesitate to ask."

"Thank you."

Maggie pulled back the curtains from the window, soaking in the fresh air, entranced by the view of the water. "You don't suppose the Colonel would sell us this place, do you?"

Duncan came over to her, a grin on his face. "We could make him an offer. It would be nice to have our own little private island."

"Wouldn't it though?"

Duncan kissed her forehead. "Ye look tired. Why don't ye take a nap? I will wake ye in time for dinner."

Maggie looked over at the bed. "That actually sounds like a great idea." She stretched out—and fell asleep as soon as her head hit the pillow.

Maggie and Duncan were the last to arrive in the parlour before dinner.

John waved them over when they came in, making formal introductions to General Clinton and some other members of his staff. Dinner, was indeed, kept lively, free of the talk of war and politics, John at his best, regaling them with his colorful stories and poetry.

As they were departing the dining room, John whispered in Maggie's ear. "Would you and Duncan like to take a walk on the beach with me later to enjoy the view?"

"We wouldn't miss it."

That evening, they met John outside. He had several blankets and a bag across his shoulder. They meandered along a pathway from the side of the house that sloped down to the beach, several large boulders hindering their view of the house. He spread out a blanket and invited them to sit. From the bag, he produced a bottle of wine and four glasses, handing them each one as he poured.

"I have news. It seems that General Clinton called me here to give me an additional title. I am now officially in charge of the coordination of British Intelligence in the Colonies."

"Oh, John! That is wonderful news! Congratulations!" said Maggie.

"Aye, it is indeed," said Duncan. "May I offer a toast?"

A voice from behind them broke in. "Only if one of those glasses is for me."

John held up a poured glass above his head, without turning around, as the man moved to take it.

"Maggie, Duncan...allow me to introduce Nathaniel Gardiner, son of our esteemed host and... surgeon for the Continental Army."

Maggie and Duncan were surprised at the very young man before them.

"You should be more careful," said John to Nathaniel. "Next time you visit, it may be best to make sure that General Clinton isn't here. I saw you when we docked."

Nathaniel took a seat next to them, grinning. "Especially," he said, "now, that the head of intelligence is here, as well. I WILL have to be more cautious. Congratulations, by the way."

"Thank you. What are you doing here anyway?"

"We are coming out of winter quarters. It was a good time to take a few days to come home and visit or so I thought."

Maggie cocked her head at John for an explanation.

"The Gardiners have become great friends to me. I could never turn young Nathaniel in; he is too much like I imagine my own son would be if I had one. Besides, he is not a soldier, he is a surgeon. He tends to as many of our own men as he does theirs."

"So, are ye hiding here?" asked Duncan.

He nodded. "There are several buildings around, as you can see. I can move around with relative ease."

"Your mother sent food for you; it's in the bag," said John.

Nathaniel rummaged around to see what he had brought.

Maggie gave him a good look over. "A surgeon? Just how old are you, anyway?"

He looked at John. "I just turned 20."

"A little young to be a surgeon, aren't you?" mused Maggie.

"Young Nathaniel joined up with the wrong army at the tender age of 16 and apprenticed in the field hospitals. He is actually very good at what he does," said John, patting him on the back. "We are all very proud of him."

Maggie raised her glass. "Well, here's hoping that this is over very soon, for both sides."

"Hear, hear...and to friendship. May it survive above all else," said John, and the four of them clinked glasses.

They all turned to watch the most magnificently colored sunset Maggie ever recalled seeing. They lingered until Maggie started to shiver from the chilly breeze.

Duncan wrapped her in one of the blankets, and they bid farewell to Nathaniel, before heading towards the house.

"Any word on Gabe?" asked Maggie.

"I have not found the right moment to bring it up yet; however, I will before we leave," replied John.

By the time they reached the house, Maggie was so tired that she could barely stand. Duncan escorted her upstairs and put her to bed. John stood in the doorway, a look of concern on his face.

Duncan closed the door and stepped out into the hall with him. "She is exhausted from the trip here," said Duncan, as if he could read John's thoughts. "I think everything that has happened over the past few weeks has finally caught up with her."

"That is understandable. Maggie is a remarkable woman, but everyone eventually hits a point where it all becomes too overwhelming. She spends so much time seeing to the needs of everyone else, that she forgets to care for herself."

Duncan looked back at the bedroom door. "Ye have no idea."

Maggie slept in late the next morning. When she finally opened her eyes, Duncan was propped up on one elbow, stroking her hair, while smiling at her.

"Good morning, or should I say, 'afternoon'."

Maggie yawned. "What time is it?"

"A little before dinnertime."

"Seriously?" asked Maggie. "Why did you let me sleep so late?"

"You seemed like ye needed it. Besides, we have no pressing matters that need attending."

"Just one," she replied.

"John and General Clinton have been otherwise occupied, so there was no need to bother ye." Duncan kissed her forehead. "Ye are allowed a day to take it easy, ye know."

"No rest for the wicked," she replied and got up to dress.

After dinner, they strolled around the grounds, enjoying the beach while waiting for John to finish his work so they could speak. Maggie picked up seashells that had washed up on shore, showing them to Duncan. It wasn't long before John came out to join them on their walk, a grave look on his face.

"I spoke with General Clinton about Gabe," he said. "I am afraid it did not go well."

Maggie stopped, "What did he say?"

John sighed. "While he does sympathize with Gabe's situation, the information that he can glean is far too valuable to overlook. I did my best. I am sorry. General Clinton is determined to end this war as soon as possible, and he is leaving no stone unturned. I have Gabe's papers here."

Maggie took the packet, looking at it as if it were an abomination. "I know, John. We are grateful that you tried, but we understand that some things are out of your control."

John nodded. "I know it is not much, but I can secure a place for Gabe in New York, at a private home, so that he may bring his daughter and her nanny, and there will be plenty of room for all of you, as well."

"Thank ye, John," said Duncan.

John touched Maggie on the arm. "We will be departing tomorrow."

They watched John walk away.

"So, that's that," said Duncan. "Gabe will be recalled and there is nothing we can do."

"I am not so sure about that."

When they returned from their walk, John and the Colonel were on the porch.

"Maggie, Duncan, you are just in time. Abraham was just about to take me out to the stables to show off his new foal. Care to join us?"

Maggie rubbed Duncan's arm. "Why don't you go? I think I am going to nap some more."

"Are ye feeling unwell, Maggie?" He touched her forehead, like a worried mother.

"No, I just want to rest up before the trip tomorrow. Go!"

He kissed her and Maggie watched them leave.

She slipped into the house and noticed General Clinton in the parlour pouring himself a glass of sherry.

"May I offer you a drink, Mistress MacGregor?"

Maggie smiled, "Please! I was actually hoping to steal a moment of your time, in private."

He handed her the drink and escorted her to his office, offering her a seat as he took his own. "What can I do for you, Mistress?"

"I wish to speak to you on behalf of Colonel Asheton."

"Yes, Major André and I have already had this discussion. I do feel terrible about having to call him back to active duty, but we are currently in need of his...special talents."

Maggie looked down at her drink. "You are making a liar out of me, General Clinton. You see, I made a promise to a very special little girl that I would ensure that she would not lose her new father after losing both of her birth parents. I do not take these matters lightly."

"I appreciate your devotion to standing behind your word, but this business of war is none of your concern. We have all had to make sacrifices on the home front."

Maggie took in a deep breath, seeing nothing but a picture in her mind of Gabe, Kat, and Quinn together and happy. "What if I told you that I could get you what you needed to win this war? End it completely, once and for all."

He looked intrigued. "And, what might that be?"

Maggie leaned forward. "General, I have made it a point to avoid this conflict as much as possible. I have maintained friendships on both sides, and, in that unique position, I have become aware of a great many things that others have not. I have recently heard rumblings of a high-ranking official in General Washington's innermost circle who is somewhat disgruntled with his current state of affairs. He may be...ripe for the picking...if you take my meaning?"

General Clinton leaned forward; his eyes narrowed. "And, who might that be?"

Maggie sipped her drink. "That particular information will cost you, sir."

He leaned back, eyeing Maggie. "Let me guess. All it will cost me is Colonel Asheton's complete release from the military."

Maggie smiled. "That's a small price to pay for victory, wouldn't you say?"

He sat thoughtfully for a moment. "You could give me any name and I would have no way of verifying it. Then, I am out the information and Colonel Asheton. I think it is safer for me to lay my bets on him."

"Fair enough, but what if I can give you proof?"

"What kind of proof?"

Maggie looked him straight in the eye. "What if I can have delivered, a letter from this high-ranking official, with his seal, offering his assistance to your side. I am sure he will expect to be compensated, but the details will be up to you. I can offer you a better chance in one shot, than all of your people and their knowledge brought together."

"That would put you in a great deal of danger from the other side if they found out what you were doing."

Maggie shrugged. "Then it seems that I am the one taking all the risks. Make no mistake, General, this is a one-time thing. I deliver one letter, and my hands are washed clean of the whole affair, my name kept out of it. I will simply make the introductions; the rest is entirely up to you."

"Mistress MacGregor, I need information as soon as possible, not something that you may produce months from now. Colonel Asheton can gather a great deal of intelligence in that amount of time."

"That is the best part. I will have your letter delivered in less than six weeks, and if I fail to deliver, you still have every right and reason to recall Gabe."

The General looked thoughtfully at Maggie. "I think you need to sweeten the pot, ma'am."

"What did you have in mind?" Maggie asked as she folded her arms.

He stood and moved to look out the window. "If you are unable to deliver, not only do I get Colonel Asheton..." he turned to face her. "I get you!"

He laid his hands flat on the desk.

"And, all the information you seem to pick up from your 'rumblings' as you say, from the other side. It will help to account for the six weeks of time I am not receiving information from the Colonel."

Maggie took in a deep breath, reminding herself that this was the only way to keep Gabe out of uniform and clear of the British side for when this war was over.

"That is acceptable."

General Clinton stroked his chin.

"Alright Mistress MacGregor, six weeks, a delivered and verified letter in exchange for Colonel Asheton's complete and permanent release from the service of the Crown...and yours, on my word."

"Thank you. You will not regret this." Maggie stood to go.

"Major André will be your contact. Deliver it straight to him so he can verify the information before it is presented to me. I trust that is agreeable?"

Maggie nodded. "Perfectly."

Maggie had dozed off on the bed, when a rather loud banging jolted her awake, causing her to sit up, blinking. "Come in."

John stormed through the door. "Damn it, Maggie, what did you think you were doing?" he demanded in an angry tone.

"Well, I WAS trying to take a nap."

"You know good and well what I am talking about."

Duncan appeared behind him. "What's going on?" He looked back and forth between Maggie and John, puzzled.

John stepped back and closed the door. "Are you going to tell your husband what you have done, or shall I?"

Maggie closed her eyes and yawned. "I was having such a nice dream."

John turned to Duncan. "She offered herself up in Gabe's place to General Clinton."

Duncan turned to Maggie. "Ye did what?"

"The two of you are overreacting," she said, "and giving me a headache in the process. PLEASE, stop shouting."

Duncan moved to her side. "Tell me he is lying."

Maggie sighed. "I am merely upholding my word to Gabe and Kat."

"Maggie, for God's sake!" exclaimed Duncan, taking her by the shoulders. "This is ludicrous!"

"What are you playing at, Maggie?" asked John. "Who is the person in Washington's camp you have promised to General Clinton?"

"Let me secure the letter, and I will tell you everything. Right now, that name is the only thing keeping Gabe with his daughter and I am the only one who knows it. If General Clinton gets it before I get the offer, he will back out of this deal."

"How did you even get it to begin with, and how do you know that it is... real?" demanded John.

"I just do. I hear things John, and I listen."

John turned to Duncan. "Can you please talk some sense into your wife before she gets herself killed?"

"He is right, Maggie," said Duncan, "Ye are putting yourself in far too much danger. Ye are not alone anymore, and the decisions ye make affect us both. I thought we were clear on this!"

Maggie could feel Duncan's anger growing.

"Duncan..." started Maggie, but he placed his fingers over her lips to shush her.

"I am your husband, and ye will OBEY me! This deal is off!" he commanded.

Maggie held up her hand in a defensive posture. "I'm sorry. Did you just say that I will 'OBEY' you? 'OBEY' you? You do not make decisions for me simply because we are married."

"I AM making this one!" he shouted, as he stood.

"NO! You are NOT! This bargain is struck, and I will abide by it. The two of you can like it or lump it, I really couldn't care less. Now, if you will excuse me, I am very tired, and I am going back to sleep. The door is over there, and you two can show yourselves out." Maggie rolled over face down on the bed and covered her head with the pillow.

Duncan and John turned to each other, unsure of what to think of her odd behavior.

"This conversation is NOT finished, Maggie," ordered Duncan in a perturbed tone.

Maggie reached her hand from under the pillow and waved him off in a dismissive manner.

Duncan's fury rose and he stormed out of the room, slamming the door behind him.

John watched him leave before he moved to her bedside and took a seat just on the edge. "Maggie," he said softly, gingerly placing his hand on her back, "we all love you, and are just concerned about you…and as your husband, Duncan did not deserve that."

Maggie rolled on her side towards him. "None of us deserve any of this, John. I am just trying to do the best that I can for the ones that I love. Is that such a crime?"

"No! And, it isn't a terrible thing when your husband tries to do it for you either," he pointed out.

Maggie sighed. "You are right. I owe him an apology." She covered her face with her hands, "I am just not feeling myself the past few days."

She sat up. "I should go and find him."

John leaned towards her, "I think that is an excellent idea, right AFTER you void this deal with General Clinton."

"I am sorry, John, but I cannot do that." Maggie slipped off the bed and went to look for Duncan, leaving John to worry as he watched her go.

She found him down by the water, staring at the ocean, still as a statue, his arms folded with his back to her. Every muscle in his body was clinched tight with anger, which made him sexier, if that were even possible. Maggie slipped up behind him and wrapped her arms around his waist as she kissed his back.

"I did not mean to be so harsh with you. Please, forgive me."

He didn't move and wouldn't acknowledge her. She squeezed him tighter from behind.

Nothing.

Maggie moved around to stand in front of him, but his gaze never left the water. He was furious. She tried to unfold his arms, but he would not give an inch.

"Duncan, I am trying to apologize."

He would not even look in her direction.

She slipped her hand over his thigh and he still rebuked her. *Damn! He really IS mad.*

An impulsively wicked idea of how to overcome his anger struck her. She shrugged in defeat. "Well, if you won't talk to me, I might as well go for a swim while I am here."

Maggie started undoing her dress and began dropping each piece of her outfit on the sand as she removed them. "Of course, I do like to swim in the nude."

He swiftly cut his eyes over to her, before he resumed his view of the ocean.

She continued taking her ensemble off, piece by piece, until she was only in her shift. Walking to the edge of the water, directly in front of him, she grabbed it by the hem, as if she were about to pull it off; he still did nothing to stop her.

Maggie started slowly drawing it up, making it almost up to her thigh before she stopped and waved, "Oh look! There is John with several of the other men, headed this way."

He ignored her ruse.

Maggie smirked, continuing to lift, and as the bottom of the shift was just about to completely expose her private area, she goaded him. "You know I have NO shame."

He stood firm.

Maggie winked, and started to pull her shift over her head.

Just as she was about to reveal herself, out of nowhere, Duncan unexpectedly rushed her, picked her up, and threw them both into the frigid ocean water, landing with a 'splat'.

Screaming from the initial shock, Maggie coughed and sputtered as her head went underwater and came back up, Duncan right there beside her.

"That should cool off your 'hot' head," he said, angrily, roughly grabbing her by the waist and pulling her into a deep, hard kiss.

When they finally broke apart, they were both out of breath and in primal need of each other.

"Actually, I think it just heated me up." She pulled him back into the kiss, laughing and biting his lip, running her hands down the length of his body.

He lifted her in the water, splaying his hands over her backside, as she locked her legs around his waist, her hands grasping the back of his head, fervently kissing as if their very lives depended on it. He moved her to an outcropping, where the water was deep enough to come up to their shoulders. He untangled her from his body, then turned her around to face the rocks, placed her hands flat against the stone, and readied her to receive the retribution that she severely craved. He took her from behind in one swift, abrupt move, savagely crashing into her repeatedly until he spilled himself deep within her. She leaned forward, recovering from her own orgasm, resting her forehead against the rock, as he wrapped both arms around her protectively, kissing the back of her neck.

"Ye are mine, Maggie MacGregor, and I will not lose ye for anyone or anything in this world," he growled.

Maggie turned and took his face in her hands. "You may lose me to frostbite if you do not get me out of this water soon," she said, her teeth chattering.

His eyes widened, realizing with horror, that her face was starting to turn a shade of blue. "Christ, Maggie! I'm sorry, I did not realize the water was this cold."

He scooped her up and toted her to the beach. Moving her to an overhang where she would not be seen, he slipped off her shift and put her dry clothes back on her, rubbing her extremities to warm her. Then, he picked her up, carried her to the house, up the stairs, and laid her onto the bed. Stripping her naked again, he covered her with several blankets and went to stoke the fire, removing his own wet clothes. He slipped into bed next to her, feeling her still cold, clammy skin, and pulled her tight to his warmer body, wrapping his arms around her, giving her his own body heat.

"Why are you not freezing?" asked Maggie, shivering.

"Highlander blood, I suppose," he replied.

"Duncan, I am sorry about earlier, but you overreacted without knowing the details."

He rubbed her back. "This is as good a time as any to tell me."

Maggie explained the deal she made with General Clinton as she snuggled against him under the covers.

"So, you are trading sides now, and selling out Washington who, I might add, you just risked your neck, to save?"

"No! I will give them their information, but only what I know they will already receive."

"I don't understand."

"Duncan, I know, from my history, who the traitor is that turns this war, and I know, that he is disillusioned enough with Washington at this time to reach out to John very shortly with an offer of his services. I just need to intercept that, and make it appear that I was the one who delivered it. As long as that correspondence makes it to John, Gabe is a free man. I promised him one letter of introduction for Gabe's release, that's all, and then my hands are completely clean of it."

"And, how are you going to get this letter?"

"That's the beauty of it. This whole thing is already in motion. The only issue is that I cannot remember the timing of the letter. I know it will come, what it will contain, and where it will go, I am just not sure WHEN it will get there."

"So, what do we do?"

"We give things a little nudge to speed them along, and I know exactly how to do that. It will require a short trip to Philadelphia, once John leaves for New York, but this should be easy-peasy."

Maggie sat up to look at Duncan. "I really am sorry about earlier. I'm not sure why I acted that way. It's just that, I have felt very strange the past few days, like I am not quite myself."

"What do ye mean?" he asked with a great deal of concern in his eyes.

"I don't know. I just feel out of balance...it's hard to explain."

"Maybe ye should see a doctor, or do ye think it is Fae related?"

"Honestly Duncan, who knows anymore? It's a topsy-turvy world. I just know that I will feel better when we are back in our own bed in Virginia," she said, just before she fell soundly asleep.

10 CHAPTER TEN

Two days later, they were back in Oyster Bay. John rode ahead to the Townsend house while Maggie and Duncan stopped to check on the repairs to the ship.

"Permission to come aboard," shouted Maggie in jest.

"Permission granted!" answered Gabe, leaning against a doorway with his arms folded, a broad grin on his face.

"Gabe!" Maggie rushed to him and they embraced. "I am so happy to see you!"

"What about me?" asked Quinn, coming up behind Gabe.

"And, you too!" she replied, hugging him next.

Duncan came over to greet Gabe and Quinn, as well.

"What are you two doing here?" asked Maggie.

"Quick and easy trip? Ring a bell?" asked Gabe, in a sarcastic tone.

"When ye didn't return, we became worried, so when we received Captain Russell's letter, we thought it best to bring the supplies ourselves," replied Quinn.

"It has been an interesting time, to say the least," said Duncan, dryly.

"What happened?" asked Gabe.

Maggie glanced over at Duncan. "Well, Duncan got arrested..."

"And, Maggie got kidnapped..." retorted Duncan.

"And, there may be a disgruntled officer looking for me...."

Duncan folded his arms. "And, Maggie may have inherited her mother's goddess abilities..."

"But we think we have your problem figured out..."

"Because, Maggie sold her soul to the British army to get you released from duty," finished Duncan.

Maggie rolled her eyes at that last one.

Gabe and Quinn looked back and forth between them before they turned to each other and tried to sum up everything that was just said.

"Maggie did what?" asked an astonished Gabe.

"It's fine, Gabe. We have a plan all worked out."

Gabe stepped closer. "Is this plan anything like all of your other 'simple' plans?"

Maggie leaned against the wall, rubbing her temples, not wanting to have this argument. She decided a change of topic was in order. "Where is my goddaughter? Did you leave her in Virginia?"

"No, of course not. She and Cora are at the tavern, where we took rooms."

"Can we please go see her? I have missed her terribly."

Gabe started to argue before he took a good look at Maggie and realized that she did not look well at all.

"Certainly," he said.

They started off the ship, and Gabe shot Duncan an anxious, concerned look, which Duncan reciprocated. Duncan, and Quinn found a table and ordered, allowing Gabe to head up to get Kat while Cora rested for a bit. Kat grinned and kicked her feet as soon as she saw Maggie, who took her in her arms and hugged her tight. "Oh, I have missed you, little one."

Maggie turned to Gabe. "She has gotten so big since we left."

"Yes, she has. She is already growing up far too fast," said Gabe. "She is crawling all over the place."

"We are having a hard time keeping up," laughed Quinn.

Kat reached for Duncan, who snatched her up. "Your Uncle Duncan has missed ye too, lass." He sat her in his lap and bounced her up and down, making her squeal with delight.

Maggie smiled; her heart warmed seeing her favorite three men making such fools of themselves to entertain one precious little baby.

After eating, they retired to one of the rooms that Gabe and Quinn had taken so they could speak in private. Maggie and Duncan filled them in on everything that had happened with Duncan's arrest, the 'kidnapping', and Wilson's escape.

"Ye two weren't gone long enough to get into this much trouble," said Quinn.

"We do seem to attract more than our fair share," replied Maggie.

"That's an understatement," added Gabe. "Now, tell us about this deal you made."

"Before you go all crazy, just know that this is all well in hand."

Gabe shook his head. "The fact that you are telling me ahead of time not to lose my mind, already tells me that this is a bad idea." But he listened as Maggie explained about her agreement with General Clinton to free him from his service.

The blood drained from Gabe's face. "You were only supposed to speak to John. I did not ask you to make a deal, to put yourself in an enormous amount of danger to save me. I didn't want you to come here in the first place. Maggie, what the hell were you thinking?"

His harsh tone cut Maggie straight to the bone. It was not unusual for him to become frustrated with her unorthodox ways, but he had never become angry with her before.

Maggie's shoulders slumped. "I was thinking that I did not want to see you and your family separated," she said softly. "I was just trying to protect the three of you."

"I am a grown man, Maggie. I do not need your protection. I am beginning to think that you are the only one who needs protecting…from yourself."

Her head dropped and a few tears slipped down her cheek. She didn't say anything, just got up and left the room, feeling emotional and alone.

Gabe's heart sank when he saw how much his words had hurt her feelings.

"Maggie…" he said gently, and he started to apologize, but she was already gone.

Duncan got up to follow her when Gabe caught him by the arm. "What's wrong with her? This is not like Maggie."

"I wish I knew, Gabe," replied Duncan fearfully. "There are other issues the two of ye need to hear about as well."

"What issues?" asked Quinn.

"She seems to be developing abilities that her mother had as a goddess. I am afraid that may be what's affecting her. She is not herself." Duncan looked back gravely at them and started towards the door. "I need to find her. We will further this discussion later."

Duncan located Maggie at the stables, leaning against Onyx, the horse's neck stretched around her, as she tried to pull herself together. He started towards her when Onyx snapped at him.

"Whoa there, beast! Ye will not keep me from my wife."

Onyx stretched out his neck and tried to bite him.

Duncan sneered, and pointed his finger at him. "I still haven't forgotten what ye did to my horse. Be grateful I let ye live."

Onyx snickered at him, and stuck out his tongue, infuriating Duncan even more.

Maggie laughed, the tears still in her eyes. "Stop it you two. I can't deal with this right now."

Onyx let Duncan by, but they eyed each other very closely.

Duncan grabbed Maggie and pulled her to him, while keeping Onyx well within his sight.

She leaned her head against his chest and let him hold her. "The more I try to help, the more people I upset," she whispered. "I only wanted Gabe to have the family he always deserved and needed…and Kat…she has already lost both her birth parents—I can't let her lose Gabe, too. She is just a little girl, and she doesn't deserve that."

"The way ye didn't deserve to lose YOUR parents?" Duncan asked softly.

Maggie nodded against his chest.

"Oh, Maggie," he whispered, rubbing over her tense back to soothe her.

"I lost mine as an adult, not even as a child, and look how I turned out. A red-hot mess just trying to hold it all together on the outside, while I am completely falling apart on the inside. Somedays, I swear, I question my own sanity."

Duncan kissed the top of her head. "I am rather fond of this 'hot mess', as ye call it, and sanity is greatly overrated. Ye have me now, my love, ye do not have to handle any of this alone anymore. Let yourself fall apart anytime ye feel the need, and I will always be there to pick up the pieces."

Maggie leaned back and gazed into his eyes as he stroked her hair. "No one understands me the way that you do. I am so grateful every day to who or whatever decided to give you to me. I honestly don't know how I ever managed before I met you." She kissed him. "Even if I do anger you on occasion."

Duncan laid his forehead on her shoulder. "It just makes 'making up' more fun."

She laughed. "Let's not 'make up' in the freezing water next time."

Duncan winced. "Och! I feel bad enough about that."

"I don't," she whispered.

"Come on my love, we need to finish filling in Quinn and Gabe," he said as he wrapped one arm around her shoulder, escorting her back into the tavern, and up to Gabe's room.

Gabe was anxiously pacing when they came back in. "Mags!" he said, reaching for her, and taking her into his arms. "I did not mean to upset you."

"I know, and I'm sorry," she replied. "I just needed a minute. Things have been a little overwhelming the past few weeks."

Kissing her forehead, Gabe made her take a seat, and they picked up where they left off.

Duncan informed them about the apple orchard incident.

Maggie leaned on her propped-up elbow on the table, blowing a strand of hair out of her face.

"Ye say it was the same type of shock ye felt before?" asked Quinn.

"Yes, just more powerful. It caused me to black out this time."

"I even felt it all the way here in town while I was in the gaol," said Duncan. "Which means, it was definitely Fae related, and very strong."

"I wonder if that is what he meant," pondered Quinn.

"Who?" asked Gabe.

"Finn. When he said that he gave Maggie something to remember her mother by. Maybe he passed along some of Danu's abilities, as a gift, if ye will."

"Och," said Duncan, searching his memory. "I had not even thought of that."

"Why would he do that? And then, not even tell me about it?"

"The Fae," replied Duncan, "have their own reasons for everything they do. They do not see fit to consult with humans on such matters, and have been known to do bizarre things, simply for their own amusement."

"At any rate," added Quinn, "we should probably keep a close eye on ye. If he did give ye Fae powers, there is a good chance that it could take a physical toll on your body when ye use them."

"Quinn is right. There may be something in the books back at home that could shed some light on things. We should check them as soon as we are able."

"So, we just need to get home," said Gabe.

"That would be nice," replied Maggie. "The sooner I settle up with General Clinton, the faster we get there."

"Speaking of," said Gabe, "what, or rather who, did you promise him?"

"One of Washington's most trusted people?" mumbled Maggie while covering her mouth.

Gabe folded his arms and gave Maggie a disapproving look, expressing his discontent, but holding his tongue, afraid of upsetting her again.

Maggie sighed. "I am giving the British what they will already get as history dictates, a Continental general who will betray Washington, eventually attempting to give up West Point before his treachery is discovered. I am just moving up the timeframe by a tiny bit to work to our advantage. I know that Benedict Arnold will turn, and that initial contact will be with John in the next few weeks. I just need to encourage him to do it sooner, rather than later, and make it appear that I had a hand in it."

"How do you plan to do that?" asked Gabe.

"It will involve a trip to Philadelphia. Now is about the time that General Arnold will be marrying someone that you and I both know very well."

"Who?" asked Gabe.

"Miss Peggy Shippen."

"The judge's daughter? Marrying a Continental general?"

Maggie nodded. "There were always rumors that she had a hand in converting him to the British side, primarily because of her 'fondness' for John. If we go there, insert ourselves into one of the dinner parties, and poke a few bears, so to speak, it should speed things up a bit. That is, if you think you can handle such a mission," said Maggie sarcastically.

Gabe narrowed his eyes. "What do you mean by that?"

"John told me about how valuable you were to the army," replied Maggie, pointing her finger at Gabe's chest, "and, by the way mister, how is it that we have known everything about each other all this time and you never once mentioned that you were so neck deep in intelligence for the British? I think you should enlighten all of us."

Gabe rolled his eyes. "You do know that intelligence involves secrecy, right?"

"As does your choice in lovers, but you trusted me with THAT information."

Sitting down, Gabe crossed his legs and sighed. "It was only those few years I was in New York. I simply traveled in social circles, gathering information from the gossip around town and investigating it. New York has lots of loose lips."

Maggie knew that was more to it than that. She narrowed her eyes. "You are not telling us something. I know you too well, Gabe Asheton."

"I don't know what you mean," he denied.

"What KIND of social circles did you travel in?"

"The upper and...an occasional lower."

Quinn folded his arms, looking at Gabe with suspicion. "Aye, Maggie is right. What aren't ye telling us?"

"Spit it out, Gabe," demanded Maggie.

Gabe looked at Quinn before he closed his eyes and made an annoyed face. "I gleaned information from...the ladies around town. I would...romance them, and get them to spill all the current gossip, before moving on to the next one."

"Did ye sleep with these women?" asked an astounded Quinn.

"Absolutely not! I didn't have to. That is why I was so good at my job."

"Gabe IS excellent at that kind of thing, I mean look at him," said Maggie. "Women have always drawn to him like flies to honey, falling all over themselves to offer up their... 'special' services, so to speak."

Quinn looked at Maggie and then back at Gabe. "Oh really?"

Gabe shot Maggie a dirty look before he took Quinn's hand, and kissed it, reassuringly. "There is only room in my bed for one, and that is you, my dear husband."

"And, it had better stay that way," ordered Quinn.

Maggie and Duncan grinned at each other.

"So, how did you end up on paperwork duty in Philadelphia?" she asked.

"Oh, that! I simply ran out of women and they were starting to talk. It was only a matter of time before they would begin to compare notes, the way that most women do, and not taking a whore on the occasions that I needed to go to the brothels, well, it was becoming suspicious. I asked for desk duty for a short time to regroup. I had planned on concocting a story about taking and losing a wife, so when I returned, I could move back into the upper circles, play the inconsolable widower with a broken heart and start all over again. That was before you came back into my life."

"'Oh, what a tangled web we weave, when first we practice to deceive,'" quipped Maggie.

Gabe held out his hand. "Hello Pot, my name is Kettle. It's nice to meet you," countered Gabe.

"Sounds like we both missed our callings in the theatre," said Maggie dryly.

"Indeed," he replied.

"We need to plan our cover story before we go. John will be leaving in a few days for New York; we can detour to Philadelphia once he is gone and, if things go as planned, meet him there later with what he needs to give Clinton to release you. If we are very fortunate, perhaps the ship will be ready to sail home by then."

Cora interrupted them with a knock at the door. "Pardon me, sir. Kat just woke up from her nap and is a little fussy. Is it alright if I take her for a walk?"

Gabe took Kat in his arms. "Are you a little cranky, sweetheart?"

Kat instantly calmed at the sound of his voice.

"It is not a good idea for you to wander around alone in this town, Cora. The soldiers are not very kind to the women here," said Maggie.

Gabe looked at Maggie, his concern for her growing.

"Why don't you and Quinn take her out for some fresh air?" Gabe suggested to Duncan. "It will give Maggie and I a chance to catch up."

Duncan nodded his understanding. "I think that is a wonderful idea." Duncan kissed Maggie, as Quinn took Kat and they disappeared, leaving Maggie and Gabe alone.

Gabe pulled a chair up close to Maggie to sit directly across from her, face to face. He took both of her hands in his. "Okay Mags, we are alone. What is going on with you?" he asked softly.

Maggie shook her head. "Gabe, I have no idea."

"Does it have anything to do with seeing Ben?" he asked.

Maggie looked down. "Ben and I... we worked through our issues and he now knows there is no future for us. I was able to give him some closure and find some for myself that I did not even realize that I needed until I saw him. He was hurt, but I think he will move forward from here."

Gabe furrowed his brow. "Maggie, no offense, but you look awful."

Maggie frowned. "Oh good, just what every girl wants to hear." She shook her head. "I am just really tired. I have been exhausted the past few days."

"Are you having trouble sleeping again? Quinn can make something up for you."

"Not really, I just don't feel like I am getting any rest when I do. It has me feeling very strange. I was so tired on Gardiner's island that I took Duncan and John's heads off for interrupting my nap."

"YOU took a nap?" asked Gabe.

"Yeah, crazy, I know. Maybe all of that stress has finally caught up with me."

Gabe touched her forehead to check for a fever, seeing the fatigue around her eyes. "Maybe you should see the surgeon."

"I will be fine. I think I will rest better when I am in my own bed at home."

"I think we all will."

"How are you and Quinn?" she asked.

"You mean besides not getting enough time alone? Other than that, we are good. We are very good," he smiled. "Quinn and I are perfect for each other."

"I am so happy for you, Gabe."

"What about you and Duncan?"

"Duncan is the love of my life. I could not be any happier," she said, and a tear slipped down her cheek.

Gabe wiped it away as he looked at her strangely. "Why are you crying?"

Maggie shrugged. "I don't know," she said, and a few more fell. "This exhaustion is affecting me emotionally, too. I can't seem to control any of it."

"Now, I am even more worried, Mags. You HAVE to see a doctor."

Maggie leaned her head forward on to his chest. "We'll see."

Duncan and Quinn returned with Kat a short time later.
"Why don't I send word out to John to come to join us for dinner? I know he would want to see you, and meet Quinn and Kat," said Maggie.

"That is an excellent idea," replied Gabe. "I want to see him, while we still can."

Maggie nodded sadly before she went to find a messenger. She wrote a quick note telling John that is was urgent that she saw him at dinner at the tavern.

Two hours later, John arrived.

Maggie met him outside. "John, I have a surprise for you."

"I am not sure I can handle many more of your surprises, Maggie," he replied sarcastically.

"I think you will approve of this one," she assured as she took him by the hand and led him inside.

John's face lit up as soon as he saw Gabe. "Gabe!" he exclaimed, striding across the room.

"John!" said Gabe, and they embraced. "It is good to see you."

"And you!" replied John. "You look well! Fatherhood is agreeing with you."

"Speaking of which," Gabe took Kat from Quinn. "I would like to introduce you to my daughter, Katherine—Kat for short."

John looked at her with a huge smile on his face and gave her his full attention. "Gabe, she is beautiful. You will have your hands full fighting off suitors in a few short years."

"Don't remind me."

"John," said Duncan, "allow me to introduce my youngest brother, Quinn."

John reached out his hand. "I have heard a great deal about you. I understand I have you and your knowledge of herbs to thank for getting rid of a terrible chest issue I was having."

"Ye mean Duncan actually listened to me for a change?" he laughed.

They sat down and enjoyed a lively meal together, talking and carrying on like they had no cares in the world. When they were done with their meal, Kat became fussy, so Quinn took her up to Cora to nurse. Maggie laid her head over on Duncan's shoulder, and dozed off while sitting up.

Duncan slipped his arm around her waist. "I think I will take this one upstairs to rest for a bit, as well," he whispered to Gabe and John. To Maggie, he said, "Come on, my love, let's find you a bed to lie down on."

"Uh-huh." She let Duncan led her to one of their rooms, leaving John and Gabe alone.

"I am very glad you are here, Gabe. Maybe you are the one person who can talk some sense into Maggie. God knows Duncan and I have had no luck convincing her to abandon this insane idea of hers."

Gabe set down his drink. "I am afraid it is pointless, John. When Maggie decides that someone she loves is in jeopardy, she is relentless and unstoppable. Besides, I have already tried. She thinks she is doing this for Kat, and nothing will get in her way when it comes to that little girl."

"I am very worried about her, and not just about this deal she made," said John.

"I think we are all in agreement there."

"Does she really have this person that she claims she can deliver, Gabe?"

Gabe sighed. "I believe she does."

"If she does not, General Clinton will never release her."

Gabe looked at John strangely. "What do you mean by that?"

John shook his head. "She didn't tell you, did she? Of course, she didn't."

"Tell me what?"

"If General Clinton does not have that legitimate letter of intent in six weeks, not only will he recall you back to service, but he gets Maggie and all the information that she has picked up in her travels, as well, as part of the deal."

Gabe braced his hands on the table, reeling from what he just heard. "She agreed to that? That CANNOT happen. If the other side finds out, she is a dead woman."

John leaned close. "You cannot let her fail. I will do all that I can on my end, but she must give him what she promised in that time frame."

Gabe nodded. "I will make sure of it, John. You have my word."

11 CHAPTER ELEVEN

A few days later, they bid John a fond farewell as he left for New York, promising to see him soon.

A week later, they arrived in Philadelphia.

Maggie had managed, with the help of Mr. Townsend, to rent a home near Judge Shippen's house that belonged to a relative of his that had not yet returned after the British occupation. They were all surprised to find the house in a relatively good state, the servants even still there. Maggie employed them on the spot, paid them in advance, and sent them to stock the house for the next month. They dined at a nearby tavern that evening while the bedrooms were made ready for them.

Later that night, after Cora had gone upstairs to put Kat to bed, they all sat around the fireplace discussing their plans.

"I think Duncan and I should take a stroll tomorrow and see who we can run into. We need to wrangle an invitation that puts us on a direct path to Arnold," said Maggie.

"What are we going to tell people about your marriage to someone else?" asked Gabe. "The last time we were here, we were still engaged as far as everyone knew."

Maggie shrugged. "We will just say that we realized that we did not want to ruin our friendship by marrying."

Duncan gave Maggie a strange look. "Are we not friends?"

She patted his cheek. "We are so much more than that, my love."

She looked at Quinn. "I suggest you stay close to your husband...the women in this town love Gabe."

Gabe closed his eyes, and slowly shook his head.

"Is that right?" asked Quinn, raising an eyebrow at Gabe.

"You have nothing to worry about," he replied and slipped his hand over Quinn's.

"I don't know," joked Maggie. "You had just better hope that Mr. Manny is in good health, otherwise Mrs. Manny might be looking for her next husband."

"Ugh! Don't remind me," said Gabe as he leaned back.

"Then again, it may be you and I who need to keep a lookout," said Maggie, winking to Gabe. "Philadelphia hasn't been introduced to the MacGregor brothers yet. We might be the ones beating off the women."

"Speaking of which," added Maggie. "We need to be very careful here. Gabe was an officer and the opposing army is in charge now. While there are still many loyalists here, it may be best if we used some discretion."

"How do ye intend to move this defection along?" asked Duncan.

Maggie leaned against him, yawning. "At this time in history, Arnold should already be well on his way to being disillusioned with Washington, his finances will be a mess, and he is—or will be—facing all sorts of charges. We just need to pinpoint what goads him the most and focus in on it...pour a little salt on the wound."

"How do ye know so much about the details of all of this?" asked Quinn.

Maggie yawned again. "My dad taught history at the college. In my time, we have museums, places that hold information, and items found during a certain time period. He used to take me to them every chance he could. The Revolutionary War museums were always his favorites and thank goodness for that. I would have been seriously lost when I got here if it hadn't been for him."

Duncan looked down at Maggie as she started to drift off. "Come on, my love, let's get ye to bed." He gathered her up and carried her upstairs.

After breakfast the next morning, Maggie and Duncan went outside for a walk, making their way down to the shop area. Maggie pointed out the places that they knew there before, like Gabe's old office and the house they stayed in when they were there. They strolled by the window of a shop when Maggie, sure enough, saw a familiar face.

She smiled at Duncan. "Wait for me out here. I think I see our chance."

Maggie went inside and started to browse through the gowns for sale, letting herself be seen.

"Mistress Bishop? Is that you?"

Maggie looked up. "Miss Shippen! As I live and breathe! How are you?"

Peggy moved closer. "I am well. And, it is Mrs. Arnold now. I was married to General Benedict Arnold nearly two weeks ago."

"Congratulations! I am very happy for you."

Peggy looked down at Maggie's hand, and smiled. "I suppose it is Mrs. Asheton now?"

Maggie followed her gaze. "Mrs. MacGregor, actually. Gabe and I called off our engagement, but we remain great friends. I married not quite six months ago in Scotland."

"Oh! Well, I wish to hear all about it! How long have you been back in Philadelphia?"

"We just arrived yesterday. I am here with my husband, Gabe, and my brother- in- law. We had some business to attend, so we are only here for a short stay." Maggie decided to test the waters to see what sort of reaction she could get. "We were actually in Oyster Bay with Major John André before we came here."

Peggy was caught completely off guard. "MAJOR André, you say? He has been promoted then?"

"Yes, he has. Duncan and I were staying under his roof while we were having some ship repairs done."

The woman looked down. "And, how IS Major André these days?"

"John is well, for the most part. He has been recovering from an illness." Maggie stepped closer. "He actually asked about you several times."

"Me?" she asked, suddenly very curious as she stepped closer. "What did he say?"

There it was, written all over her face. Peggy still had a fiercely strong crush on John that her marriage to Benedict Arnold had not cooled in the least bit. She was still the same spoiled little girl that was used to getting everything she wanted, no matter what the cost.

"Oh, we were just reminiscing, fondly, about our time here in Philadelphia." Maggie pretended to have a sudden thought. "You should write to him. I am sure he would love to hear from you, in fact, I am certain of it."

Peggy took in a deep breath. "I wouldn't know what to say to him. Unfortunately, we have not been in contact recently."

Maggie touched her shoulder. "Anything you would write to him would be a welcome distraction, I am sure. He is so burdened these days. He is diligently working to end this terrible war by attempting to locate a few brave Patriots who wish to bring this conflict to a swift close, reuniting our country. The casualties on both sides keep the poor man awake at night. John is very 'grateful' to anyone who brings these people to him." Maggie leaned in, whispering, "And when I say grateful, I mean EXTREMELY grateful, if you take my meaning."

Maggie smirked and let out a devilish sigh as she lifted her hand to her breast. The look on Peggy's face told her that she knew exactly what she meant and that she was more than a little interested. She whispered close to her ear. "There is nothing quite as...satisfying...as being on the receiving end of John's... 'gratitude'. That man is an expert at what he does. And after this is all over, he will have plenty of time to... 'show his appreciation'...over and over again."

Peggy bit her lip, and it was apparent that she was lost in a fantasy. Maggie could read her like an open book. "You know, we will be stopping by to see John on our way back to Virginia. If you wish to send him any sort of correspondence, I would be happy to deliver it. You would not have to worry about it being read by the other side, and I will make sure it goes directly into his hands. And, of course, I will be the epitome of discretion."

Peggy smiled. "Perhaps I will send him a little note."

"Excellent!" said Maggie. "I know John will be thrilled to hear from you."

Maggie looked outside. "I should get back to my husband. He is waiting."

Turning to look his way, Peggy gasped, staring. "Is THAT your husband?"

Maggie smiled. "Yes, he is."

Peggy was unable to break her gaze while she spoke. "Mistress MacGregor, my husband and I are hosting a party on Friday evening. Why don't all of you join us? It will give us time to catch up and we would all love to see Colonel Asheton. He has been greatly missed since he left and besides, we would very much like to get to know your new husband better."

Maggie smiled. "Thank you for the invitation! We would be delighted to come."

Maggie exited the shop and took Duncan by the arm, planting a kiss on his cheek.

"Ye seem very pleased," he said as they started up the street.

"I am! I just planted a seed that should come to fruition very soon."

"Good! The sooner we get out of here, the better."

A short time later, they were back at the house and, as they came inside, Maggie and Duncan could hear Gabe and Quinn arguing in the parlour.

"Hey! Hey! Hey! What's going on in here?" asked Maggie as Duncan closed the doors.

Quinn shook his head, not answering.

Gabe turned toward the window, silent.

Maggie and Duncan looked at each other, both immediately recognizing what the real problem was.

"When was the last time you two were alone...really alone?"

"That's a bit personal," said Gabe.

Maggie rolled her eyes. "I am guessing it has been a while?"

"Aye," answered Quinn. "A very long while, now that I think about it."

"That's obvious," said Duncan. "Why don't Maggie and I take Kat and Cora out for dinner to give ye two some privacy?"

Maggie nodded. "I will dismiss the staff for the afternoon. You two go 'work out' your frustrations."

Gabe and Quinn looked at each other, the anger in their faces already dissipating.

"That would be wonderful actually," answered Quinn.

Gabe moved to his side. "Yes, it would!"

When they returned that evening, Gabe and Quinn were on the sofa in the drawing room in front of the fireplace, their clothes disheveled, drinking and laughing, completely relaxed, with all signs of their earlier tension gone.

"Well, you two look much better," said Maggie, plopping down in a chair.

"We are!" said Gabe, coming over to kiss her on the top of the head. "Thank you," he whispered.

Quinn poured two more drinks and handed them to Maggie and Duncan.

Maggie sniffed the drink, the smell causing her to wrinkle her nose, and set it on the table. "We have news. I ran into Peggy Arnold this morning and we have been invited to a party at her house on Friday."

"That is good news. We have a foot in the door," replied Gabe.

"More than that," Maggie toed off her shoes. "I am fairly certain that Peggy will do anything to gain John's favor and I informed her how personally grateful he would be to anyone bringing him a Patriot willing to trade sides. She obviously still has a thing for him."

"Ye think it will work?" asked Quinn.

"If history is right, it will."

Duncan moved next to Maggie, and she looked up, a disgusted look on her face. "How are you drinking that stuff?"

He looked at his glass, "What do ye mean?"

"The whisky...it smells bad."

Duncan smelled his glass. "Nay, it does not."

"Mine did."

Gabe reached across the table, picked up her glass, and waved it under his nose. "It smells fine, Mags." He took a sip. "Tastes fine too."

"Would ye like something else?" asked Quinn.

"Just a nice warm bed with my husband in it."

Duncan set down his glass. "Consider it done."

The night of the party arrived. Maggie was getting changed into a beautiful blue gown she had found at one of the local shops while Gabe helped Quinn and Duncan get dressed. She could hear them downstairs laughing and joking while they waited on her. Taking a final look in the mirror, she stepped out onto the landing, peeking over. The sight of the three stunning men below took her breath away.

"I am the luckiest woman in Philadelphia to have the three most handsome men in town escorting me tonight," she said and descended. "All of the ladies are going to be jealous."

Duncan looked up with a wide smile across his face. When she reached them, he took her into his arms, and kissed her thoroughly.

"I am the lucky one," he growled, "to have the most beautiful woman in the world all to myself."

Maggie placed her hands on his chest as they stared into each other's eyes adoringly.

"What do you say we just skip the party and go back upstairs," she whispered. "You look very good in those clothes, but I bet you would look even better out of them."

"I am all for that," he said, kissing her neck.

Gabe and Quinn looked at each other and shook their heads.

"Break it up you two." Gabe placed his hands on their shoulders. "There will be plenty of time for that later, but right now, we have work to do."

"Is there a plan for tonight?" asked Quinn, as he stopped to adjust something on Gabe's coat.

"Let's just play things by ear, and see how it goes," said Maggie. "Just remember, if you get the chance, needle in on his money issues, his failing relationship with Washington, and his bruised ego. It shouldn't take much to push him over the edge."

A short time later, the three of them were in line waiting to greet their hosts.

"Mistress MacGregor! We are so happy you could come," Peggy greeted them with a wide, near-feral smile.

"Thank you so much for the invitation," replied Maggie. "Meet my husband, Duncan."

Duncan took her hand, kissing it. "A pleasure to meet ye."

Peggy stared at Duncan a few seconds longer than socially acceptable. "Allow me to introduce my husband, General Benedict Arnold," she said, never taking her eyes off him.

Arnold offered his hand to Duncan, who firmly shook it. "A pleasure, and welcome to our home."

Maggie stepped to the side. "You remember Gabe, and this is my brother-in-law, Quinn."

They both stepped forward.

"Colonel Asheton, how good it is to see you again."

Gabe flashed that smile and took her hand. "Mrs. Arnold, I must say you are as lovely as ever. Allow me to offer my congratulations on your marriage."

Arnold held out his hand. "Colonel is it? I do not remember hearing your name."

Gabe shook his hand. "That is because I served on the side of the Crown, but I have retired to a much simpler life these days."

Arnold nodded. "Well, no matter. All are welcome in my home and in this city."

"Thank you, sir."

Arnold shook hands with Quinn. "Welcome."

"Thank ye. It is a pleasure to be here."

They moved along into the party to allow their hosts to continue their greetings.

Maggie noticed that every woman in the room stopped to gawk at the three newly arrived gentlemen.

She sent Duncan a silent message. *Make sure you flash that wedding ring around tonight. I would hate to have to cut some bitch for trying to steal my husband.*

Duncan looked down laughing. *Ye are the only woman for me, Maggie MacGregor. Besides, I would hate to have ye angry with me the next time ye shave my neck with the straight blade.*

She smiled at him, touching his face. "I love you!"

"I love ye, too."

The four of them moved to the refreshment table. Duncan handed Maggie a glass of punch. Maggie sniffed it and set it back on the table.

Gabe gave her an odd look. "Giving up drinking?" he asked.

Maggie wrinkled her nose. "It just smells strange to me."

Quinn picked it up, took a whiff and tasted it. "It's perfectly fine; delicious actually," he said.

Maggie shrugged.

"Maggie?" a voice said from behind her.

Maggie turned to see Margaret Shippen, Peggy's mother.

"Margaret!" she said, leaning in for a hug.

"I thought that was you." The woman turned to Gabe. "And Colonel Asheton, how good it is to see both of you."

Gabe bowed. "Mrs. Shippen, always a pleasure."

"Allow me to introduce my husband, Duncan MacGregor, and my brother-in-law, Quinn."

Margaret looked around confused. "Oh! I am happy to meet both of you. Maggie, apparently you and I have some catching up to do." She looked around at the group. "Do you mind if I steal her?"

"As long as ye bring her back," said Duncan, and he kissed his wife on the cheek.

Margaret led her over to a group of chairs.

"I am surprised Maggie, that you and Colonel Asheton are not married. What happened?" Margaret asked.

"We decided that we were better as friends than we were as a married couple. Gabe and I are still very close, but then I met Duncan while we were overseas. We have been inseparable ever since."

Margaret looked over in the direction of the men. "My dear, I wouldn't let him out of my sight, either."

Maggie smirked. "I am a little surprised myself, Margaret, to see that Peggy married a general from the Continental army."

"Yes, well, Peggy seems to be in love with the man, and what Peggy wants, she gets, no matter how much her father and I disagree with her choices." Margaret looked down at her glass. "We have tried very hard to remain neutral by maintaining friendships on both sides, just to survive."

Maggie covered her hand with her own, sympathetically. "Oh Margaret, I think we all have, and it is not an easy thing to do."

"I have missed you, Maggie," she said.

"I have missed you too." Maggie leaned back in the chair, listening to some of the ladies nearby, who were eyeing her escorts.

"Oh my! Would you look at the blonde one? Where has he been hiding?"

Maggie looked at Margaret who had heard them as well. She was smiling back at Maggie.

"Sara, look at the other one. I wouldn't mind meeting him in a dark alley," she giggled.

Maggie turned around to see that the two men had already been surrounded by at least seven women. Gabe and Quinn were playing the parts of the eligible bachelors to the hilt; Gabe must have given Quinn a few pointers.

Wasting your time, Ladies.

Duncan slipped off to a corner and was leaned against the wall, watching his wife, while sipping his drink. He smiled and winked when she caught sight of him.

Margaret leaned over. "Oh Maggie, do you know how many women wished their husbands looked at them that way? That man has it bad for you."

"Not nearly as bad as I have it for him. Speaking of which, I should probably get over there and protect my husband from the lovely ladies of Philadelphia before one tries to steal him away... if you will excuse me." Maggie went to stand, but felt a little lightheaded, and immediately fell back against the chair.

"Maggie?" asked Margaret, "Are you alright?'

Duncan was kneeling by her side before her head cleared. "What happened?"

"I just stood up a little too fast, that's all."

Duncan looked more than a little concerned.

"Would you like to lie down somewhere?" asked Margaret.

"No, no! Really, I am perfectly fine. A little fresh air is all I need."

Duncan looked at Margaret. "I will take care of her." He helped her up and out of a side door into the garden.

She leaned against Duncan. "It was a little warm in there. I am better now."

"Maggie, I am very worried about ye. Ye have not seemed well for weeks now. It is past time to see a doctor."

Maggie nodded. "As soon as all this is over, I will, I promise." She glanced towards the door. "But right now, we have work to do and I am pretty sure Gabe and Quinn could use some assistance."

Duncan laughed. "Let them squirm. I was rather enjoying the show."

When they returned inside, Peggy was speaking with some of her guests while Arnold was getting a drink.

Here's our chance.

Duncan nodded.

They made their way over to the table where the General stood, and Duncan poured Maggie a drink.

"General Arnold," she said. "You have a lovely home."

"Thank you. We like it very much."

"The Continental army must be paying well these days," added Duncan.

"I am afraid no one joins the army for the pay," said Arnold, seemingly irked. "They are full of more promises than money as of late."

"If the monetary compensation is not there, I am sure General Washington rewards your loyalty in other ways, does he not? Why, I am willing to wager he hangs on your every word and takes each of your suggestions straight to heart," Maggie spoke in a conciliatory tone.

"The General has many advisors around him. He does not need me anymore," he replied, a tinge of spite in his voice.

"Well, surely he must think highly of you to put you in charge of Philadelphia, trusting you so very far away from...him...and all of the fighting," nudged Maggie. "Your SAFETY must be high on his priority list."

"I am afraid my leg injury limits me, ma'am. I would much prefer to be on the front line."

Maggie noticed Arnold's jaw start to tighten, and his hand gripped his glass tighter.

"It's just as well General, combat is a young man's game. Who needs all the guts and glory on the battlefield, when you can stay here, out of harm's way? Soldiers our age, well, our better days are behind us. Who wants to take all those unnecessary risks anymore?" added Gabe, joining them. "It's best for all concerned that they put all of us old war horses out to pasture to live out our few remaining years in peace."

"I would prefer to be in the thick of it." Arnold looked down at his drink. "I would feel useful at the very least."

Maggie noticed that Peggy was working her way over to them. Catching Quinn's eye, she nodded her head to signal him that he needed to run interference.

He acknowledged and struck up a conversation with Peggy to distract her. He looked back, winked, and escorted her in the opposite direction.

Maggie took a step closer to Arnold and whispered. "If you want to feel useful, there are... others who might be more appreciative of all the knowledge and experience that you have to offer. Ones who already speak very highly of your military accomplishments and are willing to pay a great deal of money for your valuable service."

"I am afraid I do not take your meaning," he replied with a curious look on his face.

"I think you do, General." she sipped her glass. "We have a great many friends in the very highest of places. If you ever cared to reach out to the other side, we would be more than happy to carry a letter of interest."

Gabe nodded. "And, we can be discreet. It would pass into no other hands other than where it is intended."

Arnold looked down at the floor, speaking in a low voice. "Are you suggesting I betray my General and my country?"

"Sounds to me, like your General has betrayed ye, sir," answered Duncan.

"I think we all know who the winner will be when this war is over," said Maggie. "Wouldn't it be best for you to be on the victorious side? You have a wife to support now and an expensive lifestyle that she has become accustomed to. You owe it to her to make the right decision. Talk it over with Peggy. We will be here another week or so before we leave for New York, if you decide that it is indeed what you wish to do."

Peggy excused herself from her conversation with Quinn and headed in the direction of her husband.

"If you will pardon us, General, I believe your wife is looking for you."

They started to move away from the table, but he called out, "Who would that letter go to, out of curiosity?"

Maggie smiled without turning around. "Major John André, the head of intelligence. He inspects and verifies all information before it is personally handed to General Clinton. It merely needs your intent and your seal."

Maggie smiled as she passed Peggy on their way to meet Quinn at the fireplace.

"Did ye have enough time?" he asked.

Gabe handed him a glass. "I think we got our point across."

"Now, we wait," said Maggie.

A loud female voice came out of nowhere. "Colonel Asheton!"

"Oh...dear...God." Gabe closed his eyes and blew out a deep breath.

Maggie burst into laughter; she recognized the voice immediately and whispered, "I cannot be your fiancé anymore. You are on your own."

Gabe gritted his teeth as he shot her a look of disgust.

Maggie turned. "Mrs. Manny, as I live and breathe."

Mrs. Fannie Manny, the woman who had been the cause of their long-term engagement, came straight towards Gabe. This evening, she was wearing a bright purple dress, topped with actual feathers, making her appear even more as a short, stubby bird than usual.

She nodded to Maggie. "Mistress Bishop," her tone was curt before she turned to Gabe. "Colonel Asheton, I thought my eyes deceived me. Imagine my delight, when I heard someone say it was indeed you."

"Mrs. Manny, how good to see you." Gabe forced the words out.

Duncan and Quinn exchanged amused looks.

"I am so excited that you have returned," she said and took Gabe's arm.

"Mrs. Manny, where IS your husband? I wish to say hello."

She frowned. "Unfortunately, he passed away from a heart attack three months ago. I have been terribly lonely ever since then."

Gabe shook his head. "My condolences. Shouldn't you still be in mourning? Perhaps in your own home? Away from parties and the such?"

"Yes, well. I look horrible in black. It washes me out so, and I could not look at those four walls another moment.

It must be fate that my first outing brings us back together."

Maggie stifled a snicker. "Mrs. Manny, allow me to introduce my husband, Duncan MacGregor and my brother-in-law, Quinn."

She turned to Maggie. "Your husband? You and Colonel Asheton did not marry?"

"No, I am afraid it didn't work out."

Gabe stood behind Mrs. Manny's back, and held up his hands, as if in prayer, mouthing the word 'please'.

"Well, Mrs. MacGregor, allow me to offer my sincerest congratulations. I am so very happy for you," she said, face beaming with joy at the thought of Maggie not being with Gabe.

Gabe slipped behind a grinning Quinn for protection.

The woman turned back, trying to see Gabe through Quinn. "Colonel Asheton, perhaps we could...take a walk?"

"I am so sorry, Mrs. Manny, but I cannot."

"Well, why in the world not?" she asked in a flustered tone.

Maggie felt bad for Gabe and decided to help the poor man out. "There is a new woman in his life, Mrs. Manny, and I am afraid he is hopelessly in love with her."

"Who?" she demanded.

"Her name is Katherine," replied Maggie, "and he will never love another as he does her."

Gabe nodded. "She is right. I am sorry, Mrs. Manny, but my heart belongs to my sweet Katherine. I cannot live a day without her."

"Well, where is she?" she asked, suspiciously, looking around.

"She is...with her chaperone," Quinn offered as a possible excuse, with the wave of a hand in Gabe's direction.

"Yes!" Gabe caught on to the idea. "She was very tired and decided to retire for the evening early. She becomes very cross when she does not get enough rest."

Maggie turned her face to Duncan, attempting to keep a straight face. "She really does keep Gabe on his toes," added Maggie. "That young lady has him hopelessly wrapped around her little finger."

"Hmp!" said Mrs. Manny, before she turned and stomped off.

"Oh, thank God," said Gabe, relieved. "Maggie, I love you, in case I have not told you today."

Maggie chuckled.

"So, that is the infamous Fannie Manny," laughed Quinn. "I must say, your descriptions do not do her justice."

"Careful, Quinn," teased Duncan, "Gabe may steal off in the middle of the night with her. You should lock the windows before you go to bed."

Gabe rolled his eyes, "It's all fun and games until she sets her sights on you. I may need to keep an eye on you,

Quinn. She is on the prowl for her next husband; no man is safe."

They spent the rest of the night mingling and chatting. Maggie kept watch on Arnold, who seemed to be sullen, and in deep thought. He would occasionally glance over at Maggie, then quickly look away. At the end of the evening, they said their 'goodbyes' and departed for home.

Maggie woke up around midnight that night feeling ill. She managed to slip out of bed and made it to the water basin bowl on the side table before she vomited.

Duncan was immediately beside her, holding her hair back.

When she was done, he poured some water from the pitcher onto a cloth and sponged her face.

"Something I ate at the party didn't agree with me," she said, letting him help her back into bed. As soon as she laid down, she sat right back up, and returned to the basin to vomit again.

Duncan stepped into the hall, after hearing Quinn and Gabe still downstairs. "Quinn!"

Quinn and Gabe both appeared at the doorway as Duncan leaned over the rail.

"Maggie is unwell. Do you have anything that can help calm her stomach?"

"Aye!" he answered and took two steps at a time, quickly grabbing a bag from his room, and darted back down to the kitchen.

Gabe came into their bedroom as Duncan helped her back to the bed.

"Mags?"

She was curled against the headboard, Duncan sitting next to her, placing a cold rag on her face.

"I must have had something that wasn't cooked well."

"We all ate the same thing and none of us are sick," said Gabe, concerned.

"Maybe one of your admirers poisoned me...again," said Maggie, sarcastically.

"Again?" asked a perplexed Duncan.

"Don't even joke about that," said Gabe. "That was one of the most terrifying nights of my life."

Quinn returned with a cup of herbal tea. "Try this and see if it helps."

"Thank you." Maggie took one sip, closed her eyes, and handed the cup to Duncan before running to vomit again.

Quinn, Gabe, and Duncan all exchanged very uneasy looks.

Maggie sat on the edge of the bed.

"Would ye like some water?" Duncan pulled her hair back out of her face.

"No. I hope that was the last of whatever disagreed with me. I just want to go back to sleep."

Duncan gently helped her underneath the covers, settled her, and stroked her face.

"Please don't touch me," she said. "The movement is making me nauseous."

Duncan stopped and withdrew his hand. "Sorry," he said. "Is there anything I can do for ye?"

Maggie shook her head. She was asleep in a matter of minutes.

Duncan motioned Gabe and Quinn downstairs. He left the door cracked so he could hear her if she needed anything.

Downstairs, Duncan sat with his head in his hands; Gabe handed them all drinks, then took a seat himself.

"I am sending for the doctor tomorrow," said Duncan, "whether she likes it or not. I should have made her leave the party when she became dizzy."

"Dizzy?" asked Gabe. "Tonight?"

"Aye. She said she just got overheated, but I knew there had to be more to it."

Gabe stared into the fire, his mind finally starting to put some pieces together. He smacked his forehead. "Gentlemen, we are complete idiots."

They looked up at him, puzzled.

"Pardon?" asked Quinn.

Gabe leaned forward. "We are idiots! Think about it. For the past few weeks, Maggie has been too tired to stand up, she is dizzy, nauseous, vomiting, and EXTREMELY emotional." Gabe looked over at Duncan. "Are her courses late? Maggie has never been even a day late in all the time that I have known her."

Duncan shot Gabe a perturbed look. "How do ye know about my wife's courses?"

Gabe rolled his eyes. "How can anyone NOT know? Maggie becomes downright insane during that time." He turned to Quinn and pointed to his upper side. "That scar above my rib cage...I received that from her when I made the mistake of having sword practice during her time of the month. She came after me as if her very life depended on it, like one of those Highland...what do you call them...BERSERKERS! Her eyes were wild, her teeth were clenched, and she had bloodlust in her eyes. I haven't seen anything like that, even on the battlefield, and she didn't even feel bad about the fact that I had to be sewn up. I learned that day when to avoid her lessons. Oh, and I warn you both now, if Kat is anything like Maggie when she matures, the three of us are done for."

"She does become more than a little unreasonable around that time," agreed Duncan. "She threw a bottle at me on the ship home from Scotland when I asked her why she was a little moody one day. It's a good thing I ducked, or she would have caught me right on the side of the head. Then, she broke down into tears for no reason whatsoever. I have no idea how to deal with her when she is like that."

"Rum!" answered Gabe, a faraway look in his eyes. "Just slide the rum in her direction, and slowly back away."

"I will remember that," said Duncan, lifting his glass.

Gabe took a sip of his drink. "And then, she starts babbling on about needing a Doctor Pepper and a Mister Good Bar."

"Who are they?" asked Quinn.

"Not who...what," replied Duncan. "Apparently, Mister Good Bar is some sort of candy that contains chocolate, sugar, peanuts, and something women crave during that time of the month."

Gabe leaned back. "And Doctor Pepper is a sort of sweet drink, according to her, that contains sugar and some other things that seem to make women feel better."

"Do ye think ye might able to figure out how to make that?" Duncan asked Quinn. "It would be most helpful...and greatly appreciated."

Quinn shrugged, "I suppose I could try if Maggie can tell me what's in it."

Gabe leaned forward again. "Duncan, you did not answer my question. Are Maggie's courses late?"

Duncan searched his thoughts for a moment before his face slowly broke into a wide grin. "Aye! They are!" He laughed, his eyes lighting up. "I am going to be a father."

Gabe smiled. "It all makes sense. We were so absorbed in thinking that her new Fae abilities were affecting her, the obvious answer didn't even occur to us."

"But, why hasn't she told me?" asked Duncan.

"Duncan, she doesn't know herself."

"How could she not know?" asked Quinn.

Gabe took his hand. "Maggie was devastated over losing the baby before. Her mind probably has refused to acknowledge what her body is telling her now, afraid to let herself believe for fear of what may happen."

Duncan's mind was reeling with the news. "She has been so afraid that she would not be able to get pregnant or carry to term after what happened."

Quinn squeezed Gabe's hand. "Didn't she find out she was with child after she was shot?"

"Yes!" answered Gabe.

Quinn looked at them both. "So, she had the lead fragments in her body when it happened. The lead slowly poisoning her Fae half may very well have caused her to lose the baby."

"Aye, ye are probably right," said Duncan, and stood. "We have to tell her."

Gabe chuckled as he stood up too. "Give her a few days and see if she figures it out on her own. She will want to tell you herself."

Duncan nodded, "Oh! Aye!"

Quinn got up and refilled their glasses. "A toast to my new niece or nephew," said Quinn. "Congratulations, Brother!"

They clinked glasses and celebrated.

12 CHAPTER TWELVE

Maggie woke up the next morning to find Duncan stretched out beside her, propped up on one elbow as he smiled at her.

"Good morning, my love," he said. "How are ye feeling?"

Maggie groaned. "Still a little nauseous. Remind me to skip any and all future dinner party invitations."

"Can I get ye something? Some tea, maybe?"

At the word 'tea,' Maggie's feet hit the floor and she ran for the basin bowl, only to retch again.

Duncan winced, moving to stand next to her. "Maybe we should move the bowl closer to the bed," he said, sympathetically.

"There cannot possibly be anything left in my body to throw up." She collapsed in a nearby chair.

Duncan kneeled in front of her. "I am so sorry that ye are this sick."

She leaned her head on his shoulder. "It's not your fault. It's not like YOU did this to me."

He grimaced. "Tell me what I can do?"

"You are already doing it. You are the best husband ever."

He picked her up and laid her back on the bed as a soft knock was heard at the door. It was Quinn and Gabe.

"We heard you up," said Gabe.

Quinn brought a cup over to Maggie. "I found an apothecary this morning. This is a different tea brew. Try it and see if it helps."

"Thank you, Quinn." Maggie closed her eyes as she took a sip...and it managed to stay down. She breathed a sigh of relief and looked around. "Did no one else get sick from the food last night?"

They all shook their heads.

"We are all fine," said Gabe.

"That's odd," she said. Maggie looked around the room again, the three of them staring back her with stupid grins on their faces.

"Why are you all looking at me like that?"

"Like what?" Gabe averted his eyes.

Quinn turned and pretended to play with something on the bureau, while Duncan looked down at her hand, picked it up, and kissed it. They were all trying to hide the glee on their faces.

Maggie furrowed her brow. "What's up?"

Before anyone could answer, Maggie slapped Duncan on the shoulder and pointed to the bowl as she covered her mouth with her hand. He swiftly grabbed it, and placed it on her lap, just as she threw up again.

"Quinn's tea, it would seem," answered Gabe, sarcastically.

Quinn frowned. "I'll take that mixture off the list. I will see what else I can come up with."

Maggie laid back against the headboard while Duncan wrung out a cool cloth and placed it across her forehead.

"Maybe ye should try to rest some more," said Duncan, obvious pity in his voice.

She closed her eyes and Duncan kissed her on the cheek.

"Come on, Gabe," said Quinn, "We need to go back to that apothecary."

Duncan looked down at Maggie and smiled, pulling a quilt over her.

She slipped her hand out from underneath the covers and took his.

He sat down on the edge of the bed, held her hand and watched her; he felt more blessed than he ever thought possible.

Maggie slept until the early afternoon. She managed to get up, slip on a robe, and make it downstairs.

"Maggie, what are ye doing up?" Duncan met her in the doorway.

"I can only lay down for so long."

He helped her to the sofa.

"Where are Gabe and Quinn?"

"They took Kat out for a walk down to the shops. Quinn is determined to find the right mixture to settle your stomach."

"That is very sweet of him. I do not recall ever being this sick, even when I was poisoned."

Duncan smiled. "Just let me know what I can do to make ye feel better."

She laid against him and he wrapped his arm around her shoulders.

"I don't suppose there has been any word from Benedict Arnold?"

"Nay, nothing yet, but it has not even been a day. Ye worry about feeling better, we will figure out the rest later."

Gabe, Quinn, and Kat returned.

Kat reached for Maggie, who was too weak to take her.

Duncan grabbed her instead and sat her on his lap so she could see Maggie.

"Any better?" asked Gabe.

Maggie shook her head. "Not really."

"Well, let's see what I can cook up," said Quinn, smiling as he headed to the kitchen.

"Enjoy your walk?"

"Philadelphia is a very different place than it was when we were here last, and its citizens are not very pleased with Benedict Arnold. Everywhere you go, people are complaining about him overseeing the city."

"That can only work to our advantage. The more isolated he feels, the better our case. Let's just hope that we were able to convince him to move things along last night."

"We definitely got to the man," said Duncan, making faces at Kat so she would laugh. "He was wound up pretty tight by the time we were done with him."

Maggie smiled at them. "We shall see." Her stomach started to lurch again, just as Quinn reappeared, handing her a cup. "Thank you, Quinn, for all the concoctions you have been mixing up."

"Thank me when we find the one that works for ye," he grinned.

Maggie took a sip, then waited for a moment. She looked hopefully at him. "So far, so good. Let's see if it lasts." She leaned back against the sofa.

Gabe moved behind her and placed his hand on her shoulder. "I asked the cook to make up a batch of soup. You should really try to get some of the broth down."

She patted his hand. "Maybe later."

Kat reached up for Gabe and he took her from Duncan. "I am going to take this little princess up for her nap. I will be right back."

Maggie finished her tea, set the cup down, and laid her head over on Duncan's lap.

He stroked her face, and she closed her eyes. "It looks like Kat isn't the only one who needs a nap. Would ye like me to take ye upstairs?"

"No," answered Maggie. "If I lay very still, I may not be sick again."

Duncan kissed her head. "Then, we shall stay here as long as ye like, my love."

Maggie fell into a deep sleep.

About an hour later, Gabe stuck his head in. "Gone numb from the waist down yet?"

"Aye, about a quarter of an hour ago," he chuckled.

Gabe came over to them. "Let me take her upstairs. I can do it without waking her," he said, and gingerly picked her up.

"Oh, thank ye, Gabe. I did not want to disturb her when she was so peaceful."

"And not vomiting," laughed Gabe softly.

"Aye, that too."

He slipped her into bed, which caused her to stir slightly. Gabe shushed her back to sleep, covered her up, and tucked her in, before going back downstairs.

Duncan was stretching to work out the cramps. "Gabe," he asked, "Was Maggie this ill the first time she was with child?"

"No! I mean, she did have some mild sickness, but it was nothing compared to this, and she was not sleeping this much either."

"Do ye think something is wrong?" he asked, concerned.

"I do not have an answer for that. Maybe, it IS time we consulted a doctor."

Quinn paced the floor. "Ye two are forgetting the most important part of all of this. Maggie is half-Fae and when her blood is combined with whatever amount of Fae blood that runs through our veins, it very well may cause some exaggerated symptoms in her body. We have already seen how using the abilities that her mother had has adversely affected her...this just might, too."

Duncan nodded. "Quinn is right. We are in uncharted territory here." He folded his arms. "I wish Mother were here. She would know what to do."

Quinn squeezed his shoulder. "I know ye are worried, Brother, but Maggie has the three of us, and we will get her through this. Although, I would feel much better if we had access to the books right now."

"Agreed. The sooner we settle all of this business and get home, the better."

Maggie woke just before supper, as the smell of food wafted up the stairs. She sat up, and reached for the bowl, getting sick again.

Duncan heard her from downstairs. "Maggie?" he called, rushing to her side, "Again?"

Maggie felt horrible and looked even worse. She laid back down on the pillow, on her side to face him; tears streamed down her face.

"Oh, Maggie," Duncan wiped them away. "I wish I could do something to make ye feel better."

"I rarely get sick, Duncan, and I have never been this sick in my entire life. I thought it was passing, but it's not. I think it is time you sent for the doctor."

Quinn and Gabe came through the door with more tea.

Maggie sat up, accepted, and sipped it gratefully. "I seriously think I may be dying," she said, and more tears fell.

Duncan looked at Gabe and Quinn questioningly.

Gabe sighed. "She is your wife. The decision is yours."

Quinn nodded in agreement. "Aye, it's all up to ye to tell her."

Maggie looked back and forth between them. "What is his decision? What don't I know?"

Duncan took her hand and smiled at her, pushing the hair back from her face. "We know why ye are sick."

Maggie was dumbfounded. "What do you mean? I don't understand."

"Maggie, my love...think about it. Ye have been dizzy, nauseous, tired…"

She looked thoroughly confused and shrugged.

"Your courses are late…."

She shook her head. "My courses are not lat…" She stopped mid-sentence, a stunned look on her face as she searched her memory. She opened her mouth, then closed it, a sudden realization washing over her.

"Oh... my... God...I AM late. With everything going on, I hadn't even noticed."

Gabe and Quinn broke into wide smiles.

"There is a reason, my love." Duncan cupped her face with his hands.

Maggie looked at Duncan with tears in her eyes. "You are going to be a father," she whispered.

"And, ye are going to be a mother."

They embraced each other tightly, crying and laughing at the same time.

"And, Gabe and I are going to be uncles. Congratulations ye two," said Quinn.

"We are thrilled for you," added Gabe.

Maggie sobbed and Duncan smiled at her. "I can't believe it. I didn't think I would be able to even get pregnant again." She looked at Duncan with trepidation in her eyes. "It is still very early on...and the last time..."

Quinn cleared his throat.

"We have a theory. We think that since ye became pregnant when ye had the lead still inside ye from the bullet...and since lead is poison to Fae, it may have caused ye to lose the baby."

Maggie looked at him, a look of slow understanding crossing her face. "Maybe? It does kind of makes sense, I guess?"

Duncan squeezed her hand. "I think our child is going to be just fine."

Gabe moved to the other side of the bed and took her other hand. "This child has two of the strongest parents I have ever known."

Maggie nodded and pointed to the bowl, which Duncan grabbed just in time. Once finished she gasped, "Surely, I shouldn't be this sick."

Quinn moved closer. "We have another theory. We think that after seeing what using your mother's Fae powers did to ye, that between yours and Duncan's Fae blood, that it may greatly exaggerate your pregnancy symptoms."

"Oh goody! I get to puke out my guts for the next three months? I won't be able to keep anything down if today has been any indication."

"Don't worry, Maggie," said Quinn. "I have a whole host of herbs to help, and we will not rest until we find the right combination."

"Wait! How did you three know before me?" demanded Maggie.

"You have not tried to kill any of us this month. We knew your courses were off," chuckled Gabe.

"I am not THAT bad," retorted Maggie.

Gabe lifted his shirt. "I have a four-inch scar that says differently."

"And, I have not had to duck any bottles lately," laughed Duncan.

She scoffed, "You have not seen anything yet. Wait until the pregnancy hormones kick in, and if they are worse than a normal woman's, you three are in serious trouble."

"I'll see about picking up some armor," teased Gabe.

Maggie looked at Duncan, the tears flowing again.

"That's our cue, Gabe. Let's leave them alone for a while." Quinn kissed Maggie's cheek, as did Gabe, before they left, closing the door.

Duncan slipped into bed next to her and took her into his arms. "I am so excited, Maggie," he whispered, pure joy on his face. "I mean, I feel horrible that ye are so ill, but I cannot wait to meet our bairn."

"This is much better news than dying," she burst out, laughing.

"Aye!" said Duncan. "I love ye so much, Maggie."

"I love you more than anything, Duncan."

He slipped his hand over her belly. "And we love ye little one."

Maggie was unable to get anything down that night, so they sent for the doctor the next morning. After checking over Maggie, he came to speak to Duncan.

"Your wife is perfectly healthy other than the pregnancy sickness."

"Is this normal? Maggie cannot keep anything down, not even water."

"Some women have it very bad, although she does seem to have the worst case I have ever seen. Get as many liquids and broth soups down as you can, even if she is vomiting them back up, make her keep taking them. She also needs plenty of rest. It will get better once she gets through the first few months."

"Thank ye, doctor," said Duncan and he escorted him out.

Maggie spent the next two days moving between the sofa and the bed, still extremely sick. Quinn's tea concoctions were helping, but she still wasn't holding much down. She was curled against Duncan in the parlour when a messenger arrived.

Maggie opened the note. "Well, this is a good sign," she said.

"What is?" asked Duncan.

Maggie waved the note. "An invitation to tea with Mrs. Peggy Arnold. Let's hope she has something for me."

"Uh, I hate to point out the obvious," said Gabe, "you aren't going anywhere in the shape you are in."

"I know," sighed Maggie. "But I bet if the very charming Colonel Asheton called on her, explained the circumstances, and invited her here instead of there..."

"I do not think ye should even try," said Duncan. "Ye are supposed to be resting."

She took his hand. "I know, Duncan, but we need to wrap this up if we are ever going to get home. I can drink the tea that Quinn makes, and I will manage to get through it. We are running out of time, especially since we have to factor in how long traveling to New York will take."

"I will go speak to her now," said Gabe.

The next afternoon, Maggie, with Duncan's assistance, managed to get cleaned up and dressed.

"I will be close by if ye need me," he said, helping her to get situated on the sofa. "I love ye, and please do not overdo it."

Maggie kissed him. "I love you too, even if the smell of your soap is making me nauseous," she smiled.

"Is there any smell that doesn't make ye ill?" he teased.

"No!" she smirked, wrinkling her nose at him.

Gabe greeted Peggy at the door and escorted her into the parlour where Maggie was waiting.

"Mrs. Arnold! How good to see you. Please, come in and thank you for coming to me."

"How could I not when Colonel Asheton told me of the difficulty you were having, and congratulations!" she smiled.

"Thank you. Please, sit down."

"I will leave you ladies to your tea," said Gabe. "If you need anything, please let me know." He winked at Maggie and closed the doors.

Maggie poured a cup for Peggy and handed it to her, then sipped her already prepared cup. "I am afraid I have my own special blend," she indicated. "Quinn has some sort of herbs that he mixes to help settle my stomach."

"Handsome and handy," said Peggy. "There was not one lady at the party the other night who was not jealous of the three very attractive men on your arm."

Maggie smiled. "They are fairly easy to look at."

They politely chatted about various things, before Peggy got down to business.

"I must say, it was fortuitous that you came back to Philadelphia when you did and with such an interesting suggestion for my husband. You see, Benedict and I had just been discussing that very thing that you mentioned. He has taken your arrival as a sign, so to speak."

"Am I to assume that he is interested in taking me up on my offer?"

"Is it still good, given your current condition?"

"It most certainly is. We will be leaving for New York in a few days."

Peggy reached into a bag that she brought and produced a leather bundle. "You give me your assurance that this will go directly to Major André?" she asked. "There is a great deal of treachery about these days."

Don't I know it, sister?

"On my word."

Peggy looked at the parcel for a moment, before she handed it to Maggie. She then pulled out a separate letter and hesitated before handing that one over as well. "This is a... personal note...for Major André. I trust THAT will be kept between you and I?"

Maggie smiled. "Of course. I am sure John will be beyond excited to hear from you."

Peggy pointed to the bundle. "Since I am assuming you will be retiring to Virginia for the birth of your child, Benedict has included the name of a man who can travel easily between here and New York. We trust him completely. His name is Joseph Stansbury and Major André can depend on him as well."

"I will tell him."

Peggy stood to go. "We will look forward to hearing from the Major. I wish you the best of luck with the birth of your child, Mrs. MacGregor."

Maggie stood, albeit slowly and with care for her stomach. "Thank you, Mrs. Arnold and I wish you all the best as well." She escorted the young woman to the door, and waved goodbye, before returning to the sofa.

Duncan and Gabe appeared in the doorway.

"How did it go?" asked Gabe.

Maggie held up the bundle, shaking it. "You should probably check it to make sure it has everything we need. I trust you have mastered the art of opening and resealing letters."

"Who do you think taught John?" Gabe grinned. "I will be right back."

Duncan sat down beside Maggie and she reclined against him, exhausted.

Gabe returned a few moments later.

"Well?" asked Maggie.

"Pack your bags, we are getting the hell out of Philadelphia." Gabe kissed the top of her head. "Have I told you how wonderful you are lately?"

Duncan noticed Maggie looked a little sad. "Ye aren't happy about this?"

"Not really. I mean, I am happy that Gabe will be free, but this is the beginning of John's end. The traitor will walk free, living a long life while John hangs for being loyal and doing his job."

Gabe laid his hand on her shoulder. "I know," he said softly.

"It's one thing to read about these people and the revolution in history books, but it is entirely another to know and love them, especially when you know how unfair fate is in the end."

Duncan pulled her tight, as the tears streamed down her face.

13 CHAPTER THIRTEEN

They departed Philadelphia two days later, arriving in New York City a week and a half after they began, since Maggie could only travel a short distance at a time in the carriage. They stopped at each tavern along the way, to let her rest as much as possible. Quinn managed to come up with a tea that helped her to sleep a good deal along the way, but she continued to be extremely ill.

They took rooms at the Underhill Boarding House, cleaned up and got a good night's sleep before locating the house John was staying in the next morning. The four of them arrived around noon the next day; a servant answered the door.

"We are here to see Major André," said Gabe.

The servant looked a little nervous. "Major André does not wish to be disturbed."

Maggie closed her eyes, not in the mood or the shape to hear those words. "I did not want to spend ten days in a carriage vomiting every three hours to be told he was too busy to see me. GET HIM!" ordered Maggie, a wave of dizziness and weakness hitting her, causing her knees to buckle.

Duncan and Gabe both reached for her at the same time, holding her up.

"Ye should have stayed back at the boardinghouse," fussed Duncan.

"I made this deal, and I will see it through to the end."

The servant knocked on the closed door to the parlour. "Major André? There are some people here to see you?"

"Go away!" shouted John in response, outraged at the interruption.

Maggie was on the verge of collapsing. "John André! Get out here, NOW!" she shouted back, her stomach lurching.

John flung open the door, while adjusting his clothes, angrily. "WHAT?" he demanded, enraged. His gaze fell to Maggie, the look on his face instantly switching from anger to horrific concern, when he saw the state she was in.

"Oh God, bring her in here!" He stepped back and out of the way.

Duncan scooped her up, as Maggie touched Gabe's arm. "Get me something to throw up in."

Duncan sat her down on the sofa, as Gabe grabbed a bowl from the sideboard.

A woman in the dining room adjusted her dress and discreetly slipped out the side door, as Maggie vomited into the bowl.

"Where is your kitchen?" asked Quinn.

John pointed him in the right direction.

Maggie leaned back.

"Forgive us for barging in so quickly," Gabe said to John. "We are never quite sure when this is going to hit."

John grabbed Gabe's arm, pulled him to the side, and whispered, "Maggie looks like she is on death's door. Is she...?"

Gabe shook his head. "No, although she has expressed a desire for someone to put her out of her misery. This has been going on for almost three solid weeks now. I have never seen anything like it in my life."

"What's wrong with her?"

Gabe grinned. "Ask her. She should be the one to tell you."

John looked at him strangely, but he turned and moved closer to her. "Maggie, why are you so ill? What ails you?"

Maggie sighed. "Nothing that won't be cured in nine months, if I manage to live that long."

John's eyes widened as he looked her up and down. A slow smile spread across his face. "You are with child?"

She nodded.

John slapped Duncan on the back, then leaned down to kiss Maggie on the cheek. "Ha! Congratulations! This calls for a celebration."

"We have two things to celebrate." Maggie handed him the leather bundle.

John looked down in astonishment. He opened the parcel and read over it quickly. He looked at her in disbelief. "General Benedict Arnold? He is one of Washington's closest men."

"He is all yours, now," said Gabe. "I trust he is a big enough fish for General Clinton to be satisfied with Maggie's part of the deal?"

John sat down slowly. "Most certainly!" He looked over at Maggie. "How did you manage this?"

Maggie shrugged. "I told you that he was not happy, and it was not difficult to convince him. He has also taken a wife, Miss Peggy Shippen."

"Judge Shippen's youngest daughter? She is merely a girl."

"Not anymore."

Quinn returned, and handed Maggie a cup.

"Bless you, Quinn," said Maggie, taking a sip. She looked back at John. "There is a man who can carry messages back and forth easily. His name is Joseph Stansbury. They trust him completely."

"Maggie, I don't know what to say to all of this. General Clinton will be delighted by all that you have brought to him in such a short amount of time."

"This is all yours now, John. As long as General Clinton abides by his agreement, we are completely out of this."

"I will see him the day after tomorrow."

Maggie leaned against Duncan.

"We should get ye back to the boardinghouse to rest, my love," said Duncan.

"Boardinghouse? Absolutely not!" said John. "You do not need to be in a place like that in your condition. The house I originally reserved for Gabe is two doors down. The owners are not here, but their servants are. You will stay there as long as you are here. It is closer, more comfortable, and there is a doctor on the street if you need him."

"It may be a while," said Duncan. "Maggie is in no shape to travel, and there is no way she can manage to sail home even if our repairs are complete."

"The house is yours as long as you need it. Go, get your things and your daughter," said John to Gabe. "Maggie can stay here and rest while you do." He got up and wrote down the house information for Gabe.

"I do not want to leave your side," said Duncan to Maggie.

Maggie took his hand. "It's alright. There are a few other details I need to fill John in on anyway. It won't take the three of you long to gather everything."

"I will look after her," assured John.

"You might want to keep some bowls handy," warned Gabe.

Duncan kissed her forehead as he cupped her face. "We will be right back, my love. Rest!"

"God be with ye," Duncan nodded to John with a consolatory look, and started out of the room.

When they were alone, Maggie turned to John who was sitting next to her and took his hand.

"I am so very sorry that we interrupted your 'company'. I feel horrible about that," she said as she winced.

John kissed her hand. "Do not give it another thought. You and your well-being are far more important to me than anyone I may have been momentarily entertaining."

"I have something else for you," she said as she pulled out Peggy's note, and placed it in his hand.

"What's this?"

"A letter to you from Peggy. I am afraid I may have fibbed a little bit. I told her that you had asked about her, and that you would be thrilled to hear from her."

John looked at her questioningly.

"She has always had a crush on you, John, you know that, and she still does. I may have used that to my advantage in getting her to nudge her husband along a little. She was the one who brought me the correspondence. If she thinks she holds your favor, she will be able to influence him in whatever direction that is advantageous to you. Whether you choose to use that information or not is entirely your decision, but I thought you should know."

John leaned back as he crossed his legs and looked down at the letter in his hand. "You are a little too good at this job, Maggie," he whispered.

"Whatever it takes for the ones that I love," she said, looking down at her teacup. Maggie could feel herself becoming a little emotional thinking about John's fate yet to come.

John watched her for a moment, seeing a tear form in the corner of her eye. He leaned toward her to wipe it away.

Maggie tried to pull herself together as her stomach rolled; she covered her mouth with her hand.

John saw her about to get sick and handed her one of the bowls.

When she was done, he lent her a handkerchief to wipe her face and called for one of the servants to take it away. "My God Maggie, how often are you sick like this?"

"Pretty much every hour of the day? Quinn's tea helps some, but I cannot keep anything down. The carriage ride from Philadelphia was ten of the most brutal days of my entire life."

"Is it normal to be this sick?"

"It can't be, otherwise women would stop having babies. The doctor said that I seemed to have the worst case of it he'd ever seen."

John smiled. "Are you excited about the child?"

"I really am, and so is Duncan. I never let myself get my hopes up after what happened before."

"You are going to make a wonderful mother."

Maggie squeezed his hand and laid her head over on his shoulder.

He reached his arm around her so she would be more comfortable.

John caught her cup, just as she dozed off. He leaned his head against hers and enjoyed the feeling of her being in his arms once more, even if she were just sleeping. She was still in the same place when Duncan, Gabe, and Quinn returned.

"Did she get sick again?" whispered Duncan, kneeling in front of her, brushing the hair out of her face.

John nodded.

Duncan picked her up, and she settled against him once he had her in his arms. "Thank ye, John. I am taking her to the house to rest."

John came by their temporary residence the morning after his meeting with General Clinton. They were all gathered in the family room.

"I come bearing news," he said.

Gabe handed him a drink. "I hope it is good news."

"It is. General Clinton was very pleased with the letter that you brought him. After reviewing it, he agreed that Maggie had held up her end of the bargain, so he is holding up his." John removed a letter from his coat. "Permanent release papers for Gabe and a verbal release for Maggie from her service to the Crown."

"Oh, that is wonderful news," said Maggie. "Thank you, John."

He took a seat. "He was reluctant to let you go, Maggie, after seeing what you could do. He was very close to asking you to stay on until I told him of your news and of your desire to return to Virginia to give birth. He asked me to pass along his well-wishes along with his sincerest gratitude for your service."

"Maggie is hereby retired," said Duncan.

"Just in time," teased Maggie. "I am afraid all that I would be good for now is getting sick all over the enemy's boots."

"A week of that and they would be running for the hills to surrender," mumbled Quinn.

"No doubt about that," agreed Gabe.

Maggie cut her eyes at both of them.

"I am afraid I must be going," said John and he stood, "I will check in on you later. I just wanted to bring you the good news, personally."

"Thank you again, John...for everything."

After John left, Maggie had Duncan help her upstairs. They lay in bed on their sides, facing each other. Duncan brushed the hair out of her face when he noticed something.

"Maggie, your eyes!"

"What about them?"

Duncan scooted closer. "The gold flecks are back."

"What?' exclaimed Maggie.

He nodded. "They are faint, but they are there."

"More weird pregnancy symptoms? The next few months should be... interesting."

"Aye, I think they may be."

The next few weeks consisted of Maggie being violently sick. She lost a great deal of weight and was barely able to keep anything down.

Duncan's concern only grew by the day.

The doctor visited each week and insisted that she and the baby would be fine, although Maggie wasn't completely convinced.

Gabe sent word to Captain Russell, who responded that the ship repairs should be completed by the second week of June. He would sail for New York City as soon as they were finished and wait until Maggie was well enough to travel to leave for home.

14 CHAPTER FOURTEEN

It was the first week of June when Maggie woke up around three in the morning feeling very different than she had in the prior weeks. She shook Duncan to wake him up.

"What is it? Is something wrong?"

"Do you hear that?" she asked.

"Hear what? I do not hear anything?"

"Exactly," she smiled. "That is the sound of me NOT vomiting."

Duncan wiped the sleep from his eyes. "Oh, aye. It has been a while."

Maggie rolled over and rubbed his shoulder. "I am actually really hungry."

He eyed her warily.

"Maggie, it is the middle of the night."

"I know, but I am starving! Let's go see what is in the kitchen."

"Ye want to eat? Now?"

Maggie nodded, apologetically.

Duncan pushed the covers back, slipped on his tartan and handed her his shirt to put on. "Whatever ye desire, my love."

They slipped downstairs and into the kitchen. There were several loaves of bread that had been made the day before. Maggie pulled off a chunk of the first one she saw and devoured it.

She and Duncan stood there watching each other, cautiously optimistic.

Maggie smirked. "It doesn't appear to be coming back up."

Duncan smiled. "Do ye think we are past the worst of the sickness?"

Maggie shrugged. "I don't know, but right now, I am ravenous." She pulled off another chunk of bread and stuffed it into her mouth. "This is so good," she said, with her mouth full.

Folding his arms, Duncan nodded. "I am just glad to see ye eating something."

Maggie pointed to something on the table. "Is that cheese?"

He turned around. "Aye,"

"Give it to me," she said, and he handed it over.

Maggie cut off a chunk, moaning as she tasted it.

Duncan watched her with a combination of amazement and amusement on his face.

When she was done, she had finished off an entire loaf of bread in addition to the large chunk of cheese. She moved to Duncan and wrapped her arms around his neck. "I think I can go back to sleep now."

He kissed her and took her back to bed.

Maggie woke up early the next morning. Her appetite for food wasn't the only thing that was back. She ran her hand down the front of her husband's body. Kissing his lips, she tugged on them with her teeth.

Duncan kissed her back before opening his eyes. "Good morning, Maggie."

"It will be," she moaned, climbing on top of him, kissing him deeply.

He caught her hands. "Maggie, we should not be doing this."

"Why not?" she asked.

"Because ye have been terribly sick?"

"I am much better now," she growled, catching his fingers in her mouth, lustfully. She slipped her hand down the front of his body, taking him in hand.

"Maggie!" He took her face in his hands, "I will not take a chance harming the bairn."

Maggie laid her hands on top of his. "You will not. It is perfectly safe for the baby and I need some attending, or I may very well go insane."

"Are ye sure?"

"I am positive! And besides, women in the second part of their pregnancy are known for being...lascivious. If the severity of the morning sickness is any indication of how my other symptoms will be, you may not be able to keep up your husbandly duties, my love," she teased.

"Oh, I can keep up," he growled, as he pulled her down to him and flipped her over on her back. "I can't very well have ye losing your mind, can I?" He laughed and slipped under the covers, attending to her 'needs'.

An hour later, she was rushing him. "Come on Duncan, it's time for breakfast. My stomach is growling."

He looked at her incredulously. "Ye cannot possibly be hungry after all ye ate just a few short hours ago."

"But I worked up an appetite this morning," she winked.

Gabe and Quinn were already at the table when they reached the dining room.

"Good morning," said Gabe.

"Morning," Maggie said, brushing by him and Quinn, squeezing their shoulders in passing, before she grabbed a plate and filled it.

Gabe and Quinn gave Duncan dubious looks.

Duncan shrugged, throwing his hands in the air as if he were unsure of anything anymore.

Maggie was eating a piece of bread before she even sat down in the chair.

The three of them stopped what they were doing just to watch her eat.

Maggie paused mid-chew. "Why are you all looking at me like that?"

"Feeling better this morning, I'm assuming?" asked Gabe.

"I am and I'm just...hungry."

Duncan sat down, propping his elbow on the table, his chin in his hand. "Apparently, we are in the next phase," he said. "She woke me up to clean out the kitchen just a few hours ago."

"The sickness is all gone? Just like that?" asked Quinn.

Maggie nodded, but continued to eat. "It would appear so."

"It seems we are past the first few months," said Duncan with a yawn, covering his mouth and blinking.

"That IS wonderful news," replied Gabe.

"I feel so much better. It is uncanny how good I feel. I even think I feel up for a walk this morning."

"Are ye sure, Maggie? I do not want ye overdoing it."

"Yes. Getting some fresh air will be good for me."

Maggie took in a deep breath as she and Duncan strolled up the street.

Passing by a coffee shop, Maggie pointed to it. "Let's stop and get something to drink and see if they have anything to eat."

Duncan shook his head. "Ye are making up for all of those lost meals, I see."

"I AM eating for two," she smiled.

"I am just happy to see it all staying down."

Rivington's Coffeehouse was mainly full of British soldiers, who looked them over as they came in.

They went to take a table to one side, when they heard John call out from the corner. "Maggie, Duncan, please come and join me."

Maggie kissed John's cheek and they sat down.

"I am surprised to see you out of the house," said John.

"I woke up feeling like a different person this morning," replied Maggie.

"And, she is keeping food down," added Duncan.

"Thank goodness," said John.

They ordered coffee and when it was brought over, John introduced them to their server. "This is Mr. Robert Townsend, son of our host in Oyster Bay. He is a partner in the coffeehouse with Mr. Rivington."

And a soon to be member of the Culper Ring, who will be known as Samuel Culper Jr—if Maggie remembered her dates correctly, he had not yet been recruited.

"Allow me to introduce Mr. and Mrs. MacGregor."

Robert shook Duncan's hand and nodded to Maggie.

"Your father is a wonderful man. He was very kind to us during our rather abrupt and inconvenient stay," said Maggie.

"My father speaks very highly of the two of you, as well. He enjoyed having you as guests at the Homestead."

Someone called him over.

"Excuse me."

Maggie took a sip of the coffee; Duncan and John watched her closely, expecting the worst.

"I'm good," she said. "It's settling fine."

"Oh, well that is a nice change," said a pleased John.

They chatted for a bit before John announced that he had to leave for an appointment.

"Join us for a late supper tonight?" asked Maggie. "Now, that I am feeling better, I am not sure how much longer we will be here."

John stood and kissed her cheek. "I wouldn't miss it. I will see you this evening."

Maggie and Duncan finished their coffee, bid Robert a 'good day', and headed back to the house. Passing by John's home, they noticed a woman slipping inside.

"Looks like John's 'appointment' has arrived," said Maggie sarcastically.

"He has a great many of those, doesn't he?"

"John loves the ladies." Maggie shook her head. "I feel really bad that we interrupted him with our unannounced return from Philadelphia."

"Is that the same woman?" asked Duncan.

"No, it is not."

When they arrived home, Maggie announced she was going upstairs to rest. In their room, she undressed and stood in front of the mirror, looking herself over. She had lost a great deal of weight, but a little baby bump had started to emerge from her belly. She ran her hand across it, feeling a small flutter as she did. Maggie laughed.

"Hello, little one. I cannot wait to meet you."

She sent Duncan a silent message. *I need you.*

He was in the room immediately, looking concerned.

"What's wrong?"

She took his hand and placed it over the spot. "I just felt the baby for the first time."

Duncan smiled as he dropped to his knees and kissed her stomach. "Oh, my goodness, look at our bairn."

Maggie ran her hand through his hair. "You are going to be an amazing father. I love you so much."

He stood up and took her into his arms. "And, ye are going to be the best mother." He kissed her, but Maggie kissed back harder.

"Take me to bed. I want to be with you right now."

They stayed in bed making love until dinnertime.

Maggie cleaned every plate placed before her at dinner. Duncan, Gabe, and Quinn could not believe their eyes.

"How did this change so drastically overnight?" asked Gabe.

"I am not questioning it," she replied, "I am just grateful to not be puking."

When they were done eating, Maggie slipped her hand over onto Duncan's lap. She stroked his inner thigh, biting her lip while eyeing him lustfully.

He sent her a silent message. *Are you serious? Again?* She sighed and nodded.

Duncan laid down his napkin. "If ye will excuse us, Maggie needs to go upstairs."

Gabe and Quinn exchanged puzzled looks.

Duncan came into the parlour about an hour later and poured himself a large drink.

"Where's Maggie," asked Quinn.

"She finally dozed off, thank goodness."

"What exactly is going on?" questioned Gabe.

Duncan downed his drink, then poured another. "Maggie's appetite is back...in EVERY way. And it is just as strong and severe as the sickness was."

"You mean..." asked Gabe, lightheartedly.

He nodded. "Oh, yes! Do not get me wrong, I love my wife and I love being with my wife, but even I have my limits. Apparently, she has none."

Gabe and Quinn exchanged amused looks, then burst out laughing.

"I am glad ye two find this so amusing," he said, plopping down in a chair.

"I am sure ye are 'up' for the job, Brother," teased Quinn.

"Enjoy it while you can," said Gabe. "You may not have time for all of that after the baby gets here. They do not function on the most convenient of schedules." He sipped his drink. "Kat still does not sleep through the night. I am afraid that your lives are about to become very different, but for the better."

Duncan sat down his glass as he received a silent summoning from Maggie. "She's awake and wants me back upstairs."

Gabe stood. "I'll see to her. I will take her for a walk to burn off some of her excess energy." He laid his hand on Duncan's shoulder as he went by. "Take a nap while you can," he laughed.

Gabe knocked on Maggie's door before opening it. "Mags, it's Gabe. Are you decent?'

"Pretty far from it actually, but you can come in any way." She was in her shift, looking out of the window. "Where's Duncan?"

"Resting! Leave the poor man alone already. You are killing him."

Maggie winced. "I know. I can't help it. All I have thought about since I woke up this morning is food and sex, and the more I have of them, the more I want of them." She sat down in the chair and leaned her head back.

"This cannot be normal, Gabe. Other women do not have these extremes."

Gabe came up behind her chair and placed his hands on her shoulders. "You are not like other women, Maggie. Quinn and I have discussed this at great length. You are a direct descendant from royalty; you now have the abilities of a goddess and this child, between your and Duncan's Fae bloodlines, will be the closest thing to a pure Fae entering the world ever. This is a very special child. We cannot take anything for granted as normal, and we should expect the unexpected."

Maggie reached up and laid one of her hands on top of his. "I wish my mom were here," she whispered.

"I know sweetheart." Gabe kissed the top of her head. "Get dressed and let's go take a walk. Let Duncan rest up a bit for later."

Maggie stood up and grabbed his arm. "Before you go," she pulled his hand over on her growing baby bump.

Gabe looked down and smiled. "Would you look at that?" Gabe lifted his head, then pointed at her face. "And would you look at THAT?"

"What?"

"Your eyes."

"Oh, that! Duncan said that some of the faint flecks were back."

"I think you should look again."

Maggie gave him a funny look, before she turned to the mirror and was stunned to see that the pupils of her eyes had rings of gold around them, taking up about a third of her eye color.

"Holy shit!" she said. "I can only assume this is from the pregnancy?"

Gabe stood behind her. "Expect the unexpected."

Maggie met them downstairs after dressing.

Duncan held her and took a good look at her eyes. "That is very peculiar," he said.

Quinn moved in closer. "Aye, it is."

Maggie shook her head. "I am afraid to ask what comes next." She kissed Duncan, "We will be back before supper."

She leaned in and whispered, "I'm sorry. I know I am being a handful. I really cannot control it."

He chuckled. "I know. Dinna fash about me. Ye worry about yourself and our bairn."

Maggie closed her eyes and inhaled in his intoxicating scent. She groaned slightly. "Your smell is making me…." She shook her head. "I should go, or I will…"

Gabe took her arm and pulled her away from Duncan. "Come on. Maybe with any luck, we will get a cold rain shower to cool you off."

Maggie held Gabe's arm as they walked down the street.

"I have been thinking," he said. "The war will be ending soon, and this part of the country has been greatly affected. Maybe we should open an office here in New York."

"It sounds like a good idea. I have held off opening any new places, but they will be needing a great many things in this area. Why don't you start looking around for an office and maybe a townhouse?"

"A house?" asked Gabe.

"Gabe, our families are growing by leaps and bounds, and staying in taverns will be growing rather tedious, especially with children. It would be nice to have some peace and privacy when we need to come up for business. I still have many of the gems left by the previous owners of Beechcroft that we can sell if we need the money. The estate has been doing so well, that I have not needed to use them. Besides, we will not have John's kindness to depend on much longer."

Gabe squeezed her hand, knowing how horrible she felt for John. It was almost as bad as he felt himself.

Maggie stopped suddenly and turned to face him. "I cannot do it, Gabe."

"Do what?"

"Let John die like that. His friendship means too much to me...to all of us...and I cannot abide him hanging while that bastard traitor, Arnold, walks away free."

Gabe took her hand and guided her to a nearby bench. "What are you saying? I thought we were all in agreement that this had to occur for history to turn out the way it should. You said that it must be that way."

"I know," she leaned back, "but, I cannot, in good conscience, let it happen. There must be a way to save him without messing up what is meant to be. I just don't know what it is; we have a little over a year to figure it out."

Gabe leaned back and blew out a long breath. "I am so glad to hear you say that aloud," he said, relieved. "It is exactly what I have been thinking lately, as well."

"Between the four of us, surely we can find some way." Maggie leaned her head over on Gabe's shoulder. She took his arm and squeezed his bicep.

"Have you been practicing with the sword?" she asked.

"Quinn and I have been spending some time on it. Why?"

Maggie bit her lip as her hand slipped over his chest. "Your arms and upper body are becoming very firm and muscular, and your shirts seem much tighter than usual."

Gabe made a face. "Oh my God, Maggie! Seriously?"

She sat up quickly, shook her head, and groaned. "I am telling you, Gabe, I cannot help it. I do not even realize that I am doing it."

He looked at her oddly. "It's really THAT bad?"

"YES! It must be the hormones. I have got to get myself under control."

That evening, they all enjoyed a pleasant supper with John, marveling at the amount of food Maggie was able to devour in such a short amount of time.

"It is good to see you up and around Maggie," said John as they retired to the family room.

"It feels good, too. I trust your earlier appointment went well?" Maggie smirked.

"It was just some business that I needed to handle in a timely manner."

"I am sure you had it all 'well in hand'," Maggie smiled and handed him a glass.

John blushed. He realized that she knew exactly what he had been up to. "I believe you know me a little too well, Maggie."

"Is that such a bad thing?" she asked.

"Not at all. You are one of the few people who understands me."

"How are things going with General Arnold?"

"You were dead on in your advice. Peggy seems to be encouraging her husband to make a deal."

Maggie mumbled and looked down at the floor, "She might be anticipating a favor in return from you."

John smirked. "What would give her that sort of idea, I wonder?"

"I know you are dedicated to the cause John, and that you are always willing to make the ultimate sacrifice when it comes to the ladies," she said and smiled from behind her glass.

John looked at her devilishly, shaking his head. "You DO know me too well, don't you?"

"John?" asked Gabe. "Do you know of any businesses or homes close by that might be for sale?"

John sipped his glass and took a seat. "There are several vacant places around. What sort of thing did you have in mind?"

"Maggie and I are considering opening a shipping office here and purchasing a residence."

John's eyes lit up. "That is wonderful news! I will be happy to make some discreet inquiries for you."

Maggie sat down next to Duncan, leaned against him, and rested her hand on his thigh as he put his arm around her.

She silently asked, *Think anyone would notice if I straddled you right here?*

Duncan looked down. *Aye, I think they might.*

Sighing, she listened to Gabe and John, deciding to have a little fun. *They might like to watch.*

Eyes wide, Duncan looked up, affronted by her boldness. *Am I going to have to lock ye in the bedroom for the rest of your pregnancy?*

Only if ye join me. I cannot stop thinking about wanting you. Maggie turned to gaze directly into his eyes.

Duncan smiled, shaking his head at her impropriety, reaching to halt her hand that was slowly inching up his thigh.

She grinned and wrestled with him, letting out a little squeal of delight, as he attempted to stop her.

Gabe, John, and Quinn had all stopped talking and were watching them, amused by their antics.

Gabe finally broke the silence. "Maggie, you do know we have a guest, and that you are being completely inappropriate, right?"

John laughed out loud. "Do not stop on my account. Please, continue."

Duncan cleared his throat.

"I am sorry, John," said Maggie, somewhat embarrassed. "This pregnancy is making me a little emotional in more ways than one."

"And other things, apparently," said John, grinning behind his glass. "Perhaps, I should take my leave for the evening. It's getting late and I have an early day."

Maggie hung her head in shame. "I will see you out." She escorted him to the door.

He kissed her cheek as she said, "Good night."

"Duncan is a lucky man." He leaned in closer and whispered. "I should have never let you go when we were in Philadelphia. I shall regret it until my dying day."

Maggie touched him on the back and closed the door behind him, then turned to see Duncan leaned against the wall, looking down at the floor.

"Want to tell me what he meant by that?" he whispered, as his jaw tightened.

Blowing out a deep breath, Maggie realized that it was something that she should have told him a long time ago. "Yes, actually I do," she said, softly.

She led him upstairs to their bedroom, where Maggie climbed onto the bed. "Come sit next to me and let me tell you about me and John. I should have told you sooner, but I was afraid you would not understand."

Duncan looked down at her, a tense, guarded expression on his face.

"Please?"

He moved to sit down next to her; she took his hand in hers and told him her story.

"After I lost the baby, I was not in a good place at all. Gabe was doing his best to take care of me, trying so hard, and I didn't want him to know how bad things really were for me. My body had healed physically, but inside, I was dying a slow, painful death. Shortly thereafter, we received an invitation from John to come to Philadelphia for General Howe's going away party, and Gabe suggested we go because he thought it might be good for me. We also knew it might be the last time we would get to see him before his death. John and I have always been able to read each other, and he instantly knew how badly I was hurting. He took care of me; he comforted me, in the way only a man can when a woman is suffering inside. It was just those few days, but it was enough to bring me back to where I needed to be. If he had not done what he did for me, I would have never been ready to fall in love with you when I did. We left for London right after, and that was the end of it. I know it is not what you want to hear, but I owe John a great deal for what he did for me. I don't expect you to understand, but we were friends before—and we remain friends now…ONLY friends."

Duncan said nothing.

Maggie took his silence as anger. She closed her eyes and let go of his hand. "I am sorry if you cannot accept it, but it is part of my past, and it is part of who I am; there is nothing I can do to change it."

He took her hand back, and then her face in his other hand, letting out a deep sigh. He half-smiled; tenderness and pity appearing in his eyes. "I understand more than ye know...about what grief does to a person. When my father died, I was beside myself. Mother fell completely apart, and I suddenly became the man of the house. Everyone expected me to step up and take his place, but I had lost my father, my best friend, and I was drowning in misery, as well. I was 17 years old and had four brothers and a mother that needed me to take care of them."

He swallowed hard. "I met a widowed woman who was dining in the village tavern one evening after I had entirely too much to drink. She had lost her husband the previous year, and she was still trying to come to terms with her own pain. We ended up taking comfort from each other that night, and in the weeks to come. It changed me, mended that part of me, and helped me to get through the worst time of my life. So ye see, I do understand more than ye will ever know." He kissed her forehead lovingly.

Maggie leaned against him, relieved to have no more secrets between them. "What happened to her? The widow?"

Duncan put his arm around her and laughed softly. "My mother caught wind of what was going on. She marched right into that house, dragged me out by my ear, and told me that was the end of it. She had me chopping wood all day, every day for the next two weeks. She said that was a better, healthier way to work out my grief." He chuckled. "It wasn't. I much preferred the warm comfort of a woman's bed to that damned never-ending pile of wood. I still have nightmares about it."

They both burst out laughing.

"I could see her doing that."

"Aye. That woman is no-nonsense when it comes to her boys. I think it gave her something to focus on besides her own loss. She told me later that bedding a woman did not make ye a man, that if I wanted to be a real man, that I would find a woman, fall in love, and treat her with respect and love the way my father did for her every day they were together."

"Don't tell me you never bedded another woman."

He laughed. "Oh, I did. I just didn't let my mother find out about it. We all learned to be very discreet when it came to that." His laugh faded and he became serious. "The point is, I do understand, and while I may not be thrilled that I have been under the roof of a man who has had carnal knowledge of my wife, I am grateful that he healed ye enough to bring ye to me. I also know what John's friendship means to ye."

Maggie kissed him as the tears flowed down her face. "Thank you. Now take me to bed because if you do not tend to me soon, I may have to do it myself."

"Now that, I might like to watch," he teased and laid her back.

Maggie was wide awake later that night while Duncan was sleeping peacefully, and she did not want to wake him. Gingerly, she slid out of bed and headed for the kitchen, her stomach growling so loudly she could hear it.

Gabe was sitting alone in the drawing room, reading.

She stuck her head in. "I am staging a kitchen raid. Are you in or out?"

Gabe rolled his eyes and snapped the book in his hands closed. "I'm in, if only to protect you from yourself."

Maggie carved off some of the bread and handed him a slice as they sat facing each other. "So, I told Duncan about John."

Gabe stopped mid-chew. "I'm afraid to ask how that went."

"He was surprisingly understanding. He went through something similar when his father passed. I mean, he is not thrilled that John and I are so close, but he isn't angry."

"Well, I am sure that is a great weight off your shoulders."

"It is," she said, slicing off more of the loaf. "I do not like there being anything between us like that."

"Where are you putting all this food?" asked Gabe, changing the subject.

Maggie shrugged. "I guess my body is just making up for all of those weeks I was sick."

"And, all those weeks you were too sick for other things, as well," he said dryly. "I expect John left so quickly because he needed to go find a woman for himself for the night after watching the two of you at it."

Maggie laid down the knife. "Thanks. Now, I have the image of John having sex in my mind. I am going to have to go wake Duncan up."

"My God woman, do you have no shame?"

"Have we met?" she asked and went back to cutting the bread.

"I thought I heard someone down here," said Quinn, from the hall.

"I was hungry," shrugged Maggie.

Quinn came up behind Gabe and slipped his arms around him while kissing the back of his neck.

Gabe smiled and turned around to kiss him.

Quinn sighed, tugging on Gabe's collar. "Everyone is asleep if ye wish to join me in my room."

Gabe pulled him close. "Nothing would please me more. I will be very happy when we are back in our own house, just you, me, and Kat, so we do not have to sneak around."

"That will make two of us," said Quinn, and they kissed again.

Maggie waved the knife back and forth in their direction, chewing on a piece of bread, all sorts of thoughts entering her mind. "You two are so damn sexy, do you know that?"

Gabe shot her a scolding look.

"Great!" She slapped the knife down on the table. "Now, THAT image is in my mind too. I am definitely going to have to wake Duncan up now." She took a final bite and brushed the crumbs from her chest. "Enjoy your night, you two," and she kissed them both on their cheeks and headed back upstairs.

At breakfast the next morning, Maggie closed off the doors, so they could speak in private. "I have made a decision, and I know how Gabe feels, but I need to know what the two of you think."

Duncan and Quinn gave her their full attention.

"I cannot, in good conscience, let John die a traitor by hanging."

"Are ye planning on warning him?" asked Quinn. "Won't that change an important part of history?"

"I have been giving it some serious consideration. Once John is caught and put on trial, he becomes very cooperative with Washington, giving him all the information he needs and, obviously, he gets it all before John's execution. What if we were to figure out a way to save John at the very last minute, but make it appear he is dead...for history's sake? As long as his death is recorded on that day and at that time, nothing major in the war should be changed. All the information will already be relayed to the Continental army, and the resentment towards Arnold from the British side for John's death will still be in play. All the main pieces would have already fallen into place. He would not be able to stay here. He would have to go far away, probably to another country, but he would be alive."

Duncan looked straight ahead. "How do ye propose to do that?"

"I didn't say it would be easy, but the four of us should be able to figure out something." Maggie rubbed Duncan's shoulder. "I just need to know how you and Quinn feel about saving him. Gabe and I are old friends with John, and we both agree that he deserves better, but the two of you are a big part of this, and you have not known John as long as we have."

"Truthfully," said Quinn, squeezing Gabe's hand. "The idea of letting the man hang when we knew all of the details ahead of time was not settling well with me. I am all for saving him if we can."

Maggie looked to Duncan. "What say you?"

Duncan blew out a deep breath. "John means a great deal to ye, and he has done many things to help this family. Honestly, I have grown quite fond of him despite recent revelations coming to light. I have no issues with saving him if we can do it without interfering with the future."

Thank you!

"Since we are all in agreement, when the time comes, we figure out a way to keep John alive."

Later that afternoon, Duncan, Gabe, and Quinn went to check out some places that were for sale while Maggie was napping. They had not returned by the time she woke up, so she decided to pay John a visit. She left a note for the others and went to his house.

"Maggie! What a lovely surprise," he said as she came through the door.

"Hello, John. Do you have a few minutes free? I am craving some coffee from Rivington's, and I could use an escort and some company."

"I will always make time for you," he said, picking up his hat.

She took John's arm and they walked up the street. "I actually wanted to speak with you alone," she said.

"Oh?"

"Duncan overheard your comment at the door last night and asked me about it."

John stopped and turned to her, his face going a little pale. "Maggie, my deepest apologies," he said sincerely.

"Causing trouble between you and Duncan was not my intention."

Maggie took his arm. "I know that, and it's alright. I told him everything."

John looked down. "What was his reaction?"

"Surprisingly understanding, believe it or not. I was expecting much worse."

Deep lines creased his brow. "You weren't concerned that he might become violent, were you?"

Maggie shook her head. "No! Duncan would never hurt me. I have no fear of that."

They continued to walk.

"I suppose my welcome mat has been revoked at your home," he stated, sadly.

Maggie patted his arm. "Never! I told Duncan how you helped me, and that if we had not spent that time together, that I would have never been able to be with him."

"Maggie, you give me far too much credit. My time with you was very special and, in truth, probably meant far more to me than it did to you," he whispered.

She laid her head over on his shoulder as they walked. "You are very important to me, John, and I never want to lose you in my life."

He kissed her hand. "On my word, you never will. It would leave far too great a hole in my own heart."

Taking a table in the coffeehouse, Maggie noticed a woman staring at them through the window from the street and recognized her as the one going into John's house the day before. Her face was filled with scorn and rage as she glared directly at John.

Maggie tilted her head toward the window as Robert Townsend brought their coffee, Townsend following her gaze. She suspected he was paying closer attention to the things going on around him more so than anyone suspected.

He smiled and moved on to the next table.

"Your lady friend from yesterday looks a bit aggrieved. Do you wish to step out and reassure her?"

John glanced at the window for only a few seconds, before he turned his full attention back to Maggie. "No! I am spending time with you and nothing takes precedence over that," he smiled.

He cocked his head and narrowed his eyes at her. "And, how did you know about that anyway?"

Maggie sipped her coffee. "Duncan and I saw her going into your house when we left yesterday. She was not attempting to be discreet."

"Ah!" he said, acknowledging his understanding, "I will keep that in mind for the future."

Leaning closer, she asked, "John, exactly how many women are you juggling at one time?"

John's eyes widened with surprise at her boldness. "I am not sure how to respond to that question, especially from you, of all people."

"How about truthfully?" she asked, quietly.

John sat silent for a moment before his face became solemn. "I do what I must in my line of work."

Maggie laid her hand over on his. "What was her name, John?"

"Who?" he asked, with an exasperated sigh.

"The woman who broke your heart."

"Maggie was her name, and I shall never recover," he quipped with a grin before he lifted his cup.

"I mean the first one, because someone did. A man does not go through women the way that you do unless they are running from some sort of heartbreak."

John took in a deep breath and let it out, then set his cup back down on the table. "Her name was Honora...and I just received word that she has passed," he said, softly, glumly.

"I am so sorry, John." She squeezed his hand.

He cleared his throat. "Yes, well. It was a long time ago."

They sat silent for a moment.

Maggie sipped her coffee as she eyed him. "Can I ask you something?"

"I am afraid to let you ask me anything else," he replied, with a wink.

"I will make it easy," she said, trying to lighten the mood. "If you were not a soldier and could live anywhere in the world, do anything that you wanted to do, what would it be? Where would you go?"

"Ah, a game, is it?" he asked, intrigued. He thought for a bit. "Alright, let's see. I enjoyed Switzerland when I was there. It was where my father was from, and France is always nice; my mother was from Paris, but in all honesty, I would just like to see the world and all it has to offer."

"What would you do for a living?"

"Well, if I wouldn't starve to death, I would split my time between writing and my artwork."

"With nude models, no doubt," joked Maggie.

John burst into laughter. "I suppose you are not entirely wrong."

"Your turn," he said and leaned forward on his elbows. "What would Maggie do?"

She bobbed her head a bit. "Scotland felt a lot like home when I was there. I actually do miss it. Duncan's home had these wonderful hot springs that were amazing. We spent our wedding night there, and it was like something out of a dream."

"Ah! Maybe I should add Scotland to my list. And what would you do?"

"Honestly, I can't imagine it being any different than what I do now."

"You really are happy, aren't you Maggie?"

"I am…other than the frequent trouble that tends to find me, but it does tend to keep life interesting."

"You do find more than your fair share, don't you?"

Someone from behind them called John's name. He turned to see who it was. "Maggie, would you excuse me for just a moment? I need to speak to this gentleman about some business."

"Of course."

Maggie sipped her coffee and turned her gaze back to the window. The woman who had been staring at John had moved up the street and was speaking to a man. When Maggie looked closer, she noticed it was Robert Townsend. She remembered that there were rumors of a woman that was close to John André, one that passed information to the Culper Ring, and it made her wonder if something as simple as her coffee date with John might have been the one little thing that pushed a woman into trading information to the other side. So many little things that could happen in an instant could change an entire country's history. Her mere presence had to have already shifted a great many things. Maggie looked over at John, her dear friend, and she knew that she had to figure out a way to save him while keeping history on track as much as possible.

John returned, and they finished their coffee date. He escorted her back to the house.

Duncan, Gabe, and Quinn had returned by then.

"Where have ye two been?" asked Duncan, kissing Maggie.

"I was craving coffee, and John was kind enough to escort me over to Rivington's. Did you three have any luck finding properties?"

"We found a couple that are promising," said Gabe.

Maggie turned to John. "Why don't you come in for a while?"

John looked down with his hands clasped behind his back. "I must be getting back to work. Thank you for the company, Maggie."

Duncan was the one who went to show him out and followed him onto the sidewalk. "I need a word with ye, John," he said.

"I figured as much."

"You mean a great deal to Maggie and, truthfully, I have grown fond of our friendship, as well. She told me about what happened between the two of ye. I also see how ye look at her, and I know that it is the look of a man in love. I cannot fault ye for that, because Maggie is easy to fall in love with, but I need ye to understand something, and let me be painfully clear; she is MY wife and I will not let anyone, or anything, come between our union. Not now, not ever!"

John nodded. "Maggie is happy with you, Duncan. She is the happiest I have ever seen her. I would never cross that line. Maggie means too much to me, and I would not risk anything that might cause her to cut me out of her life. I could not bear it."

"As long as we understand each other," said Duncan.

John smirked and placed his hand on his shoulder. "But, let ME make something painfully clear; if you are ever fool enough to turn her out, or let her go, all bets are off, my friend. I will be there, and I will not let her get away a second time."

Duncan shook his head, amused. "Well, MY FRIEND, that will NEVER happen."

John nodded with a sly grin on his face and started towards his house.

"We will see ye at supper, then?" called Duncan.

"I wouldn't miss the show," replied John, as he bowed and presented his arms out in a dramatic fashion. "I am hoping for a repeat performance from last night," he chuckled, walking away, a slight skip in his step.

Duncan laughed to himself and turned back towards the front door.

"Everything alright?" Maggie asked cautiously, when Duncan came back inside.

"Aye. John and I were just coming to an understanding."

"What kind of an 'understanding'?" asked Maggie, eyeing him warily.

"Nothing for ye to worry about," he said and kissed her forehead.

"Duncan!"

He slipped his arms around her, as he kissed her thoroughly.

Maggie pushed him back. "Stop trying to distract me. What did you say to John?" she demanded.

He just smiled, pulled her roughly back to him, and kissed her again, while sliding his hands down her backside.

"Dunc.... oh...." she moaned, as he kissed her neck, and tugged on her ear with his teeth.

He moved back to her lips, and she forgot everything that had been said.

"We are right here, in the parlour," called Gabe. "Can you take that upstairs, please?"

"That is an excellent idea," said Duncan, and he scooped her up, and toted her upstairs to the bedroom.

After supper that night, John pulled Duncan off to the side to have a word alone. "I wanted to inform you that I have received a report from the Queen's Rangers; Wilson has still not been found. He might turn up anywhere at any time. Maggie should not be left alone, or be unescorted at any point, especially given her condition."

"Thank ye John, for the information. I will inform Gabe and Quinn so that we can make sure that she is never out of our sight. There is no need to upset her with this. I know she is feeling better, but she is still very emotional."

"That is probably for the best, and of course, I will give whatever assistance you need. I will also have guards patrol the area just to keep an extra eye out."

"Our ship should be ready soon, and we will be on our way home anyway."

John looked down at his glass. "I would not let my guard down in Virginia either. Wilson was already a nasty bastard before, but I am sure he is ten times worse now. I would not put it past him to travel that far for revenge. Keep close to her at all times and make sure she is safe."

"I will."

A week later, Captain Russell arrived with the fully repaired ship. They enjoyed a final long dinner with John before departing for home.

15 CHAPTER FIFTEEN

When they arrived back at Beechcroft, Hettie met them at the door.

"It is so good to be home!" smiled Maggie.

Hettie felt the baby bump when she hugged Maggie. "Maggie?" she grinned and rubbed her stomach, "Is that what I think it is?"

"It is, indeed, Hettie!"

Hettie laughed and hugged her again. "Lord have mercy, we gonna have more babies around here than we know what to do with."

"Who else?" asked Gabe, handing Kat to Cora.

"Well, there's Sadie…she is about five months along, and Wawetseka is gonna have a baby...she is about four months along..."

Maggie stared at Hettie, brows drawn, "I thought Sadie couldn't have any children?"

"So did she, but she is gonna have one now."

Duncan searched his mind for a moment, then folded his arms and sent Maggie a silent message. *The four of us need to talk alone.*

"Hettie, we have some business to discuss, and we do not want to be disturbed."

Hettie nodded as they went into the drawing room and pulled the doors closed.

Duncan was noticeably disturbed.

"What is it, Brother?"

He turned to Maggie. "That strange thing that ye said happened when the pain shot through your body, didn't ye say it happened for the first time when ye hugged Sadie?"

Maggie nodded. "Yes, it did."

"And the next time, was in the village the night of the ceremony? Were ye touching Wawetseka when it happened?"

She looked at him oddly. "Yes, I was," she responded slowly. "The same thing happened again, at the apple orchard when it sprang back to life," added Quinn, the pieces starting to fall into place for him, as well.

Duncan and Quinn exchanged looks.

Gabe shook his head. "What am I missing here?"

"Maggie's mother, among other things, was the goddess of fertility," said Quinn.

Maggie waved her hands in front of her. "Whoa, whoa, whoa! What are you saying? That, I am the cause of Sadie and Wawetseka becoming pregnant?"

"Well, indirectly," said Duncan. "Ye said Sadie could not have children and, if my math is correct, she would have become pregnant about the time this occurred. What were ye thinking when it happened?"

Sinking down into a chair, Maggie tried to recall that day. "I was wishing there was something I could do to help when she said they couldn't have children."

"Were ye thinking anything when ye touched Wawetseka?" asked Quinn.

Maggie covered her mouth. "I was wishing there was some way I could repay her for all she did for us that night." Her eyes widened. "No! No way! This cannot be possible."

Duncan knelt in front of her, taking her shaky hands in his. "I think Finn gave ye more than the ability to produce a good harvest."

"But, the other time…" A terrified look crossed Maggie's face, another memory surfacing, and she paled. "Duncan, my love, my stomach feels a little queasy. Can you get Hettie to make me some tea?" The words spilled from her mouth, tripping over each other.

Duncan looked at her, concerned.

"I will get it," offered Quinn.

Maggie shook her head, when Duncan turned his head to look back at him.

"Please, Duncan?" she begged. "Just run and grab me some."

"Of course," he said.

As soon as he left, Maggie turned to Gabe and Quinn.

"I AM A DEAD WOMAN!" she whispered.

"What are you talking about?" asked Gabe.

"It happened one more time. I was rubbing Gavina's muzzle, wishing that I had a dozen more like her, when it happened. That's the same night that Onyx…"

Gabe and Quinn looked at each other, then burst into laughter, leaning against each other as they roared.

"Stop it, you two! I was able to quell Duncan's anger with sex before, but I am pretty sure that he has had so much lately, it just won't work this time."

"Well, ye are carrying his bairn," said Quinn, wiping the tears from his eyes, "That should afford ye some protection," he snickered.

"Laugh it up," said Maggie, folding her arms. "I wished for a dozen, and you two have mares in Gavina's bloodline."

Gabe and Quinn looked at each other, their amusement slowly fading.

Duncan returned to the room with a cup. "Here ye are, my love."

Maggie took a sip and pulled Duncan down to sit next to her. She cupped his face. "You know I love you more than anything in this world, right?"

"Aye, of course. I love ye too."

She set down her tea. "And, you know that I would never do anything to intentionally hurt you…and I didn't know I could do all this; this is all very new to me...and remember, I AM carrying your child..."

Duncan tilted his head. "What are you not telling me?"

Maggie pinched the spot between her brows. "It happened one more time that you have forgotten about." Maggie winced.

"When? Who?"

She closed her eyes and covered her face with her hands. "When you were saddling Gavina the morning after the ceremony at the tribe. She is so sweet and wonderful...I wished...for...a dozen more like her."

Maggie cringed, bracing for the worst.

"Gavina? But, she...wait...that was the night...the stable..." Duncan's eyes flew wide open with rage, his face bright red. His bellow was enough to make the glass panes shudder. "ONYX!" His face contorted. "Are ye trying to say that beast..."

"Well, we don't know for sure," said Maggie, optimistically.

Duncan got up and stormed out of the house, headed straight for the stables, Quinn following close behind him.

Maggie threw herself across the sofa. "This is so bad," she said.

Gabe slipped in to sit next to her. She laid her head in his lap. "He cannot blame you, Maggie. You had no idea."

"Duncan may love that horse more than he does me."

"I seriously doubt that."

Maggie covered her face with her hand. "So, how does this work now? I touch women and they get pregnant? It sounds even more ridiculous when I say it aloud."

Gabe looked down at her sympathetically and stroked her hair. "Everything will be fine, Mags. You should not upset yourself in your condition."

She raised up. "I am suddenly extremely tired, physically and mentally. I think I am going to go lay down for a bit."

Gabe helped her up. "Anything I can do?" he asked.

Maggie shook her head, looking very despondent and weary. She went upstairs, crawled into bed, curled into a ball, and fell fast asleep.

Awakening, she sensed Duncan near her. Opening her eyes, she noticed him sitting in a chair pulled up next to the bed, watching her.

Realizing she was awake, he stood, came to the bed, and slipped in to face her, wrapping his arms around her. "Are ye feeling unwell?" he asked softly.

"Just a little bit overwhelmed with this new information."

"That is understandable," he said and kissed her forehead. "I did not mean to upset ye. What happened with Gavina is not your fault. Ye had no way of knowing."

"Is she?" asked Maggie, cautiously.

"Aye," he forced out through clenched teeth, disgust in his voice.

"I'm so sorry, Duncan."

"Dinna fash yourself. It is not good for ye or the bairn, and I could never be angry with ye, Maggie. Onyx yes, but never ye."

"Duncan, I don't know how to deal with this. I am afraid to touch anyone for fear of what it might do."

He looked down at her. "We will figure this all out." He kissed her. "We are finally home. Why don't ye take a nice, long hot bath and relax before supper?"

"That actually sounds like a wonderful idea."

"I will come scrub your back for ye."

Maggie disrobed and slipped into the tub. It felt more amazing than she remembered. She soaked for a while before Duncan came in. He helped her wash her hair, dried her off, and assisted her as she stepped out when she was done.

He put his arms around her from behind and ran his hands over her ever- growing baby bump. Just as he did, they both felt it; a tiny, very subtle, kick. She craned her head back to look at him, smiling.

"Did you feel that?"

"Aye," he laughed. "Our baby is a strong one, Maggie."

Maggie nodded, a few tears slipping down her cheek.

They all gathered for supper that night, Hettie having gone straight to the kitchen as soon as they got home to whip up all of Maggie's favorites.

"I have missed your cooking, Hettie," Maggie said, digging in.

"Ye might want to keep the kitchen stocked at night," said Duncan. "She usually cleans it out around three o'clock in the morning."

"Well, I will leave plenty out waiting for you then," said Hettie.

"Be glad you missed the first few weeks," added Gabe. "She couldn't even keep tea down."

"They say the sicker you are, the healthier your baby will be," replied Hettie.

"This baby should be as healthy as a horse," mumbled Quinn.

Duncan growled at the word 'horse.'

"Just look at it this way, Brother," teased Quinn, "Your baby and his or her horse will grow up together."

Maggie touched Duncan's leg under the table. "A horse for our child with Gavina's temperament and Onyx's sense of protection might not be such a bad thing."

"What if the horse has Onyx's temperament?" asked Duncan, with a frown on his face.

Maggie winced. "If it does, we should probably get Harm some help and lay in a massive supply of gates and doors."

The next day, they got back to work. Maggie and Gabe spent the morning going over the books for the shipping company and making future plans for new offices, while Duncan and Quinn went to check on the crops and the rest of the estate with Abel.

Joshua came in while they were working. "Welcome home, Ms. Maggie and congratulations on the baby."

"Thank you, Joshua, it is good to be home."

"How is the house for my nanny coming?" asked Gabe.

"We haven't started on it."

"Why not?" asked Maggie.

"Mr. Percy asked us not to until you came back. He said he wanted to talk to you first."

"Any idea why?"

"No, but I can ride over and let him know you are home."

"Please! If you don't mind," said Maggie.

"I wonder what that's all about?" asked Gabe.

"I have no idea."

David Percy arrived a short time later.

"Welcome home!" he said, striding in. "I understand 'congratulations' are in order."

"Thank you, David. Come in and join us."

He sat down, trying to conceal his obvious nervousness.

Maggie and Gabe exchanged a curious look.

"We were wondering why Cora's house has not been started," said Maggie.

"Yes...about that. I was waiting for you to return home. We expected you much sooner." David pulled at his collar as if he were warm.

Gabe folded his arms. "Go on."

"I wasn't sure who I needed to speak to since she has no family here, and I know you are not her father or brother, but there really isn't anyone else to ask..."

Maggie shook her head. "David! What is it? Spit it out, man."

He turned very pale, let out a breath and stood, squaring his shoulders. "I wish to ask you for permission to... marry Miss Roberts."

Gabe was stunned. "You wish to marry my nanny?"

"Well, yes. It would not affect her position with you unless she chose not to work, but you see, if we were to marry, there would be no need to build another house. She would just live with me. Young Katherine is getting older, and no longer needs a wet nurse around the clock, so she could come in the mornings and leave in the evenings. If you need to go out of town, the baby would be welcome to stay with us. I am actually quite fond of her. Katherine, I mean...and Cora, too, of course."

He was so nervous that he started to perspire.

Maggie poured him a drink and handed it to him. He drank it down in one swallow.

"Have you thought of asking her?" asked Maggie. "I mean, she is the one you actually want to marry."

"Not yet...I was waiting to speak to the two of you."

Gabe stared at David with a stern look on his face, making poor David start to tremble slightly. Gabe sighed. "It is not my decision. If she wishes to marry you, then you will have my blessing, not that you need it."

David let out a nervous giggle and stuck out his hand to shake Gabe's. "Thank you, Gabe. And thank you, Maggie. I will ask her today."

He rushed out, more excited than he had ever been.

"I did not see that coming," said Gabe.

"Me, either. But, lucky for you, if she says 'yes,' you and Quinn will have the house all to yourself even sooner."

Gabe turned to her. "You are right. God, I hope she says 'yes'."

And she did. Cora and David came by later that afternoon to announce their engagement.

"Congratulations!" said Maggie, going over to hug Cora, but was intercepted.

Gabe stepped in front of her and whispered while pointing his finger at her. "Do NOT touch my nanny with your...fertile hands. I need her too much."

"Oh right!" remembered Maggie, sticking her hands behind her back.

They celebrated with a late dinner that evening, and Cora and David were married at the house two weeks later. Gabe, Quinn, and Kat finally had the house to themselves and were free to be together in their home without worry.

Askuwheteau, and his wife Wawetseka, came to visit a few days after the wedding.

Maggie and Duncan welcomed them inside to the drawing room.

"We came to thank you," said Wawetseka.

"Thank me? For what?"

"Powaw says that you are the reason we are having a baby," smiled Askuwheteau.

Maggie laughed. "I didn't have anything to do with it. That is all on you two."

"He says that you did. That you have the power to help those who want to, but cannot have, a child."

Wawetseka nodded. "We have hoped for a very long time. Powaw has performed the fertility ritual so many times, and we have always been disappointed. He said that the night you came for the ceremony, that your spirit was different than before, and that you held great power to help things take root. We conceived that very night. I felt it when we did."

Maggie looked at Duncan before taking Wawetseka's hand. "I look forward to our babies growing up together."

Maggie laid her hand on her belly.

Askuwheteau and Wawetseka smiled with excitement. "As do we."

Maggie spent the next few months eating—and keeping Duncan busy. The swell in her belly continued to grow exponentially.

By the end of her eighth month, Maggie had grown to an enormous size, unable to sit, or stand, without assistance. Her eyes were now almost completely gold.

Several women had come up from the tribe and asked for her help with conceiving over the course of the previous few months after hearing what she could do. She laid her hands on each of them, wished for them, felt the electrical shock, though it bothered her less each time, and each of those women conceived shortly thereafter.

Sadie gave birth to a healthy baby boy in September. Askuwheteau and Wawetseka welcomed a beautiful baby girl in October.

Maggie had grown so big that she could not get off the sofa by herself, and she was becoming bored being stuck inside the house.

"Duncan, I am going out to see Onyx," she announced one morning. "I need some fresh air."

"I will take ye to see the filthy beast," he grumbled. He helped her up and escorted her to the stable.

Harm met them at the gate when he saw them coming down the path. "Powaw is visiting with Onyx."

"What?" asked Duncan.

"He comes up about once a week just to talk to him."

"What do they talk about?" he asked curiously

Harm scratched his head, confused, unsure how to answer. "I don't rightly know."

Powaw came out just then, and came over to Maggie, smiling. He had not learned English, but they had managed to find a way to understand each other. He stood in front of Maggie and indicated that he would like to touch her stomach.

Duncan was about to protest, when Maggie held her arm out to stop him. "It's fine, Duncan. He means no harm."

Maggie nodded to Powaw.

Powaw gently laid his hand on her belly and said a few words in his language; a blessing of some sort. When he was done, he looked down with his head cocked, as if confused at first, before his face split into a wide grin that morphed into a chuckle. He laid his hand on Maggie's shoulder, and began to laugh even harder. He nodded and left, still laughing.

"Should we be concerned about that?" asked Maggie.

"Maybe ye should ask Onyx."

Maggie went out and had a visit with her horse, while Duncan went to check on Gavina. Onyx was happy to see her and gently nuzzled her belly. After a short visit together, Duncan helped her back inside and onto the sofa.

Maggie groaned as she settled in. "How can I be this big, Duncan? I feel like I won't fit through the door much longer."

"Ye are beautiful, Maggie." He rubbed her stomach, then kissed it. "We will be meeting our baby very soon."

Maggie sighed, then gave him a wicked look. "You know, they say sex will bring on labor."

Duncan raised his eyebrows at her. "Ye still have two weeks."

"And, you will not be able to lay with me for several weeks after. You should have me while you can," she winked.

"Maggie!" he scolded.

She shrugged. "Maybe Gabe will take pity on me and help me out," she teased.

"You would do that?" he quipped.

"You would deny the mother of your child this tiny request?" she retorted.

He stared at her for a moment before shaking his head. "Nay, I will not."

He took her hand and led her upstairs. He undressed her, and made love to her slowly and gently, taking her from behind while she leaned forward on the bed, too large to do it any other way. Later that night, Maggie's water broke.

She woke Duncan. "It's time."

He sent for the midwife, and the rest of the family. As her labor progressed, Duncan, Gabe, and Quinn took turns walking with her and holding her hand, while kneading her back and massaging her tight belly.

Maggie leaned against the windowsill as a contraction hit.

Duncan held her hand and rubbed her back until it passed.

She turned to face him. "I don't think I am strong enough to do this."

He brushed the hair back from her face. "Ye are the strongest woman I know. I have no doubt that ye can."

She leaned against him as the pain seized her again. She cried out, tears streaming down her face.

Duncan held her tight, not wanting her the see the agony in his own face from seeing her in such a state.

Gabe stuck his head in the door when he heard her. He could see the toll it was taking on Duncan as well. He entered the chamber, went over, and laid his hand on Duncan's shoulder. "Why don't you let me take over for a bit?" he asked. "You have been up here for hours."

Duncan looked at Maggie and she nodded. "Take a break. One of us should be able to and I'm out of luck on that front."

Gabe nodded. "Hettie has food ready downstairs. You may not get a chance to eat later."

Duncan kissed her, told her he wouldn't be long, and that he loved her as Gabe took her arm.

When Duncan was gone, Maggie pointed to the settee. "Help me over there." She sat on the edge of the seat, another contraction gripping her, which caused her to break into a sob. "It hurts too much! Gabe, I can't do this."

"It's a little late to change your mind," he said, sarcastically.

"At least in the future, we have drugs for this. They can put a needle in your back, so you feel no pain whatsoever. How do women in the 18th century do this? Why would they even take a chance by having sex? You and Quinn are the smartest people in the world. You do not have to worry about getting pregnant."

He wrapped his arm around her, in an attempt to hush her ramblings. "It will all be worth it once you are holding that baby."

Maggie leaned back, panting, focusing on the ceiling. "Duncan is NEVER touching me again; I don't care how good it feels."

Gabe softly chuckled. "Have you broken the news to him yet?"

"No, but I am about to."

"Somehow, I think you will change your mind," he whispered, amused. "You two can't keep your hands off of each other."

"At the very least, we need to figure out some kind of birth control. Is that a thing now? There has to be something that works, right?" she asked, desperation in her voice.

"You're asking me?"

"Oh right," she nodded. "I almost forgot."

Maggie leaned forward, the searing pain slamming into her again.

Gabe held her against him, rubbed her back, and whispered encouraging words while she dug her fingers into his arm, causing him to wince and curse under his breath.

When it passed, she leaned back and looked at Gabe. "I don't know how to be a mother. What if I screw this kid up? What if I leave him or her somewhere out in the snow and forget where? What if I sleep straight through feedings and the baby starves to death? What if a dingo eats my baby? What if..." she rambled.

"What the hell is a dingo?" he asked.

"It's like a wild dog that eats babies. Do we have those here? I mean, we have wild wolves and we have dogs and...and..."

Gabe pulled her over on his chest to stop her blathering. "Stop it! Stop doubting yourself this instant! You are going to be the best mother ever, and everything will come naturally once you hold this child for the first time."

"Gabe, I am terrified," she whispered in a weepy voice.

He touched her face. "I am going to let you in on a little secret, Mags; all parents are terrified of everything you just said, and a thousand other things, except dingoes. I don't know what they are, and neither does anyone else." He wiped away the wetness on her cheeks with his thumbs. "When I found out about Kat, I didn't think I would be able to care for her or love her as much as her own parents would. I had no idea what I was going to do, but when you placed that little girl in my arms, I fell in love so fast, and I knew that I would do whatever it took to make sure she was taken care of."

"You are a wonderful father to her...you and Quinn both are."

"And, you and Duncan will be, as well. You wait and see," he said and kissed her forehead.

As the contractions became stronger, Maggie was confined to the bed by the midwife, the pain becoming more intense by the moment. She was in labor for ten hours before she was fully dilated, already well past the point of exhaustion.

When it came time to push, the midwife told the men in the room to leave.

"No!" ordered Maggie. "They stay! I cannot do this without them."

The midwife started to protest, until Maggie shot her a death stare that shut her down quickly. "I said THEY STAY!"

"Alright. Let's get this baby into the world. You need to push, Maggie," said the midwife.

Maggie had Duncan holding onto one hand and Gabe holding the other.

Duncan pushed back her damp hair. "Ye are doing so good. I love ye so much!" he whispered into her ear. "And, we are going to meet our baby very soon."

She screamed in agony, nearly breaking both Duncan and Gabe's hands in the process. The two men exchanged looks behind her back, feeling each other's pain—literally. Maggie gritted down, and bellowed, finally pushing the baby out.

"It's a boy."

Duncan and Maggie both cried as they saw their beautiful baby for the first time.

"We have a son," exclaimed an ecstatic Duncan.

The midwife wrapped the baby in a blanket and placed him in Maggie's arms.

Maggie and Duncan looked down at him in amazement, checking all his fingers and toes one by one.

"Welcome to the world, my sweet baby boy," said Maggie, tears streaming down her face.

Duncan's eyes filled with wonderment as he touched his son's tiny face. He kissed Maggie and embraced her and their son.

Gabe and Quinn smiled, looking on.

They were enjoying the moment, when a sudden, intense pain slammed into Maggie's body. She leaned forward, wailing.

The midwife looked concerned, glancing over to Gabe and Quinn. "One of you take the baby," she instructed.

Quinn moved quickly to take him, rocking him in his arms, watching Maggie, greatly concerned.

"What's wrong?" demanded a distraught Duncan; he held Maggie and she cried out again.

The midwife shook her head and grinned. "Nothing! There's just another one coming."

"What?" asked Maggie and Duncan at the same time, turning to each other, utter astonishment on their faces.

"What did you do to me?" Maggie asked Duncan, smacking his chest.

The midwife laughed. "Get ready to push again, Maggie."

"I cannot." She shook her head and leaned back. "I am too tired. Can't I take a break first?"

"You have no choice," said the midwife. "This baby is coming whether you are tired or not.

Duncan slipped his arm around her. "You can do this, my love."

Maggie leaned in, and screamed out, the next contraction hitting hard; she felt the baby coming.

Gabe took her other hand and rubbed her back. "Come on, Mags. This baby needs you."

She sobbed again… and the second MacGregor baby arrived into the world.

"It's a girl," said the midwife.

"We have one of each," cried out, Duncan.

Maggie laid back, her tears mingling with the sweat on her face. "I can't do anymore."

Before the midwife could hand the baby girl to them, the pain overcame Maggie again. She was too exhausted to make a sound, only curl forward and grunt.

The midwife handed the girl to Gabe. "There's a third one coming."

Maggie and Duncan exchanged horrified looks.

"No! You MUST be mistaken!" panted Maggie. "You had better look again!"

"I am not," she laughed, "I already see the head."

Gabe moved next to Quinn, each holding a baby, looks of joyful amusement on their faces.

Maggie burst into tears. "I cannot do this again," she cried, burying her face into Duncan's chest. "I do not have any more strength." She closed her eyes.

Duncan kissed her. "Take my hand, my love. Look into my eyes and focus on me."

She sat back up as the next contraction hit.

Duncan climbed onto the bed behind her so she could lean against his chest, while squeezing both of his hands. He whispered words to her as Maggie managed to somehow find the fortitude to push out the third before collapsing back against the bed, too spent to even open her eyes.

"It's another girl."

"Please, tell me there are no more," whispered Maggie, reaching out blindly for Duncan.

"That's all of them," said the midwife.

Maggie and Duncan both cried as he kissed her.

"We have three beautiful babies, Maggie. I love ye so much."

Maggie patted his face. "You are never touching me again, my love." She drifted off to sleep, too drained to do anything else.

The midwife looked up. "Let her rest for now. She is worn out, and she has earned it." She handed Duncan the third one.

He moved next to Gabe and Quinn, all of them with huge grins on their faces.

"You two are never sleeping again," chuckled Gabe.

"Or, doing anything else for that matter," laughed Quinn.

"Three," said Duncan, looking around in amazement. "How did we end up with THREE?"

Quinn leaned in close and whispered, "That's what happens when ye marry the daughter of the goddess of fertility."

Duncan looked down at his new family. "We are very blessed indeed. I am the happiest man in the world right now."

"At least ye are off the hook with mother for grandchildren," laughed Quinn.

The midwife shooed them out so the women could get Maggie cleaned up.

Duncan stepped out onto the landing to see a group of people gathered in the foyer below, anxiously waiting for news.

"Well?" asked Hettie. "Is it a boy or a girl?"

"Take your pick," he grinned, as Gabe and Quinn joined him. "Ye have three to choose from. One boy and two girls."

Hettie's mouth dropped. "Three? Lord have mercy. We sure enough gonna have a full house around here."

Everyone downstairs laughed and offered their congratulations.

"How's Maggie?" she asked, peeking over at the babies when they came downstairs.

"Exhausted," answered Duncan. "She is resting."

"Sounds like she needs to."

Maggie slept for a few hours. When she woke, her body was wracked with pain and soreness.

Duncan lay next to her, watching her, and smiling.

"Where are the babies? Are they well?"

He nodded. "The babies are perfect. Some of the ladies, who are nursing, came up and helped, so ye could rest. They are well in hand and their uncles are keeping a very close watch over them. The midwife said that you lost a great deal more blood than ye should have and did not need to be moved or disturbed for any reason. She will check in on ye later."

"Three, Duncan. Three babies at one time. We are so...SCREWED."

Duncan burst into laughter and slipped his arm around her, kissing her. "Aye, we are—and I couldn't be any happier."

Maggie touched his face. "It is pretty wonderful, isn't it?"

"I am so proud of ye, Maggie, and I love ye so much."

"I love you too." Maggie snuggled against him and dozed back off to sleep.

Later that evening, after she was awake, Duncan, Gabe, and Quinn brought the babies up to meet their mother. They laid them all on the bed next to her; Duncan lay on the other side. Gabe kissed her forehead before he and Quinn left them to be alone for the first time as a family.

Maggie looked around in awe at what their love had created. Each baby was born with Duncan's dark hair and Maggie's golden eyes. They were breathtaking.

"Look at what we did," she said, her eyes welling up.

"Ye did the hard part."

"How are we going to manage all of them?"

"We have plenty of help. Everyone on the estate has already started pitching in. Sadie and Wawetseka are assisting with feedings, Cecile and some of the other ladies are taking care of the changings, and Joshua and Abel are already working on additional furniture for the nursery. This is the first time these babies have lain down because they have been passed around, and in someone's arms, the entire time. They are already loved by so many."

A little while later, Gabe knocked softly on the door. "The midwife ordered us up to take the babies. She wants you to have complete rest."

"I am not exerting myself," said Maggie softly, never taking her eyes off them. "I am just laying here watching them."

"What are ye going to call them?" asked Quinn.

Maggie and Duncan looked at each other.

"We do not know yet," replied Duncan. "We weren't expecting to need so many names."

"I think we should name our son after your father," said Maggie.

"Are ye sure?" asked Duncan. "We could name him after your father."

"These are Celtic babies. They need Celtic names."

"What was your father's name?" Gabe asked Quinn.

"Kendric."

Maggie took her son by the finger. "What do you think? Is your name Kendric MacGregor?" She could have sworn he smiled. "I think he likes it."

"Well, that's one," said Duncan. "What about our two beautiful girls?"

"Give it some thought," she said. "We will discuss it tomorrow. Right now, I can't hold my eyes open."

Duncan kissed her head. "I will be back soon."

They each took a baby, and left Maggie to rest.

The next morning, Maggie woke with Duncan curled around her protectively. He opened his eyes as soon as she did.

"How are ye feeling, my love?" he asked.

"Like I lost a match in a bullfight. I do not think my body will ever be normal again." Maggie groaned, trying to stretch out. "How are the babies?"

"Perfect. We had people in and out, all night, caring for them. I had to fight to get to see my own children."

"Enjoy it while you can. They will disappear when the middle of the night feedings come along."

"Given any thoughts to names?" she asked.

"Aye, a bit. How do ye feel about Morgan...for the maiden name your mother used?"

Maggie smiled, her eyes watery, and she nodded. "I would like that very much."

"Our oldest daughter will be Morgan," he said, wiping her tears away. "And, I am at a loss on the third."

Maggie looked at him thoughtfully. "Our mother's first names are very alike. Ana, Aurnia...can we combine them somehow?"

Ana, Aurnia...Alanna? It is very close, and it is the Gaelic word for beauty."

Maggie smiled. "I like it.

"So, do I," he said and kissed her. "We have officially named our children."

"We had to start somewhere," she joked.

"Now, I need to take care of my wife. Ye did not eat at all yesterday and ye need to rebuild your strength. I am going to get Hettie to make something for you and bring it up."

"I can go downstairs," she said, attempting to move.

Duncan stopped her. "Nay, ye will not. The midwife said your blood loss was substantial. She does not want ye moving until she says it is alright, and it may be a good while, so prepare yourself."

"Duncan..."

"No arguing," he cut her off. "The babies and I need ye healthy and well. I cannot care for them alone...I am sorely outnumbered." He kissed her nose. "Stay! I will return shortly."

Gabe came to the door as Duncan left. "Up for some company?"

"For you, always," she said.

Gabe came in and sat on the edge of the bed. "How are you feeling today?"

"I feel like my insides have been ripped in half and if I move the wrong way, everything might just spill out." She looked down at her chest. "I also appear to be leaking."

Gabe made a face. "Sorry I asked."

"Other than that, I am over the moon, and a little shocked, but thrilled to have my three babies here and healthy."

"To think, you were worried that you couldn't even get pregnant," he winked.

"That will teach me, won't it?" she retorted. "I cannot believe that I am actually a mother now."

He took her hand. "What of your doubts about motherhood yesterday?"

"You were right, Gabe. I will do anything to make sure those three are taken care of. Thank you for reassuring me as you always do. I could not make it through this life without you."

"Did you two figure out the other two names yet?"

"Yes! Morgan for the oldest girl, after my mother's last name, and Alanna for her and Lady Aurnia."

"Kendric, Morgan, and Alanna...I like your choices."

16 CHAPTER SIXTEEN

Maggie was in bed for two solid weeks recovering. She was able to start nursing on a limited basis a few days after giving birth. The babies were happy and content, rarely fussy, and patient with their new parents—who were still learning.

Joshua and Abel surprised Maggie and Duncan with a large crib big enough for all three to sleep together, and as they did, they would always reach out to touch the others. Joshua also made a cradle big enough for all of them to place in the drawing room, which came in very handy.

Kat was fascinated with the babies and wanted to be with them all the time.

Gabe and Quinn spent more and more time at the main house.

About six weeks after their births, now in a steady routine of madness, Maggie laid the last one back in the crib after a 'middle of the night' feeding. Duncan always got up with her, helping any way he could.

"They are settled, let's go back to bed before they are back up in a couple of hours," he said yawning, both feeling much like walking zombies from lack of sleep.

"Go ahead," she said. "I will be right there."

Duncan kissed her. "Don't be long," he said and went into the hall.

Maggie leaned her arms on the crib, watching them peacefully sleeping, wondering how she ever got so lucky. She felt a strange tingle up the back of her spine.

"You can come out now. I know you are here," she whispered. "My Fae senses are tingling."

Finn appeared by her side, leaned on the crib the same as her, and smiled down at the babies. "I could not stay away. I had to come visit my great grandchildren."

"What do you think?" she whispered.

"I think they are magnificent, and I think their mother is quite a wonder. Ye did very well. Your own mother would be proud."

"Thank you for the portrait, and the one you delivered to my parents. Are they truly alright?"

He nodded. "They are. They now believe their daughter is living a happy life, just somewhat far away from them."

"I am," she said. "Although, it would have been nice if you had warned me about the little gift you left me with. I would have liked to have known about it before I got half of the estate knocked up, including Duncan's horse. He still hasn't forgiven Onyx, and I am not entirely sure he has forgiven me."

Finn chuckled softly. "Wait until he sees the foal. He is really going to have a conniption."

Maggie couldn't help but laugh. "You really are bad, aren't you?"

"I have to amuse myself somehow; being immortal gets a little boring at times."

She turned to him. "Why did you give me those abilities?"

The Fae shrugged. "I didn't. I simply awakened what was already there, given to ye through your mother's bloodline, your birthright as the granddaughter of the King of the Fae. And, look what ye have done with it, my dear. Women who had given up hope of ever having children of their own now clutch their precious babies to their bosoms. Land that lay decimated by cruel and careless acts of mankind, spring back to life wherever ye touch." He looked down at the babies. "You have brought into this world, the greatest hope that it has seen in a millennium. You are a blessing everywhere ye go, Maggie."

Maggie looked down at the babies. "They have abilities too, don't they?" she asked softly.

He nodded. "They will not come into them until they are older, but ye may see a few...unusual things here and there."

"Like what?" demanded Maggie. "These surprises are getting a little out of hand."

"Spoilers!" he winked.

Maggie frowned, shaking her head. "What will they be able to do?"

"More than ye ever thought possible. They, and their siblings, are the hope of this world."

"Always cryptic...wait...what...siblings? Did you say siblings? What siblings?"

A wide grin spread across Finn's face.

"Oh, he is definitely never touching me again now," grumbled Maggie, shaking her head.

"Don't kid yourself, Maggie. Ye two can't stay away from each other. Besides, the future depends on it."

"About the future Finn...what if I made a few...changes. Saved someone who wasn't meant to be saved."

Finn turned to her and placed his hands on her shoulders. "I told ye before, I completely trust that ye will make the right decisions for the situations placed before ye that need your attention."

"What if they are for completely selfish reasons?"

"Then, ye will handle the consequences, as well. Ye are a wonderful soul, and ye do far more good in this world than ye do harm, but, if things get too far off track, a correction may need to be made."

Maggie sighed.

Finn smiled. "I like the 'gold eye' look on you."

"Is that going away?" she asked.

"Do you like it?"

"Actually, I think maybe I do."

"Good, because it's never going away. It will just make the babies look more like ye." He looked down at them. "Which reminds me, I have a gift for ye."

Maggie rolled her eyes. "Does it involve a trojan horse and a few Greeks? Your gifts tend to have more surprises than a box full of Cracker Jacks."

"Oh, I think ye will like this one," he smirked. He waved his hand over the crib.

"Are you going to tell me what you just did, or do I have to figure it out, because honestly, I am too tired these days to remember how to put on my own shoes?"

"I will tell you this one time. Your gift is that your babies will now sleep completely through the night, never being hungry or needing changing while the sun is down. Ye and your husband will be able to get a full night's sleep from now on."

"Huh?" said Maggie. She stepped over and embraced him. "Have I told you that you are my favorite grandfather ever?"

He laughed softly and hugged her back, lingering for a moment. "You are going to need all the rest ye can get. These three are going to be a handful."

"I already had THAT feeling."

Finn squeezed her hands, kissed her cheek, and turned to go. "Be well, Maggie."

"Finn?"

He stopped and turned.

"You don't have to stay away. You can come by and visit whenever you wish...use the front door...maybe stay for supper and drinks sometime. I wouldn't mind seeing more of you, and I would really like my children to know their great-grandfather."

Finn looked down. "I will keep that in mind. Take care of those babies, Maggie." He turned and disappeared before she was able to see the tear drop from his eye.

Maggie returned to the bedroom and slipped into bed next to Duncan.

"What took ye so long?" he asked, wrapping his arms around her.

"Finn stopped by for a visit."

Duncan raised his head, concerned. "What? Are the children..."

"They are fine," she said, placing her finger over his mouth. "He delivered a gift for us."

"I am afraid to ask."

Maggie grinned. "He gifted us with babies who will sleep through the night."

"Seriously?"

Maggie nodded and snuggled in. "I did not turn it down."

"Nay, I wouldn't have either."

"I will tell you the rest tomorrow. Apparently, we need all the rest we can get before the next batch of babies come along."

Duncan raised up, looking down upon her. "What did ye say?"

Maggie was already asleep.

The next morning, Maggie filled in Duncan on the previous night's information.

He slipped his arms around her waist. "Siblings, ye say?"

Maggie gazed into his eyes. "That's what he said. But I told him, you were never touching me that way again."

"Oh really?" he growled, kissing her neck, working his way down to her breasts. "Never is a long time. Are ye sure I can't change your mind?"

Maggie moaned and pulled him closer, biting his lip. "Nope...no way....no more of that for us," she said, kissing him.

"Even if the future depends on it," he teased, burying his face against her chest.

"Well, maybe one time…or twice…if we are very careful," she said softly, laughing and running her hand down his backside.

They were in a passionate kiss when they heard a ruckus downstairs.

Duncan laid his forehead against hers, groaning. "I should check on that. We will continue this later."

They went out of the bedroom onto the landing.

"What's going on?" demanded Duncan.

"Gavina is foaling," Harm called up to him.

Duncan and Maggie headed for the stables to join Gabe and Quinn who were already there.

"Are ye excited to be a grandsire?" laughed Quinn, as Duncan approached.

Duncan sneered and shoved him, stomping by.

Maggie and Gabe laughed, and Gabe slipped his arm around Maggie's waist. "Good morning, sweetheart."

"It is a good morning," she replied.

Onyx came over to join them, keeping a close eye on Gavina.

Maggie rubbed his muzzle, though Duncan shot him a loathing look.

"How is the father-to-be today?" she whispered.

Onyx nodded his head and appeared to grin.

A short time later, a brand-new life entered the world. When the young colt stood, they all got a good look at him. He was strong and stout, solid black and the spitting image of Onyx, with the exception of a single white spot, in the perfect shape of a heart, right on his rear rump. Onyx went to greet his offspring, licking his face as they appeared to speak their own language. The new colt looked at Duncan and appeared to laugh, the same way Onyx always did.

"Oh Lord!" exclaimed Harm. "There's two of them now."

Duncan gritted his teeth in disgust. "Aye, there are."

Maggie lovingly greeted the new foal. "You are a wonderful addition to our family, and you will be perfect for our son."

Duncan moved beside her.

"How can you hate this adorable face?" she asked Duncan.

He rubbed his mane. "I cannot. His mother is my favorite horse," he softened, "despite his sire. If he protects our son the way that beast looks after ye, I have no complaints."

Maggie turned to him. "Now, our daughters will need horses."

"I don't think that will be a problem," said Harm from the side of the stable. "Onyx broke down the gate last week and... well...he and the other two white horses...."

The look on Gabe and Quinn's faces were priceless.

Duncan pointed at them and broke into laughter. "Not so funny now, is it?"

"We will be bursting at the seams here soon," grinned Maggie.

"Especially, when ye are with child again." Duncan didn't bother whispering.

Quinn and Gabe each folded their arms, shooting Duncan a chastising look.

"For God's sakes man, she just gave you three," said Gabe.

"Leave the poor woman alone. Can ye not control yourself, Brother?" asked Quinn.

Maggie chuckled and told them of Finn's visit.

Later that night, Duncan went out to check on the new colt. He found himself growing attached to him, despite how he came to be.

"He will be your son's protector, the way his sire protects his mistress. Consider it a small baby gift."

Duncan turned around. "Ye must be Finn."

"I am," said Finn, approaching to greet the new foal, Onyx close on his heels.

"I suppose the heart on his arse was your idea?"

Finn chuckled. "No, that idea was all his sire's."

Onyx laughed over his shoulder and Duncan shot him a dirty look.

"He will have Gavina's temperament, so do not fear him around your children. He will serve your son well, as will the next two born especially for your daughters. Those three babies upstairs are very special."

"So, I have heard. What exactly are ye trying to do here, Finn?"

"Just spoiling my great-grandchildren. I am entitled, am I not?"

Duncan glared at him. "That's not what I am talking about. What are ye doing to Maggie?" He stepped closer. "I see the changes in her. The color of her eyes, the tiny gold streaks appearing in her hair, the way those abilities no longer cause her pain when she uses them. Exactly, what are your plans for my wife?"

Finn folded his arms. "Maggie is very special, and she has a purpose here beyond extending the MacGregor line, but she needs to discover it on her own."

"What purpose?"

"All in good time." Finn smiled looking up at the window. "She is missing ye. Ye should go see to her."

Duncan jaw tightened. "I am not sure what your game is, but I will not allow ye to harm my wife."

Finn smirked. "I would never harm, Maggie. She means too much to me, and I do admire your loyalty to each other. In fact, I am DEPENDING on it."

Duncan opened his mouth to say something, but Finn was already gone.

"Damn it."

Duncan stomped back into the house, and up to the bedroom.

Maggie was standing by the window, fresh from a bath, in a long white nightgown, looking much like an angel. "There you are," she said.

He forgot everything as he took her in his arms.

"The midwife released me this afternoon and the babies will be sleeping all night."

Duncan looked her over, sighing. "I thought ye weren't going to let me touch ye anymore."

Maggie shrugged. "A woman is entitled to change her mind." She chewed on her lip, teasing. "Unless, you don't WANT to touch me anymore. My body is not exactly what it used to be."

Duncan ran his hands down the length of her back as his lips lightly grazed hers. "Your body is beautiful. Look at everything it has given me. The day will never come when I do not want ye in my world and in my bed. I cannot imagine my life without ye."

He took her to bed and showed her exactly how much she meant to him.

17 CHAPTER SEVENTEEN

In May of the following year, Maggie had just laid the babies down for a nap while Duncan, Gabe, and Quinn were on the estate checking on the crops that had been put in for the year. Thanks to Maggie's magical touch, everything was growing faster than anyone could have ever imagined. She had just come downstairs when there was a knock at the door.

"I will get it, Hettie," she called out.

Maggie opened the door and was beyond thrilled to see John's smiling face. She rushed into his arms as he embraced her tightly, kissing her cheek.

"John!"

"Maggie! You look wonderful."

"What are you doing here?"

"I was on my way back from Charleston and thought I would make a quick stop off...if you can spare a room for the night."

"For you, always! What a lovely surprise! Everyone is out, but they will be back for dinner soon."

"So?" asked John excitedly. "I have not been back to New York for the post lately to find out...is it a boy or a girl?"

Maggie laughed. "Come let me show you." She led him upstairs to the nursery.

John's face filled with delight when he looked down at the little sleeping angels. "Triplets?" he whispered, careful not to wake them. "Oh, my goodness, Maggie! How marvelous! Duncan must be beside himself with pride."

"He is! We were both taken a little aback, to say the least," she said, and they stepped out of the room, "but we cannot imagine our lives any other way now."

They went back to the drawing room and Maggie poured him a drink.

"Your house is something else and so big. I had no idea."

"It's filling up quickly," she laughed.

"How are Gabe and young Katherine?"

"They are good! Kat is almost two years old now. She is walking, talking, and into everything."

John set down his drink. "I have missed you so much, Maggie. New York has been so boring since you left."

"I have missed you too, John," she said and squeezed his hand.

Maggie heard the men come in through the kitchen. "Wait here!" she ordered.

She met them in the foyer. "We have a special guest," she smirked.

Duncan came over and kissed her. She took him by the hand and pulled him to the drawing room as Gabe and Quinn followed.

"John!" said Gabe, and they embraced.

"Welcome to our home," said Duncan.

John spent the rest of the day and the night with them before he had to catch a ship to New York the next morning. Maggie hugged him tightly when it was time for him to leave, promising to see him soon. When he was gone, Maggie turned and looked at the rest of them.

"It's time we started planning out how we are going to save John. October will be here soon, and we cannot fail him."

They all nodded in agreement and filed into the drawing room to lay out their ideas.

Scotland

Lady Aurnia watched the dark-haired little boy eating at the table. His mother had just passed a few hours before, but she had not had the heart to tell him yet. Logan, Evan, and Reade all stood with their arms folded, whispering among themselves.

"Are ye sure, Mother?" asked Logan.

"The woman confessed it on her deathbed. She would not have lied knowing she was about to meet her maker. Besides, look at him. There is no doubt that he carries

MacGregor blood. He is the spitting image of your brother at that age."

"How old is he?" asked Evan.

"Seven. His mother said she was working as a barmaid in the tavern in the village on the outskirts when it happened."

Logan searched his thoughts. "I remember that. It was the day we buried Dougal. We went in to share a drink in his memory."

"Aye," added Reade. "He was so upset that he became as drunk as I have ever seen him. It was so out of character for him, and there was a barmaid there flirting with him that night."

"He did disappear for a while," recalled Reade.

"What are we going to do with him?" asked Logan.

"The only thing we can do," replied Lady Aurnia. "I will take him to his father."

"Is that a good idea?"

"We have no choice. The boy will need him, and he deserves to know that this child is his."

"I will escort the two of ye," nodded Logan. "It is a long journey to Virginia, and we are not sure what we may find when we get there. Evan and Reade can hold down things here."

"We will leave after his mother's burial."

Lady Aurnia went to sit next to her newly found grandson, smiling and roughing up his hair the way she had his father's so many years ago.

Finn slipped into the house. He could hear them making love in the room across the hall. He smirked to himself, shaking his head.

Those two were made for one another, and they were going to need each other desperately in the days to come.

He opened the door to the nursery and moved to look down into the crib as he leaned over it. "The boy is on his way and very soon, all of ye children that have the MacGregor Fae blood flowing through your veins, will be in one place. Then, the real magic can begin," he whispered.

The Fae King smiled, reaching down to push the hair out of Kat's face. He loved watching her sleep. She had so many of the MacGregor features, yet no one had even noticed.

"Sleep well, little one. I will see ye soon."

A thick fog surrounded him, and he disappeared into the night.

TO BE CONTINUED....

ABOUT THE AUTHOR

Tempie W. Wade is a lifelong resident of Virginia and currently resides in Williamsburg. She has a love of history, old architecture, and travel. The author likes to incorporate historically accurate events with a touch of fantasy, in hopes that the reader will become interested enough to do their own research into the past. The author can be reached by email at TempieWade@cox.net.

The Timely Revolution Book Series in Order:

Book One-A Timely Revolution

Book Two-More

Book Three-The Complicated Life of Maggie MacGregor

Book Four in The Timely
Revolution Series will be
coming soon.

Follow the author page of Tempie W. Wade
on Facebook for upcoming information or
visit…

www.TempieWade.com